Praise for The Sam Austin Chronicles:

"Impressively well written and thoroughly entertaining from beginning to end, *Target Citadel* is the anticipated sequel to *Destination Citadel*, the first installment of Robert Adrian's Sam Austin Chronicles."

—The Midwest Book Review

I0679032

Titles by Robert Adrian

Destination Citadel

Target Citadel

Checkmate Citadel

THE SAM AUSTIN CHRONICLES
CHECKMATE CITADEL

ROBERT ADRIAN

ISBN: 099061042X
ISBN 13: 9780990610427
Library of Congress Control Number: 2015914489
Cambrian Park, LLC, San Jose, CA
AKM 9-3

To Hannah, Grace, and Olivia,

Who remind me that love comes in
large and small packages.

PROLOGUE

Courtney Harrington had lived a charmed life in some ways, including having been elected president of the United States. Even though she'd been impeached and convicted of war crimes, she'd managed to escape any further punishment so far. Her partners in those war crimes had all been convicted and shipped to the planet Citadel, where they'd been hanged. People in two solar systems used the term "Harrington's War" as a derisive reference to the unjustified acts she'd initiated against Citadel in a desperate bid to be reelected.

Two things her experiences had taught her were to never admit wrongdoing and to always keep fighting. She came from wealth and could afford lawyers whose sole purpose was to ensure that she stayed on Earth and out of prison. Although she was, in theory, under some form of house arrest, she actually had a lot of freedom while her attorneys did their work, at least as far as her travels were concerned.

I'm entitled to all the perks that every other former president receives, she thought with a smirk. *I'm sure as hell not the only one to have bent the rules while in office. I just happened to run afoul of Sam Austin.*

A feeling of rage welled up within her as she thought about Austin, who was the president of Citadel and a former United States president, but she was distracted from that rage as soon as someone entered the room. "What do you want?" she asked with no attempt at warmth or even civility.

"You asked for an update, Ms. Harrington," the man began.

Harrington whipped her head around sharply as she snapped, "I'm still *Madame President* to you!"

The man regarded her without reaction and replied calmly, "You *were* President Harrington. You have been removed from office, so the title is no longer yours to claim. I'm not under a potential death sentence, and I don't have any interest in catering to your whims. Your toadies did that, and they're all either dead or in prison."

"Money can always buy new toadies, or at least people who will do what I tell them to do, Flynn," Harrington warned. "You would do well to remember that."

"The name is *Mr.* Flynn, and you would do well to remember *that.* Unlike you, I can leave anytime I wish and never look back. Do you want the update or not?"

Harrington's eyes flared, but she stifled the urge to tell the man what to do to himself. "Yes, I want the update," she said.

The man smiled faintly and replied, "While nothing has happened yet, our scientists believe that they have learned more about how the aliens think. They are still working on applying that knowledge to their forms of communication."

"I've heard that one before," she replied, unimpressed. "All they need is more time and money, and their promises will be fulfilled. It's been over a year since I ordered them to carry out this project."

"You've also heard that the task is extraordinarily difficult. Even with the full resources of the government during your administration, the odds were against our being successful. It was a minor miracle that you were able to fool the public into believing the project was shut down after your administration ended. It was even more of a miracle that they were able to reconstitute it with a new team of people who had the intellectual abilities needed to succeed. This gives us an advantage that no one else has, whether on Earth, Mars, Citadel, or anywhere else. In short, patience is needed, Ms. Harrington. If you have patience, think of what success could mean."

"I'm thinking of what it would mean to Sam Austin," she replied, malevolence in her eyes. Those eyes were something she'd never allowed her constituents to see. "All right, you'll have more money, but that will be all you get without results! If we can't communicate with them, then this project isn't worth a damn."

The man left without a word.

CHAPTER ONE

Flynn hadn't gotten where he was without being resourceful. Although he knew he'd never be able to understand the science behind things like warp-field generators, alien communication, and space travel, he knew how to find people who did. He also knew how to figure out what motivated such people. More often than not, he mused, it was money, but sometimes it was recognition or even the intellectual challenge itself. The motivator was money for virtually everyone in the group he had assembled, and Harrington had plenty of money to provide. Flynn preferred such people, since they were predictable and more likely to lack the scruples that sometimes got in the way of results.

Later that day, Flynn met with the men and women of that group, and they expressed some anxiety over the news he had for them. "We have good news," he said. "Our benefactor has agreed to provide additional funding, although she made it clear that there would be nothing more after this if there hasn't been any concrete progress."

One of the men, a scientist named William Spatcher, scowled. "What does she think we're trying to do, solve a challenging crossword puzzle? We've been busting our asses for a year trying to solve something that no one else can solve."

Dr. Nora Farmer frowned in agreement as she said, "We've been staring at every image of their spaceships that exists, trying to understand their thought processes, let alone how they communicate. We have to have something more to go on!"

"What more would you need, Dr. Farmer?" Flynn asked.

Farmer thought for a moment before saying, "I'd like a better sample than we have for what might pass for language, Mr. Flynn. So far, we don't have any viable physical relics to study."

"Where would you suggest we look?"

She shook her head. "I wish I knew."

"Call me crazy," Spatcher said, "but I have an idea."

CHAPTER TWO

Flynn met with Lillian Raffles, a physicist who had been fired from her last job at a research institute because she was lazy. She'd thought nothing of collecting a full-time salary for doing part-time work, which had given her time to write lousy novels that no one wanted to read. She'd managed to get a job as a manager, so she had had her people do the real work, while she'd taken the credit and pretended to be in charge. In reality, she was a poor leader, her knowledge was out of date, and her people despised her.

Although Raffles was not particularly attractive, she'd managed to stroke the ego, and perhaps other parts, of a much older man who was in a senior role at the institute. He hadn't demonstrated much competence when it came to running his organization. He regularly ignored complaints from Raffles's people and people in other departments who complained about her. In Flynn's mind, this was an indictment of nonprofit organizations in general, where talent and results weren't always demanded so long as the funding continued.

Eventually, even the institute was visited by the winds of change. While the executive's lack of competence had been tolerated for years, he was told in no uncertain terms that staying on past retirement age wasn't an option. Amazingly, the winds of change blew even more strongly, leading to the organization hiring a replacement that happened to be good at her job. It didn't take long for Raffles's lack of value to the organization to become apparent to her new boss; it didn't take much longer for her to be fired. Not only did her people shed no tears over her departure, but there were also rumors of dancing on tables for joy.

Flynn figured that Raffles needed money and would, therefore, leap at the opportunity to work on the project. He wasn't wrong. "Why don't you tell me what you need, Mr. Flynn?" she said.

"I need someone to do some work to figure out where the remains of a device that exploded in space might be found, Ms. Raffles," he replied.

Raffles's eyes narrowed as she said, "I'm sure you meant to call me *Dr.* Raffles, Mr. Flynn. You must be aware of where I earned my doctorate degree."

Flynn raised an eyebrow, almost as a sign of amusement, as he answered, "I'm also aware that doctorate was revoked later, Ms. Raffles, due to questions relating to the work you did toward obtaining that degree."

She was indignant. "That was all a misunderstanding! It's an administrative issue to get everything clarified and confirm that my degree is still in good standing." Raffles was used to such outbursts putting others on the defensive, so she found it unsettling to see that Flynn didn't react as expected.

In fact, his expression didn't change at all as he said, "You'll find that I'm not one for bullshit. There is no administrative issue holding up anything. You falsified your results and claimed as your own work that others actually performed."

"How could you know that?" she asked somewhat nervously.

"I do my homework, which includes learning about the people I consider approaching for work. I pay well, Ms. Raffles." Flynn showed Raffles a piece of paper with a number written on it. Her eyes widened at the amount, and her face paled slightly as the expression on Flynn's face changed subtly. "As I was saying, I have absolutely no tolerance for people trying to bullshit me about anything, especially when it concerns something I have paid them to do. So long as you remember this basic rule, we can talk about what I have in mind. Are you interested?"

Raffles needed money, so she set aside any misgivings as she said, "Yes, I am. You won't ever have any reason to regret using my services."

Flynn's face was again neutral as he said, "That's good to hear. I'm sure you recall back when Earth was attacked by the alien race that also attacked Citadel?"

Raffles nodded in recollection as she answered, "Of course. We probably wouldn't be here if it hadn't been for Sam Austin showing up at the right time to destroy the alien ship."

"That's precisely the moment I want to address. I need someone to work out every possible location where any debris from that ship may be located."

Raffles was confused. "I don't understand. There isn't any debris, not counting what's left of the burned-out remains of the ship itself, which haven't told us much of anything."

"It would be more accurate to state that no debris has been discovered. At the time, people were so glad to have survived the attack that they didn't worry when no debris showed up. Like you, they all assumed that there wasn't any to be found. Before I agree with that assumption, I want to know that every possible location for debris has been identified and investigated. I want you to calculate every one of those possible locations."

"To do that, I'd need an incredible amount of data from that moment."

Flynn nodded. "I've uncovered an incredible amount of data."

"How?" she asked skeptically. "Citadel isn't exactly sharing that type of information these days."

Flynn shrugged. "There isn't a lot of mystery about it. Back before things got out of hand between Citadel and the United States, there was a lot of sharing of data on the attack, as part of a goodwill gesture by Citadel. I have access to that data."

"I thought that data was already thoroughly scrutinized and locked away."

"People often see what they want to see. They see a fireball appear and consume the alien ship completely, with nothing appearing in the immediate vicinity, so they don't look very hard at the data for a different answer. Also, locks nearly always have keys. I have a key to this data." The earlier look of subtle warning flashed across his face briefly as he said, "You don't need to know anything more about the key."

Raffles decided that Flynn was right. "When do I start?" she asked, not entirely able to conceal the greed in her eyes.

"You will have the data by the end of the day. You will receive half of your fee up front, as a sign of good faith. It is important that you understand this is not an open-ended assignment, where you will have what may seem like an indefinite amount of time. The time allotted to complete your review is six months, and I do mean six months. Keep in mind that I do not reward a lack of results. For example, I will not regard your efforts as being acceptable if your findings are just guesses that include every physical object in the solar system.

"You will receive the other half of your fee when you have completed your review. In addition, there will be a bonus if we locate an artifact based on your findings." Raffles flinched as Flynn warned, "If I am not satisfied that your efforts have been everything they should be, then in addition to your not seeing the second half of your fee, we will discuss what you have already been paid. You are to present your findings only to me and to tell no one else about this matter. Also, we need to maintain strict control over the data, so you will return it to me once you've presented your findings. Do you understand everything?"

The look in her eyes gave Flynn his answer even before she nodded her head.

CHAPTER THREE

R affles was feeling a great deal of stress. It had been three months since she'd agreed to work for Flynn, yet she hadn't gotten much of anything done. She'd been astonished at the volume of data Flynn had provided. In fact, she'd felt overwhelmed by what she'd seen and couldn't get her head around how to approach it.

For once, Flynn's homework had been incomplete. Although he knew the circumstances of Raffles's departure from her last job, he had still believed she had the technical qualifications to do this assignment. Although he had understood that Raffles was lazy and willing to use her staff to do all the real work, he hadn't realized that she had allowed her technical skills to atrophy. Even she hadn't appreciated the extent of the deterioration until she'd realized she couldn't make any sense of the data.

Raffles was spending a lot of time thinking about Flynn's warning concerning what would happen if she didn't show sufficient effort toward the project. She'd already spent much of the money she'd received, so offering a refund was out of the question. After seeing the look on Flynn's face as he warned her, she wasn't sure offering a refund would solve her problems anyway.

All of this had led to her meeting with someone whom she normally avoided. Gerald Porter had been one of the people who had worked for her at the institute. She'd been happy to take credit for his work and had been something of a bully toward him as well. Since this had taken place when she'd been protected by her incompetent boss, Porter had realized that nothing would change, so he'd finally quit.

His problem was that his technical skills had always been sharp, but he hated leadership roles. This meant that he was probably never going to be anything more than a senior member of a team, and the leader would still take the credit for the team's work. Although he'd joined a team with a better boss at another think tank, he was still available for freelance work, always hoping for the recognition that had been denied to him.

"I was surprised to hear from you, Lillian," he said. "We didn't part on the best of terms."

"I've often regretted that things didn't work out well between us when we were at the institute, Gerry," she said, working hard at sounding sincere. "I really don't know what happened."

For a moment, old emotions of resentment washed over Porter's face. They subsided as he replied, "What happened was that you never gave me proper credit for my work."

"I'm sorry about that. I can appreciate how important proper credit is for any scientist. In fact, that was why I contacted you. I have an opportunity to do something that is amazing, with the chance for recognition if things work out."

"What do you mean?" he asked without enthusiasm.

"I've been approached by a private organization that has been tasked with doing an in-depth review of the alien attack on Earth. While I'm doing a lot of the work myself, I'm too swamped to be able to get to everything. I have a lot of data that needs to be analyzed and interpreted for a key part of this project."

"What is this key part?"

"We need to determine any possible locations in our solar system where debris from the alien ship might have ended up."

Porter couldn't hide the look of astonishment as he said, "How the hell could anyone do that? Ever since Harrington's War, Citadel won't tell anyone jack shit about the alien ship."

Raffles assumed a sly expression as she said, "Calmer heads have prevailed, although, for political reasons, this activity cannot be acknowledged publicly. The data has been obtained quietly."

"That's incredible," Porter said with increasing excitement. "Citadel has by far the most data. They were the ones who lured the aliens away from Earth after things had been pounded to hell here. They were the only ones around when they destroyed the alien ship. In fact, they had two of their ships there, so there may be differences in the data from the two ships that could be useful." He looked straight into Raffles's eyes. "We have all of that data?"

Raffles noted the use of the word "we" as she replied, "Yes, we have it all, Gerry. We have a limited amount of time available to do the project, so this data needs to be analyzed and findings on potential locations ready within three months." She pushed a paper toward him with a figure on it. "I can pay you this sum for the work, provided you can get the results to me within the three-month window."

Porter looked at the figure and frowned. "This is half what it should be for this work."

Raffles's eyes were never more sincere than they were as she said, "This is what I have available, Gerry. However, as a bonus, you will get to publish your findings once the project has been completed and made public. You've always wanted recognition for your work; this is a way to get it, in bright lights. Who knows? If your predictions pan out, there might even be a Nobel Prize in it for you."

"When will the project be completed?"

"That's hard to say. In addition to the science, we will need to follow up on your predictions to try to locate any debris. There will then be the political side of things, to figure out just when to make the announcement. This is a sensitive issue, and we'll have to wait until they feel the time is right." She paused for a moment to let the excitement build, before continuing. "One other condition is that when you provide your findings, you must return all of the data as well."

"Why would I need to do that?" Porter asked suspiciously.

"This project is highly confidential, and I'm bending the rules as it is to bring you on board. I have to return my data as well, so I'm not asking you to do anything that

I won't also have to do. The last thing Citadel wants is for its data to be somewhere outside of its control."

"OK," Porter replied grudgingly. "I get it that they're really sensitive about their data, considering what happened during Harrington's War. I hope that when they see my findings, they'll want me to continue to use the data further."

"That wouldn't surprise me at all," Raffles said smoothly. "Remember, no one can know about this project until it has been made public by the powers that be. You can't share this with *anyone*."

"That's fine," Porter agreed. "When do I get the data?"

Raffles rose with a smile as she said, "I'll get it to you immediately."

CHAPTER FOUR

Alan Turner knew he was supposed to be relaxing while visiting with friends at Sam Austin's place. He'd already been busted by Austin for sneaking a look at his link's display, hoping against hope for some new inspiration that would get him a little closer to understanding the images from the ancient alien derelict that seemed to taunt him. The giant, abandoned vessel had drifted into their star system two years earlier, and still denied them access to any of its secrets.

Austin had chuckled as he'd put away the display and had everyone pile into his ground transport for a trip up to his lake. An hour later, they'd reached their destination. As they'd practically jumped out of the transport, Turner had looked around at the surrounding mountains, their caps dusted with white and covered by a thin mist. Even though it was the planet's warm season, there was always clear, cold water that splashed down thousands of feet from those mountains, making its way past boulders, shrubs, and trees. The water stopped at the lake temporarily, before continuing down to the rest of

Austin's acreage in the valley below. Although the plants and trees were different from what one would see on Earth, the overall view was surprisingly Earthlike.

Going for a swim was quite a treat. While every settler's land had access to running water from rivers much like the one that coursed through Austin's property, not every plot of land could accommodate a lake. As a result, everyone had gotten out of their clothes and into the lake almost immediately. Each of the four couples there had children with them. Sam and Liz had their boys, Matt and Luke. Bret and Donna Yabuno had their girl, Maddie, and their younger boy, Tommy. Alan and his wife, Dawn, had their two kids, Marie and Albert, and they'd just learned that Dawn was pregnant again. Joe and Sara Albretti only had one child, their daughter, Gina. *That's understandable,* Turner mused to himself, *since they haven't been a couple for nearly as long as the rest of us.*

After a while, the women got out of the water to stretch out on their towels and talk about Dawn's pregnancy. Austin and Albretti were in the water with the kids who wanted to swim, while Turner and Yabuno stayed on shore and looked after the toddlers who weren't quite as adventuresome. Everyone, even the youngest, was wearing a waterproof bracelet that let the transport's security system know he or she was not an enemy.

Turner grinned as he watched Austin laugh as several little ones splashed him; then, there were shrieks of delight as he returned the favor with loud but gentle splashes of his own that got him wetter than the kids. Turner turned to Yabuno. "Isn't it amazing how Sam seems just as happy being silly with kids as he is in doing something important, like helping everyone plan a successful harvest?"

Yabuno chuckled. "I think he really lives for days like this. He's probably having a lot more fun with the kids. He's always been that way. What's amazing is that there are still people who don't realize that what we're seeing is at least as genuine as anything they've read about. The things he posts online about what's been happening rarely have anything to do with his being the leader. He's always enjoyed life, and being on Citadel has given him a chance get back to the basics of what's important."

Turner gave a mock groan. "I wish *I* could contribute something more important to the place."

"I thought Sam told you to stop worrying about that damned derelict for the day," Yabuno said with amusement.

"That's easy for you to say," he replied. "*You* haven't been gnawing at the same problem for a couple years. It's more like it's been gnawing at *me*."

"What makes you think you're the only one who knows what it's like to gnaw at a problem for years?" Yabuno asked with a grin. "Hell, it took me forever to come up with the designs we now use for the warp-field generators for our transports."

Turner chuckled. "Thank God you did, or we'd still be stuck here!" He looked around. "I'm not complaining about the scenery or the life we have here, but things would have turned out a hell of a lot differently without your designs."

Yabuno's smile of appreciation faded after a moment. "Just because we worked out the solution to the warp-field generators doesn't mean I don't still have problems that gnaw at me. I've been working on a problem since before we ever found the derelict." After seeing Turner's quizzical look, he continued, "I've been trying to figure out how to modify our warp-field generators to warp space-time around an object even if we don't want the object to go anywhere fast."

"Why do you want to do that?"

"Think of the possibilities," Yabuno said with excitement. "If we can warp space-time around an object but keep it pretty much in place, we may have an effective shield for our ships. In theory, nothing—not projectiles, energy weapons, nor even radiation itself—could get through because they would be warped past the ship along the fringes of the warp-field bubble."

"Didn't we used to do that, back when we were first developing warp-field generators? I recall that at one point, we couldn't even get a bubble that would allow anything to travel at all."

"Don't remind me," Yabuno replied in a voice that indicated he remembered the frustrations from those trials well. "If we didn't have bubbles reaching out like multiple fingers in all sorts of directions, we just had a static field that didn't do anything."

"What's the problem?"

"When we came up with the replacement design for the warp-field generators, we had to sacrifice the ability to keep things fine-tuned. Collapsing a warp-field bubble is tricky because space-time is still warping past our ship. Remember, we use two fields—the primary one and the one that reinforces the primary one."

"Yes, I remember," Turner said. He tried to bring a thought into focus but couldn't quite get past its murky streaks of gray. "You once showed us a picture you put together of what was happening." He chuckled. "I always thought that picture was rather elegant in a way. It was almost like a work of art, the way it combined the image of what was happening with the physics behind it." He sat up suddenly as some of the mental streaks dissolved. He picked up the link that Austin had teased him about avoiding and pulled up an image. He showed it to Yabuno and said, "What does that remind you of?"

Yabuno looked at it casually and said, "It looks like you drew your own version of my picture with a few tweaks." Suddenly, he scanned it more intently and demanded, "You didn't draw that! Did it come where I think it came from?" Turner didn't need to nod for Yabuno to know the answer to his own question. "If the symbols from the derelict include an image like that, then we may finally have a common point of reference, possibly for their technology, their language, or both!" He turned toward the splashing that was still engulfing the oldest man in two solar systems and said, "Sam! You're not going to believe what Alan and I just figured out!"

Austin forgot the disappointment he felt over his friends not putting their work aside when he saw the looks on their faces.

CHAPTER FIVE

Porter took a small sip from his coffee cup and made a face. He'd known that the dark-brown liquid would be cold, considering the amount of time he'd ignored it, but he needed to do something that didn't require using any brain cells. He'd stared back at his computer display countless times over the past months, determined to make sense of the seemingly endless waves of data Raffles had sent him. He thought back sourly on a recent conversation with the woman, when she'd pestered him with demands for updates on his progress.

"It's been nearly three months since I gave you the data," she'd reminded him needlessly, as her image appeared on a display. "You must have some idea by now of what it all means."

"What it means is that the amount of data you sent me is a lot more than I imagined."

"What do you mean?"

"You told me that what you were giving me is just what you couldn't get to, which sounded like overflow work. If what I have is overflow work, what you must have would be almost unimaginable. At some point, you'll need to integrate my findings with yours, to create a complete picture." He'd shaken his head. "I don't mind saying that I'm glad I'm not the one who has to do that work. You're really going to earn your money!"

She'd put some of her fake honey into her voice. "I was hoping you could walk me through the methodologies for analyzing your data, Gerry, as well as your conclusions, so that I can make sure it jibes with what I'm doing with my data. While I could do it by myself, having that conversation would be a big help."

Old alarm bells had started to ring in Porter's head. "What are you talking about, Lillian? You asked me to handle the data you sent over, which I'm doing. I shouldn't need to walk you through the methodologies; those are things that we already discussed, at least generally, when you sent me the data. The basis for my conclusions should be clear when you review what I've done with it." A nasty headache began to throb its way through his skull as he asked, "Or will it? Just how much of the data that they gave you did you send to me? A tenth of it? A quarter? Half?"

Raffles hadn't answered.

The truth had begun to dawn on him as he'd said, "You sent *all* of it to me, didn't you? You're not actually doing any of the work yourself, are you? Do you even understand anything I discussed with you back then?"

"I admit I'm a bit rusty, Gerry," Raffles had answered in a light tone, "but I'm sure you can bring me up to speed."

"Bring you up to speed?" Porter had said, almost in shock. "Lillian, if you're that rusty, why would you even take on the assignment? Come to think of it, why did anyone even come to you?" He'd bitten his lip as the answer came, one that had haunted him previously. "Someone came to you because of your background, even though it's based on the work of people like me, instead of your own efforts."

The shock had turned to bitterness. "You were never going to share my work with anyone, were you? You were going to do what you've done before, which is present my findings as your own and collect your fee. You were hoping to talk me into creating a summary that would make it seem like you knew what you were talking about, weren't you?"

"That's harsh, Gerry. You would have gotten credit at the right time."

"I've heard that before"—Porter had snorted—"only it never happens. I swore that I'd never be your patsy again, Lillian. While I've failed on that score by spending a lot of time on this data, at least I can have the satisfaction of knowing that you've placed yourself in a deep hole, with no way to get yourself out of it."

"Wait!" she'd said in desperation. "I need that analysis, and I'm running out of time to deliver it."

"That's the best news I've heard today," he had replied as he'd reached for the button that would end the call.

"What do you want?" The panic in her voice had been real. "Name it."

Porter hadn't bothered to hide the distrust on his face. "I don't want anything that requires me to rely on any more of your promises. I told you once that you were offering me half of what it should have been for this work. By tomorrow, you will pay me the fee you should have agreed to pay me in the first place."

"I don't have that kind of money."

"That's not my problem. Beg, borrow, or steal it, but if it isn't in my account by the end of the day tomorrow, then you can go back to the people who hired you and tell them you have no idea how to analyze the data."

"All right. I'll figure out a way to make it happen."

"That's not all."

"What else do you want?" she'd asked nervously.

"You're going to make sure that I get credit for my work this time by having me there to present and explain the findings. I'm not going to stand there like a flunky to prompt you on what to say, either. *I'll* do the talking."

"You don't want to do that, Gerry," she'd said, trying to hide a growing sense of uneasiness. "Trust me, these are not people to deal with if you don't have to. Let me present the findings. I'm saying this for your own good."

Unfortunately, she'd said similar things to Porter too many times over the years for him to take her word on anything now. He'd brushed her comments aside, assuming that she was, as usual, operating from self-interest. "Don't bother trying to sell me a story about how some people are intimidating, scary, etc. We had the real deal during Harrington's War, and they've been dealt with.

"I get it that having me there makes it look like you've been doing nothing to earn their money. You'll probably tell them that the problem was even more complicated than you guessed and you needed to bring someone on board with a lot more skill to do the work. That isn't far from the truth anyway," he'd said dismissively.

Raffles had tried reasoning with Porter, but he wouldn't listen. "You need me to be there anyway, Lillian, since I'm not about to share a detailed explanation of my findings with you at this point. There's one other thing too."

"What is it?" she had asked resignedly.

"I'm going to publish my work once this project is complete, and I'm not going to wait around for permission from anyone to do it."

"You can't do that!" she had exclaimed. "Secrecy is an explicit part of the deal."

He'd thought for a moment. "OK, I'm willing to wait awhile to publish, while a search is made for any artifacts. I'm only willing to consider it because it would be nice to have my findings validated. Once we have the validation, I'm going to publish." He'd looked at her image expectantly.

"You win, Gerry," she had said, "but God help us both if your findings don't pan out, whatever they are."

Porter smiled at the memory of the conversation's conclusion. He had an additional reason to be pleased over how events were turning out because of what he had learned from the data. Things were definitely looking up.

Flynn was furious, although the look on his face scared Raffles more than any shouting would have done. "What part of my instructions were unclear, Ms. Raffles, particularly the ones about you telling no one about the project?"

"Your instructions were clear, Mr. Flynn," she began, "but I didn't have any choice but to bring in someone to help. The data was too much for me to handle on my own."

"Why didn't you check with me first, if the job was too much for you?"

"It took a while for me to understand fully just how large the project would be. By that time, it just made sense to bring in someone that could make sure I met your deadline."

"I once told you I didn't tolerate bullshit. Nothing that you just told me answered my question. However, I'll deal with that problem later. Tell me about this person you showed the data to."

Later, Flynn and Harrington discussed the situation.

"Are you telling me everything has just blown up in our faces, Mr. Flynn?" Harrington demanded.

"No, Ms. Harrington," Flynn replied evenly. "I'm telling you we have a problem with someone I hired who isn't everything she seemed to be and lacks the sense to know not to cross me."

"I don't tolerate that kind of sloppiness from anyone. Not even from you," she said pointedly.

"Our options were limited, for reasons you should understand," he said, a warning of his own in his voice. "Citadel has made it clear that it will take a dim view of cooperation with the United States so long as you remain in this solar system. Reputable scientists are nervous about doing anything to cross Citadel. Besides, while we have good people on our scientific team, they don't have the background for this kind of analysis, so we have to go outside and find what's available.

"While money will always be a great motivator, the images of the gallows on Citadel are still fresh in the minds of most people. Fortunately, another thing that motivates people is success. Raffles told me that the man she had do the work will have some results that will make it worthwhile."

"For your sake, I hope so."

CHAPTER SIX

Porter stood in front of a large display, waiting to begin. He knew the presentation would be monitored and wondered why people thought it necessary to keep everything so secret, especially since he was going to publish his findings. Raffles was standing off to one side, looking, for a change, like she was *his* assistant. His sense of satisfaction was tempered by the fact that she'd kept trying to cut him out of everything by letting her be the one to speak. He'd only gotten his way by refusing to share any advance summaries of his findings, so they *had* to listen to him.

The atmosphere seemed to change instantly when a man walked into the room. He was tall, fit, and showed a self-confidence in his movements that didn't rely on anything exaggerated like a swagger. His expression was neutral as he approached Porter. Porter noticed that the man seemed reluctant to clasp Porter's hand in greeting, although his words were cordial.

"Welcome, Dr. Porter," he said. "My name is Flynn. I represent the people that are supporting this effort." He gave a pointed look at Raffles as he continued. "I hope that you have some news that will be of great interest to us."

Porter missed the look on Raffles's face as he replied. "Thank you, Mr. Flynn. I think you will consider my findings to be of great interest, to both Earth and Citadel."

Flynn didn't respond, and his expression remained neutral, a sign that it was time to begin.

After introducing himself and walking the audience through the methodologies he had used to analyze the data, he got to the heart of the matter. "I know that what you want to hear is whether any artifacts could have survived the destruction of the alien ship. Based on my review of the data, the answer is I believe at least one artifact did survive from that event."

There was no need to worry now about whether he had everyone's attention as he brought up several images. "I believe that these images, along with the sensor readings taken by *Pathfinder* and *KT-2*, confirm that an artifact was ejected from the dying alien ship."

Dr. Farmer squinted at the images as she said, "I don't see any artifact, Dr. Porter."

Porter manipulated the images and replied, "Here are the images seen through different filters, Dr. Farmer. As you can see, I've managed to work with the images and remove much of the glare from the explosions." He pointed to a spot on the display. "Although it is hard to make out, those aren't flames flickering. There is a solid object passing through a flame. I'll show it to you in slow motion, with everything enhanced."

Even after scrutinizing repeated showings of the images, Farmer and the others were skeptical. "Others have checked out those images and reached a different conclusion. They believe that these are simply tongues of flame created by the intense energy that was released from the ship after the impact with the asteroids Austin and his people launched. What makes you believe that everyone else is wrong?"

Porter was enjoying his moment in the spotlight. He brought up an image of the destruction of the alien ship from another angle. "As you can see," he began, "they were able to capture the destruction of the alien ship from more than one angle."

"Unfortunately, this angle is much less useful in studying the explosion," Farmer pointed out. "It doesn't even give the same view of what you claim is more than just a series of flames. Even with the best filters, plus algorithms for cleaning up images, there isn't any way to get a clear image of that particular part of the alien ship."

"That's true," Porter said with a nod. "However, that's not why the image is important. Take a look at it in real time."

More pairs of eyes squinted at the images as the destruction replayed itself. In time, the position of the image shifted away from the alien ship as *Pathfinder* and *K-2* moved away to a safer distance. Occasional tendrils of flames still reached out, however. Finally, Farmer stood up and said, "All right, what are we supposed to have seen?"

Porter manipulated the image to filter out the flames. "You haven't seen it yet. Watch."

Farmer sat down with the others to watch the display. The looks from the audience were as blank as the wall behind the display. Porter pointed to an asteroid and asked, "What do you see?"

"An asteroid, of course," Spatcher replied, somewhat sarcastically. "They were in the asteroid belt after all."

"Where did that cloud come from, Dr. Spatcher?"

"What cloud?" he replied with a confused look.

Porter replayed the recording as its view shifted away from the alien ship. He pointed to the same spot again and said, "Note that there isn't any cloud there yet."

Farmer jumped up, feeling truly excited for the first time. "I see it! The cloud just showed up, like from an impact." She looked over to Porter, who nodded.

"Yes, it is exactly in line with what I believe to be an object in the first image. Also, I've calculated the probable force behind the explosion and the speed of an object being expelled from the ship. That cloud appears exactly when one would expect an object from the alien ship to reach it."

Flynn spoke for the first time since Porter began his presentation. "Why hasn't anyone else figured this out, Dr. Porter?"

Porter shrugged. "No one thought that part of the image had anything important in it. All anyone saw were the flames from the fireball. I'd have missed it too if I hadn't decided that I was seeing something more than flames in the first image. I'd have still missed it if I hadn't filtered out the flames and kept watching." He pointed back at the asteroid and concluded, "While I can't say what shape it might be in at this point, I'm pretty certain that a piece of the alien ship reached that asteroid."

"Couldn't it have ricocheted off into space?" Flynn asked.

Porter shook his head. "Not likely. The pattern of the cloud indicates that the artifact was close enough to the center of the asteroid that it didn't go anywhere else after impact."

Flynn continued to probe for flaws. "Why wouldn't it just drift into space, instead of resting on the surface? There isn't any gravity to keep it there."

"It's a microgravity environment," Porter explained, "so it would be more accurate to say there isn't *sufficient* gravity to keep it there if it had just been placed on the surface. However, the images and data suggest that the object was traveling at sufficient speed to embed itself in the asteroid, assuming that it wasn't destroyed outright from the force of the impact. That's what's holding it there, rather than gravity."

"Can we find this asteroid?" Flynn asked, his expression showing increasing interest.

"Yes." Porter nodded. "The authorities have been monitoring the asteroids in one form or another for over a hundred years. We know its position at the time of impact, so it should be simple enough to track down which one it must be."

Flynn looked around the room, taking note of the fact that various people were nodding in agreement with Porter's claims. It was clear that the rest of the scientists found his analysis persuasive. He nodded at Porter as well. "Well done, Dr. Porter. I assume that you're as curious as the rest of us to find out what's on that asteroid."

Porter grinned back at Flynn. "I wouldn't dream of publishing my findings until there's been an attempt to confirm my conclusions by direct observation of the site."

Flynn maintained his usual neutral expression at hearing Porter's words. As the rest of the audience gathered around Porter to offer congratulations and ask him more questions, Flynn moved toward Raffles and spoke to her softly. "First of all, you did much better than I expected in finding Dr. Porter to do your work for you. While we still need to confirm his conclusions, I'm satisfied that the money I paid you wasn't wasted."

Raffles winced as Flynn's expression went from neutral to dangerous.

"However, we now have another problem. Apparently, Porter plans on publishing his findings. Just how the hell did he come to believe that was part of the deal?"

Raffles had trouble meeting Flynn's gaze as she answered. "He wouldn't do the job unless I promised him he could publish his findings at some point. The only delay he would accept was until after we determined whether his conclusions were valid."

"You have an interesting concept of 'we,' Ms. Raffles. There is no way 'we' will allow Porter to publish anything until 'we' are ready for him to do so. In fact, 'we' might never want this information published."

"What do you intend to do?"

Flynn's expression had returned to neutral. "For now, I don't intend to do anything. While his analysis is interesting, it's still just a theory until we can confirm it with a visit to the asteroid. If he were to publish anything without that confirmation, he'd just look foolish."

"He still has the data," Raffles reminded him.

A spark flickered through his gaze as he asked, "Did you tell him the data had to be returned once he provided his analysis?"

"Yes," she said with relief. "He knows he can't keep it, although he hopes that if his conclusions pan out, he'll be allowed further access to it."

"Get that data back and you may yet earn the second part of your fee. There may even be a bonus to come, assuming that there really is a piece of alien junk on that asteroid."

Raffles found his gaze even more uncomfortable as he continued.

"Don't confuse dumb luck with any notion of having fooled or manipulated me, and don't assume that you'll be able to do it again and try to rely on some bullshit explanation to avoid any unpleasant consequences. This is the last time I will ask this question: Is there anything else I should know about Dr. Porter or you, Ms. Raffles? Anything else you've neglected to tell me?"

Raffles merely shook her head. As Flynn walked away, she was glad to be out from under his gaze. While she still felt some uneasiness over having brought Porter into contact with Flynn, her greed overruled her misgivings at that moment.

CHAPTER SEVEN

The image on the display was of an unusual object framed by the blackness of space, interrupted by countless stars, indicating the object wasn't near a planet. In fact, it was on the edge of the Citadel system, many millions of miles away from any of the system's planetary bodies. A countdown indicator on the display was nearly at zero, and presently, the area around the object seemed to ripple.

As the countdown ran past zero, the ripples became irregular tendrils of distortion, some of which curled back on themselves and some of which appeared to reach out toward unseen targets. Sensors had been placed at various distances from the object. As the tendrils reached out, some of the sensors were brushed aside, although not without suffering strange distortions; others were transformed so severely as to be unrecognizable.

Since the image was a 3-D presentation, some of the tendrils seemed to reach out beyond the frame of the display. Several of the viewers felt the need to shift in their chairs to avoid what would have been a deadly embrace.

Suddenly, the tendrils withdrew rapidly back to their starting points. As the scene came to an end, Austin spoke in an amused tone. "Seems to me we've been here before, going all the way back to when we developed the warp-field generators that took the original *Pathfinder* and the first ships to Citadel."

Yabuno motioned toward the display. "As bad as things look in these images, they're still an improvement over where we were originally." He glanced at Turner. "Alan here knows better than anyone just how difficult it's been to translate the alien information."

Turner nodded. "What we just saw was a direct result of our efforts to translate the symbol based on an assumption that it means something similar to the one Bret created. With Bret's help, I've been trying to decipher several of their symbols that appear to be related to that first one of theirs. I hope that the process of deciphering those symbols will give us the insights we need to complete this task." He gave Austin an anxious look.

Austin chuckled when he saw the look. "Don't worry, Alan. I'm not regarding the progress to date as a sign that we should abandon this effort. In addition to the fact that this is the type of project that will help us to maintain our knowledge base, there will be some practical applications if we can make it work. Also, there's a whole new area of space-time that we could, conceivably, explore if this works out."

Austin traced his finger over several of the symbols. "We haven't talked about whether these symbols are purely mathematical in nature or are, at least in part, a language."

Turner shrugged. "It's too early to tell, but my guess at this point is that it is probably the latter. We're just not able to work out the language part at this point." He gave out a rueful laugh. "Hell, we're barely able to work out the math side of it for now, although you'd hardly think of the results so far as progress."

Austin laughed as he said, "I guess this means I'll have to tell Curly Stephens that you're going to visit her space yard and ask her to build some more components that you're going to break. It's a good thing she knows how important this project is, considering the proprietary interest she takes in anything that comes from her yard."

CHAPTER EIGHT

Although the view of the landscape was breathtaking, framed as it was by the swirls of unblinking stars that stood out against the deep blackness of space, the people who moved across that landscape in their survival suits paid the broader scenery no heed. The surface was craggy and forbidding, revealing the violence of its formation and bearing the scars from the extreme existence it had endured for billions of years. They didn't actually walk on the surface; the ancient rock's microgravity environment lacked the strength to keep them from drifting into space. Instead, they drifted over the terrain, kept on track by the thrusters in their suits.

They approached a crater blasted into the jagged surface, its age unclear in the lifeless environment. One of the people held a small device that she aimed toward the terrain. After reading the display, she motioned to her companion to look at a spot in the crater that was covered in shadows in the uncertain light.

As they walked toward the spot, the readings on the display flashed rapidly as they became more insistent.

Once both of the people pulled out and activated their flashlights, they saw that the interior of the crater had a resident. Nestled among a series of fissures was an object, over three meters long and over one meter across, in a rough, vaguely cylindrical shape. One end of the object was partly lodged within the jagged fissures. There were obvious signs of exposure to heat seared onto its surface. Here and there, evidence of the heat gave way to what may have been the true colors of the object. There was a series of browns and blacks that seemed to absorb the light without revealing themselves fully.

The edges showed signs of damage, and it was difficult to get precise readings on its appearance. What was even more unsettling was the fact that portions of the surface looked like something organic had been scorched; it was as if they were looking at something from a burn victim.

If it hadn't been for the near lack of gravity on the asteroid, they would have had a hell of a time moving the object, even as small as it was. From the readings they were able to take, they learned that it was incredibly dense. That density had contributed to the crater being so significant and was probably why the object had survived the impact.

They sent a message to their ship with their coordinates, and in short order they saw the vessel as it made its approach in silence. The ship would never win any awards for a graceful appearance; it was an ore transport borrowed from one of the mining operations. That type of ship, with a large hatch and hold for taking on cargo, made it ideal for recovering something from the surface of an asteroid.

They deployed tools for cutting away the sharp spikes of rock that held the object of their search in place. While transporting the object in space wouldn't be a problem, they weren't sure it was wise to try to take it to Earth, especially since it hadn't been vetted for any microorganisms. No need to give the aliens another chance to wipe out humanity.

The two people in the room found the image on the display fascinating, although one of them complained about it. "Why can't we get a better picture of the artifact?" Harrington asked. "I have some antique night lights that give off more light than what we must be using on this thing."

"I doubt that," Flynn replied. "We have so much light focused on the artifact that people would be melting from the heat if it were coming from any of the old-style incandescent bulbs your antiques used."

Harrington pointed toward the display with excitement. "That looks like symbols of some kind!"

"Our people think so too," Flynn agreed. "They think they've finally found the starting point they need to understand how the aliens' language works."

"What is that artifact specifically? What do our people think was its function on the alien ship?"

"It's too early to know, although one of the team members has already identified symbols that may relate to the artifact's function. If that guess is right, then we may end up with the breakthrough we need for this project."

The excitement faded from Harrington's expression as she turned away from the display. "We still have a problem though."

Flynn nodded. "Porter and Raffles," he replied. "They're the only ones who haven't been vetted thoroughly."

"What are you doing about them?"

"For now, I have Porter continuing to review the data, to see if there is evidence of any other potential artifacts."

"Why bother?" Harrington asked dismissively. "Don't we already have what we need?"

"Yes and no. First of all, we don't know yet if this artifact will be what we need for our mission. More artifacts would give us an even better chance of understanding enough about the aliens to communicate with them. Porter found this artifact after others tried and failed, and that means he has real value to us. He's probably the best chance we have to find another artifact—if there's another one to be found."

"There's more, isn't there?" Harrington asked.

"Yes." Flynn nodded. "So long as Porter's focusing on the data, he isn't focusing on publishing his findings, which means we don't have to worry about what to do with him."

A look of feral understanding flashed across Harrington's face as she nodded. "OK, I get it where Porter's concerned. What about Raffles? From what you've told me, she doesn't add any value to our operations."

Flynn shook his head as he replied. "It isn't quite that simple. So long as we need Porter, we need to avoid distractions, such as having to explain her absence. Also, she might be of help in keeping Porter in line, by promising him things to keep him focused on doing what we want."

"What were you going to do about Raffles originally, before Porter came into the picture?"

It was Flynn's turn to speak in a dismissive tone. "She wouldn't have mattered much to anyone. With the data retrieved, no one would have believed any claims about her having calculated the possible locations of any artifacts. By the time anyone might have bothered to check out any of those locations, we'd have been there and recovered anything of interest."

Flynn had a rueful look on his face. "While I overestimated her technical skills, I didn't miscalculate what would happen to her reputation. We'd have made sure to leak information about the circumstances around the loss of her doctorate. With those leaks and no proof of her claims, she'd have looked foolish and been discredited, which her ego wouldn't have accepted." His expression returned to a more neutral look. "Besides, I think she understands that crossing me wouldn't be a smart thing to do."

"Does Porter understand that?"

"That would be another one of those distractions that we want to avoid for now."

Harrington nodded. "All right, you appear to have matters in hand. We'll come back to what to do about Porter and Raffles another time."

CHAPTER NINE

A man sat in a stark room that had only two utilitarian chairs and a table. His chair and the table were attached securely to the hard floor. Although the man's wrists were tethered to the arms of the chair, such treatment was not considered unusual at the United States Disciplinary Barracks, located at Fort Leavenworth. Despite a name that suggested a place for recalcitrant soldiers to drop and do some push-ups, the place was a high-security military prison, located near where similar prisons had stood for over a hundred years. Life in this prison was far tougher than in the medium-security military prisons that had been located in the area for well over two centuries.

Most of the men in this prison were former military officers; this man was no exception, having once held the rank of major. In the past, the tethers restraining the man would have been steel chains. Today, they were made of a synthetic material that was nearly impossible to cut or disable without specialized tools.

What was unusual was the fact that the man was receiving a visitor. Most of his existence was of a solitary nature; direct contact with outsiders was discouraged. It turned out that visitors weren't much of an issue anyway; in the course of his journey to this prison, he'd discovered how few friends he actually had.

Without any fanfare, a man entered the room and sat in the other chair. The prisoner noted that the other chair wasn't secured to the floor, which was a reminder of the loss of even small privileges. He didn't bother talking; the other man had arranged for the visit and would get around to telling him the reason when he was ready.

"Good morning, Mr. Wolfe. My name is Flynn. There is something we need to discuss."

"I don't know you," Wolfe replied. "It seems I don't know many people anymore."

"That's what happens when you refuse to disobey unlawful orders, especially when they are part of a broader series of war crimes, Mr. Wolfe," the man said without emotion. "Even your friends desert you." His expression remained neutral as he continued. "You haven't had a single visitor since you were incarcerated here following your court-martial. You never hear from your ex-wife directly; everything goes through her lawyer. Your son rarely writes to you, although you blame your ex-wife for that."

Wolfe nearly dislocated his wrists as unreasoning fury overwhelmed him, urging him to leap at his tormentor and place his hands around Flynn's neck. "How the hell do you know any of my business!" he shouted. "Why are you here?"

Flynn hadn't flinched at Wolfe's outburst. "As to how I know about your business, I make it a point to learn what I need to know about people with whom I want to do business."

"What business could you possibly have with me?" he asked bitterly. "You already know why I'm here and that I'm without friends. You don't need to remind me that no one bothers with me anymore. I know it better than anyone."

"Like many people, I know that as Major Wolfe, United States Army, you were ordered by National Security Director Bering to enter the Citadel embassy and take Ambassador Preacher into custody, along with various items present in the embassy. I know that Preacher and General Choi, former commanding officer of United States Space Command, testified against you at your court-martial. I know that although you received a long prison sentence, things could have turned out even worse for you than they did. You were damned lucky not to have been sent to Citadel for judgment. If you had been, you might have ended up hanging from the gallows."

Flynn paused in case Wolfe wanted to respond, but he remained silent.

"As it happens, one of the things you did is of interest to me."

Wolfe shifted in his chair slightly. "Which one?"

"The one when you removed some items from the Citadel embassy. I want to know some information relating to one of those items. The item in question is Citadel's alternate beacon."

"Why?" Wolfe asked with little interest. "We gave the beacon back to Citadel as part of the settlement, along with all of our files."

Flynn's tone was sardonic. "I learned a long time ago that technical people like to keep copies of important data hidden away, in case they ever need to make use of it later. For something as significant as Citadel's alternate beacon, there's no way someone wouldn't have kept something back. I want that information."

"Why come to me? I'm not a scientist. I don't have a clue how that thing works."

"No one is certain who Bering was using for all of his clandestine activities, and Bering isn't likely to come back from the grave to enlighten anyone. You were the one who turned it over to his scientists, so you know who would have it."

"What difference does it make now?"

"It may make a lot of difference to you if you cooperate with me," Flynn said.

"What do you mean?" Wolfe asked warily. "I'm stuck here for a long time."

"If you tell me what I want to know, I can provide significant funds to ensure that your son receives an excellent education, along with a better lifestyle than he has currently."

Wolfe held his breath for a moment before exhaling. "That sounds interesting, Flynn, but what's even more important to me is getting to communicate with him. Everything has to go through my ex-wife, and she's not exactly been supportive of her son staying in touch with a criminal."

"What if I were to provide another channel for your son to communicate with you, one that neither your ex-wife nor her attorney would know about?"

"What if I wanted to fly to the moon?" Wolfe scoffed. "I'd have about the same chance of doing that as talking with my son."

"You don't know me, so I'll overlook the sarcasm this time, but don't question whether I can do what I say I can do," Flynn warned.

"You haven't said you can do anything yet," Wolfe replied. "You've just asked some questions."

Flynn nodded. "Fair enough. All right, if you tell me the name and location of the person who received that beacon, I will provide the funds for your son that I mentioned, and I will also arrange for a separate means for you and your son to communicate with each other.

"There are a couple of conditions. The first is that I won't guarantee that your son will have the willingness to take advantage of the resources that I make available to him; that will be up to you and him to figure out. The second is that while I can set up a private means of communication between you and your son, I can't prevent him from telling others about it, including your ex-wife."

"You have a deal." Wolfe's expression showed his distrust of Flynn. "You'll forgive me if I don't give you the name now and take your word for it that you'll do what you say. Show me that everything is in place, in a way that can't be reversed, and I'll give you the name you want."

A look of warning crossed Flynn's face. "I understand that I need to do my part first. There's something you'd better keep in mind though. If you steer me in the wrong direction, I'll know it. While I might not be able to reverse the financial arrangements, I can and will make sure your ex-wife and her attorney know about any private means of communication between you and your son. Once warned, they'll make sure nothing like that will ever happen again.

"However, that won't be the end of it." Flynn looked around the room with a gaze as hard as the concrete walls. "Interestingly, people in prison, especially a maximum-security prison, often develop a sense of isolation from the outside world and think nothing that happens on the outside affects them while in prison. In fact, they sometimes come to think they are untouchable, at least as far as the outside world is concerned. While that may be mostly true in your case, it won't stop me from getting to you and making sure your sentence is shortened permanently, but in a way you won't like."

Flynn read the challenge in Wolfe's gaze. "Don't make the mistake of thinking what happens will be by my own hand. That would be too easy; you might even be able to be on your guard against something like that. The reality is that after today, you'll never see me again. Even here, though, there are people who can be persuaded to do things. Think about it. I've already arranged for an unscheduled visit, which is almost never approved." He nodded at the camera in the corner. "The surveillance has been disabled, and my visit will never show up in any database or log. If I wanted to do something to you, I could."

"What makes you think I wouldn't turn you over to the authorities?"

"Would that be the same authorities who have placed you here to rot for an extended period?" Flynn asked bluntly. "Besides, you'd only incriminate yourself further if you admitted to having withheld any information relating to the beacon. Citadel was adamant about wanting everything back, and President Lee doesn't want the headache of dealing with any more demands from Citadel."

"I can still make arrangements with my attorney to act if I die, Flynn."

"No one knows a damned thing about me under that name, so go ahead, if it'll make you feel better," Flynn replied. "Just be sure you give me the correct name. After that, I really don't care if you rot in this place for the rest of your life."

"You still haven't told me why you want the information," Wolfe persisted. "As you've pointed out, I'm not going anywhere."

Flynn thought about it for a moment. "You don't need to know the full answer, Wolfe, but, for what it's worth, giving me this information might serve to settle the score with Sam Austin, at least a little."

Without another word, Flynn stood up and left the room. Since Wolfe couldn't rise and follow him out, he had a moment to himself. He mused over Flynn's implications. If a score with Austin would be settled, perhaps he hadn't lost everything after all.

CHAPTER TEN

"We think these symbols are the key," Dr. Farmer said as she pointed at several images on a display. "While it would be nice to have an alien version of a Rosetta Stone, we can't complain about our progress. It was a stroke of luck that the artifact came from their communications system, as several of our assumptions have been guided by the apparent function of the artifact itself. In some ways, the symbols have served as a kind of primer." Farmer made a small sound.

"Why the sigh?" Flynn asked. "I'd think this is perhaps the most exciting time ever for you, at least professionally."

"It is, of course," Farmer replied with a small smile. "I mentioned the Rosetta Stone a moment ago, and in some ways, this may be the most significant scholarly activity relating to recovering a language in over three centuries. As a key scholar involved with this project, I'm delighted to be doing what I've trained much of my life to do. However, being a scholar only goes so far, considering the stakes involved. While the world never had to worry about the return of the ancient Egyptians, we don't have the same luxury when it comes to the possible return of the aliens that made this artifact."

She rubbed her hand over her eyes as she continued. "We had approached this project originally with the notion of actually making contact with the aliens at some point. The problem is that our attempts to communicate beyond this solar system differ little from what we did a hundred years ago, and there are huge limitations with that approach. While Citadel has some significant advantages over us in that regard, they aren't likely to share those advantages anytime soon. I wish there were some way to make that artifact function, so we could know whether our efforts are even on the right track. Otherwise, this will just remain an intensely interesting scholarly endeavor."

Flynn walked over to a display and brought up an image. "I'd say this will make the project something more than a scholarly endeavor, wouldn't you agree?"

Farmer stared at the image, speechless with surprise. As her shock wore off, she began to see the possibilities.

"It's been over three months since our people started looking at the artifact," Harrington said by way of a greeting. "Tell me you have good news."

Flynn ignored the tone as he replied, "I do have good news." He brought up some images on a display. "Our people have had some breakthroughs in interpreting the symbols on the artifact. It seems the artifact itself was part of the alien communication system, and some of the symbols gave us a starting point in working out their language, at least in written form."

"Does that mean we can communicate with them?" Harrington asked, not bothering to disguise the anticipation on her face.

"Our people believe they know enough about the written language to be able to convey some basic concepts with a fair degree of reliability. More complex concepts may be more difficult to work out."

"You mentioned that the artifact was part of their communication system. Can we use it to contact them?

Flynn shook his head. "The artifact is useless for that purpose, Ms. Harrington." He brought up multiple close-ups. "What we can review doesn't look anything like what we would regard as circuitry, and it was devastated by the destruction or the impact with the asteroid. We can't begin to understand the technology well enough to do anything with it."

"I don't understand," Harrington said in a disappointed tone. "If we can't use the artifact, why do you consider this good news?"

Flynn brought up another image and said, "With this, many things are possible."

"What is that?" Harrington asked. "It doesn't look like an artifact. It looks like something from our own solar system."

Flynn nodded. "That's just where it came from. In fact, it's straight from the Citadel Group. It's the alternate beacon that your people once used to keep track of communications with the Citadel star system."

"What good does that do us? Citadel controls all of their communications between the two systems, and we don't have the encryption keys." Harrington's tone was slightly bitter. "While we could listen to their messages from Citadel, we couldn't send any of our own back to them. It would have worked out vastly differently for us if we'd been able to plant false messages in Austin's in-box."

"What if we send a message but not to anyone at Citadel?"

"No one else lives there," she said impatiently.

"Maybe not, but there's another possible destination for communications from this system."

"I'm listening."

Flynn pulled up an image of Citadel and numerous other installations. "They now have in place an extensive network for keeping tabs on the area around their system for quite a distance. Our people have reviewed what your people learned about the alternate beacon and believe that we can send messages to the network itself, for broadcast into deep space."

The enthusiasm returned to Harrington's face as she said, "Are you saying we can send messages to the aliens directly, right under Austin's nose, using his own network?"

"In theory, yes." Flynn nodded. "Not only that, but we can also receive messages coming back to us through the same network."

Harrington was skeptical. "How can we get access to that beacon? Didn't Citadel cut off that access a long time ago?"

Flynn brought back the image of the beacon, zooming in on a section. "There's another channel available on that beacon that they didn't bother with, since messages wouldn't really go anywhere. Your people learned how to gain access to that channel when they brought it online. Our people have opened up a link to it and determined that it is still active."

"When can we test everything?"

"That depends on what we want to say. We can probably generate a basic greeting, which we hope will attract the aliens' attention."

"Why do you say 'we hope'?" Harrington asked with a frown. "A moment ago, it sounded like you were sure we could do it."

"Two reasons, Ms. Harrington. The first is that we can't be sure about the extent to which we really understand their language, even at a basic level, until we try. Our people believe it to be a complex language, guided in places by mathematical concepts."

"What's the other reason?"

Flynn brought up an image showing a vast region around the Citadel system. "We aren't sure the aliens are even within range to detect any signals. For all we know, they've abandoned the place to the people on Citadel."

"I hope not," Harrington said with some heat.

"You're probably the only human in two solar systems to feel that way," Flynn said with a wry expression.

"I have more to lose than most people in two solar systems," Harrington replied. "I'm playing for the highest stakes possible, and I'm under no illusions regarding what happens if I fail." Harrington walked to the display and brought up a familiar image she regarded with distaste. "Speaking of failure, one way for everything to blow up in our faces is for Austin to find out what we're doing. Even if we're successful, how do we know that his people won't detect any reply from the aliens?"

Flynn brought up some images of the alien symbols and pointed to them. "One of the benefits of a language that is based in part on mathematical concepts is that we can provide instructions on how to generate the reply, including the frequency and access codes for the beacon. We'll also provide information on how to mask the signal, so that it will appear to be connected with natural phenomena, which will be ignored." Flynn shrugged. "There's still a good chance that we're wrong, and everything will be broadcast throughout both solar systems, so you'll need to decide whether the risk is worth it." He looked at Harrington with his usual neutral expression.

Harrington's tone was malicious as she replied, "I'm tired of being cooped up here, never really free. Austin keeps hammering that weakling Lee over my fate, and one day, he'll probably get what he wants. I want a chance to get free on my own terms, which include sticking it to Austin if possible. The aliens are my best chance to get what I want."

"What about what it means for our solar system? We know what the aliens can do, and they aren't shy about doing it."

A gleeful look appeared on her face. "We'll just have to give them a good enough reason to leave us alone. Fortunately, I can think of a great one."

CHAPTER ELEVEN

Flynn didn't spend any time on pleasantries as he entered the room. "Tell me why I'm here, Dr. Farmer," he said.

Farmer couldn't conceal her excitement as she answered. "As you know, a little over two months ago, we sent our first attempt at a message to the deep-space sensor network in the Citadel system."

"What's been the response from Citadel? Do we have any reason to believe they are aware of our activities?"

Farmer shook her head. "There hasn't been any noise from them at all."

"Couldn't they have just shut our message down once it arrived in their system?"

Farmer moved to a display and brought up an image. "If they'd done that, then this wouldn't have arrived today." Flynn took a closer look at symbols from no language he'd ever seen.

"I take it these aren't the same symbols we sent out originally," he said.

Farmer shook her head. "No. Although there are some symbols that are similar to what we sent out, this is a new message, with symbols we haven't seen before. Our assumption is that we now have the first communication between our species and the aliens."

"Any guesses as to what the message says?"

Farmer shrugged. "That's what we're already trying to work out. It's extremely encouraging that our message was recognized at all for what it was."

Flynn's expression was cautious. "Is there any possibility that the aliens tapped into the network from a different location and are actually near our solar system?"

Farmer brought another image up. "We have confirmation that our message was broadcast from these deep-space locations and that it was from one of those locations that the reply was received, all according to our instructions. Besides, the timing of the reply isn't consistent with a message that originated from our own system."

"Good." Flynn nodded. "If anything blows up on us, I'd rather they be far enough away that we'd at least have some warning before they show up. When do you expect to have the message translated?"

"We're probably looking at several weeks, perhaps longer. Keep in mind that we may not be able to come up with a precise understanding of their message," she warned. "There may be some concepts that just don't translate into our view of things and vice versa."

Six weeks later, Flynn was back, reviewing the team's translation. "The message is entirely visual, in the form of symbols," Farmer began. "There is no attempt at including any information in audio form. Some of it is still unclear, but we think we understand the key parts."

"What do the aliens have to say?" he asked.

She rolled her eyes slightly. "The first thing is that they're surprised that we even have the ability to understand how to communicate with them. Although they acknowledge that we have some understanding of technology more advanced than stone knives, they view humans as being inferior. In fact, that view is so ingrained in their thinking that they don't even seem to consider that we might be offended by their sharing that view with us."

"What else do they have to say?" Flynn asked.

"They view all humans, in both solar systems, as little more than vermin to be removed from those systems."

"Why? Do they want to colonize our systems?"

Farmer shrugged. "It isn't clear what they want to do."

"Why did they attack us in the first place? We didn't offer them any reason to view us as enemies."

"If it is possible to get a feel for the tenor of their message from the symbols used, it is that they don't feel that they have to explain themselves to us," Farmer answered in an exasperated tone. "If they want to do something, then that seems to be justification by itself."

"Clearly, they're willing to communicate with us," Flynn persisted, "so they must be prepared to offer some kind of explanation."

"It isn't so much being prepared to offer an explanation as it is to let us know what they want," Farmer replied.

"I thought we'd get to that," Flynn said knowingly. "Self-interest is usually the answer. What do they want?"

"They want us to surrender ourselves to them for eradication. That seems to be the least we can do, considering that we're inferior beings," she replied sardonically.

"Seriously? It isn't an attempt at interstellar humor?"

She shook her head. "One thing that's clear from reviewing their message is that they have no notion of humor, at least not in any way that we understand the concept. They might not even understand irony."

"What else did they say?"

"There wasn't much else to the message. They don't seem interested in talking with us."

Flynn thought for a moment and then brought up a familiar image. "I'll bet this will get their attention. Can you figure out a way to describe it to them?"

Farmer's brow furrowed. "The derelict? What made you think of that?"

"They invaded Citadel because they wanted it. They even sent ships to pursue Austin's ships when they recaptured the derelict from the aliens. Perhaps they're still interested in it."

"Isn't that risky?" Farmer asked in alarm. "For one thing, we don't even have control over that ship, and for two, lives have already been lost over it. Under the circumstances, people might wonder why we'd be discussing the derelict with the aliens."

Flynn's tone was conciliatory. "We're not trying to do anything at this point, Dr. Farmer, except maintain a dialogue with them. You already mentioned that they don't seem that interested in communicating with us. We just need something that will keep the dialogue going. Who knows? We might be able to come up with something that actually brings Citadel and the United States closer together, while putting us on better terms with the aliens. We can agree that that would be good for everyone."

"I suppose that makes sense," Farmer admitted.

"Sure, it does. Speaking of dialogue, is there anything they've asked us?"

"While they understand that translation time will be needed for messages, especially on our side, they seem to be confused by our telling them how long it would take for us to receive their message and send a reply."

Flynn was puzzled. "Why would that be confusing to them? We explained that we're piggybacking on Citadel's network." A look of understanding flashed across his face. "They don't understand that the populations in the two solar systems aren't part of the same group. They probably assume that all humans speak as one. That's most likely the way they think." His expression turned sly. "We'll work out in more detail what needs to go into our response, but we'll need to explain some things about humans, including the fact that we live separately from each other and don't necessarily speak for each other. We can emphasize that very much applies to the humans in this solar system and in the Citadel system. I don't know if the concept of 'enemies' exists in their language, but maybe we can make the point that we aren't friends."

"Why would we do that?" Farmer asked. "That might suggest to the aliens that they can do some dividing and conquering to get what they want. That certainly isn't the case with respect to Citadel and Mars or even most of Earth. While I get it that things aren't going smoothly between Citadel and the United States these days, we need to be careful to avoid undermining them where the aliens are concerned. Austin and his people are still the only ones with the means and the will to defend humans against aliens. I'd want to think long and hard about doing anything that could call that fact into question."

"Those are fair points," Flynn admitted, "but we have to have an explanation for the delay that makes sense. Get working on the response immediately."

"We definitely have their attention," Farmer reported. "They want us to turn over the derelict to them." She snorted. "While they don't understand humor, they definitely understand anger. They're clearly angry with us for resisting when they tried to take the derelict, and for following them and fighting them to recover it and keep it where they can't get at it."

"Why do they want it?" Flynn asked. "Is there some special technology in it they want? Or is it from their race and they just want to reclaim a part of their ancestral heritage?"

"Those are questions we'll have to pose to them in another message," she replied.

"That brings us to another thing that we'll want to address in our response," Flynn said. "They've told us what they want. Now it's our turn to tell them what we want. What are they willing to give us for the derelict? For example, we can point out that their warp-field generators are even more advanced than ours. Get started on the response, Dr. Farmer. I'll consult with our benefactor and let you know if there is anything else to cover in our reply." Flynn barely waited for an acknowledgment from Farmer before he started walking toward the door.

"The aliens understand the concept of a deal," Farmer reported in a subdued tone that Flynn wasn't sure what to make of.

"Tell me about it, Dr. Farmer."

"They are willing to give us their technology relating to their warp-field generators. They claim that it is self-installing and vastly easier to use than the Citadel technology."

"I take it they want the derelict in return for providing us with this technology?"

"Not quite, Mr. Flynn," Farmer replied uneasily. "While they definitely want that ship, there's something else they want too."

"What the hell else could be of value to them if they have the derelict?" Flynn asked. "The technology in that thing must be worth far more than anything."

"There are different kinds of value. It appears that humans are of value to them," Farmer said. "Our efforts to explain humans and the dynamics of human groups keep leading to additional questions on their part that we either haven't been able to understand well enough to answer or that don't translate clearly enough into their language to make sense. Instead of giving up on the subject, their curiosity has been piqued. They feel that the only way they can have their questions answered is to have some humans to examine for themselves."

Now Flynn was uneasy. "What does that mean, 'examine'? Conduct some kind of face-to-face interview?"

"'Examine' is one interpretation of what they mean. It appears that they examine things by taking them apart. It isn't clear if this is a metaphorical reference or a literal description of what they want to do."

A look of concern was in the gaze that she directed at Flynn. "Remember, this dialogue hasn't changed their basic attitudes toward humans. We are still no more significant to them than a minor creature that might wash up on a shore, assuming that such a creature might have technology. We should keep in mind how humans go about examining lower animals that we wish to study. Even in this day of advanced analytical technology, we still sometimes dissect them and analyze individual systems to understand how they function."

Flynn had arranged many deals in his time and wasn't ready to worry about a potential misunderstanding over a bargaining point. "I'll check with our benefactor, but I assume that this is a negotiation and we can provide a counterproposal, one that doesn't include handing humans over to them. Perhaps we can even get a better deal on the technology in exchange for the derelict. Get started on a response along those lines, and I'll fill you in on what else we'll want in addition to the warp-field generator technology. For example, their EMP weapon is impressive, as is what appears to be an organic approach to the construction and operation of their ships."

CHAPTER TWELVE

Yabuno and Turner walked Sam through the latest round of tests for the new approach to the warp-field generators. Yabuno brought up a new set of images on the display, saying, "Here's what happened the last time we did some trials."

A vessel appeared, surrounded by the deep blackness of space sprinkled with stars. People familiar with the patterns of stars surrounding Citadel would know that the location of the test was nearly opposite to the side of the solar system with the entrance to the radiation field, beyond the planets.

As the generators came online, the image of the vessel began to distort. Unlike previous tests, where tendrils of space-time seemed to reach out in multiple directions, it looked like the ship was being pulled in several directions, as if the bubble were competing for control over the direction in which the ship would travel.

The image of the ship seemed to move in and out of space-time. At no point did the ship vanish completely, although there were times when they seemed to be looking at a ghostly outline. Once the generators went off-line, the image stabilized. The ship looked no different than it did before the test.

Austin had a bemused look on his face. "At least this time, we didn't have to duck or pick up any pieces. Bret, tell me what happened."

Yabuno stepped up to the display and chuckled. "While there're obviously still major issues to address, it looks like a different kind of hundred-year-old science fiction from that of the first time. We're at least doing better with respect to maintaining the stability of the warp bubble itself. That means that while there aren't any more 'arms' reaching out to grab everything in sight while the ship stays still, there are forces trying to pull the ship in more than one direction while it's in the warp bubble. Unfortunately, that means we're still stuck with a warp bubble that doesn't seem to know what to do with anything in it."

"What's the risk to any ship in the middle of the bubble?" Austin asked.

Turner moved toward the display and brought up several new images. "Take a look," he invited.

They had a closer view of the ship, which had been used originally to transport ore. The ship looked less like a ship than a poorly illuminated version of the ship. They watched as the vessel seemed to move around within bubble. "If that were a boxer, I'd say it was bobbing and weaving," Austin murmured. "How is it we can even see what's happening inside the bubble?"

"That's one of the problems we haven't worked out," Turner replied. "With this approach, if everything were working properly, we shouldn't be able to see it directly at all. We see what's happening because the ship is drifting in and out of normal space-time, moving in one direction and then another, thanks to the stability problems we've been having. Because of these uneven influences, the ship can't stay on a particular 'course.'"

"What damage has the ship experienced?" Austin asked. "Is it safe for anyone to be aboard it during a test?"

"The stresses weren't great enough to do any damage, although we can't be certain what would happen if the ship were flung around more forcefully," Yabuno answered. "If we try to ramp up the power in order to form a more useful bubble, we're probably going to have more problems.

"One of the benefits of using that type of cargo ship is that it is similar in size to our interstellar transports. That means if we can solve the problem with the warp bubbles using these cargo ships, we can probably adapt the solution to the transports."

He looked back at the image. "Getting back to your question about whether anyone should be aboard during a test, I don't think I'd want to be aboard it until we've solved the drifting problem. If the ship ended up being ripped apart, I'd rather watch the images on a display than participate in being filleted or compacted. For now, we'd better stay with tests that are remote controlled and remote programmed.

CHAPTER THIRTEEN

"This has taken longer than we thought," Harrington said wearily. "I didn't think we'd ever get them to understand what we wanted. How can beings so smart also be so stupid?"

"Some concepts are difficult to convey, especially in a language we barely understand," Flynn said, the weariness plain on his face as well. "Besides, we already know they don't have a particularly high opinion of our intelligence."

"I don't really care what they think of us, so long as they understand what's at stake for both sides."

"They understand well enough what they're getting out of the deal," Flynn said, pulling up an image of the ancient derelict ship that was sitting in a space yard in the Citadel system. "If we've understood their communications, they've been on something like a holy mission to find that ship for hundreds, perhaps even thousands, of years." Flynn continued in a sardonic tone. "We sure as hell got their attention once we found a way to describe it to them." His expression looked troubled as he said, "What I didn't expect is what else they wanted."

"We brought that on ourselves by trying to describe humans," Harrington said. "We didn't realize that by failing at getting them to understand humans in physical, mental, and social terms, we would pique their curiosity enough that they would want to figure us out for themselves."

"We need to work out how we're going to pay the price they've demanded if we want to close the deal with them," Flynn said.

"That reminds me," Harrington replied, "where do we stand on what our people understand about this project?"

"They still believe that we are trying to come up with a long-term, peaceful solution to the conflict with the aliens. Not surprisingly, their egos have been boosted over the possibility of being a key part of the effort. The money doesn't hurt either," Flynn added with a smile.

"What about Porter and Raffles? What do they think about what we're doing?"

"Porter, like the others, has been lulled by the impact his work is having on finding a peaceful solution. He's become emotionally invested in the project, to the point that he's willing to hold off on publishing his results until he can do it in tandem with our announcing our break-through deal with the aliens."

"What about Raffles? She doesn't have the same principles as Porter, so what's her value to us?"

Flynn brought up an image of Porter and replied, "Her connection with Porter is her value. She's morally challenged and a weasel; plus, she can be intimidated. I've paid the bonus I promised and dangled the prospect of additional money once the project has been concluded. I didn't have to spell out that it all depends on her ability to keep Porter in line. So far, she's been worth the money," Flynn concluded, his expression showing a hint of contempt.

"Our people know about the aliens' demands regarding satisfying their curiosity," Harrington said. "How can we maintain their cooperation and still proceed with the deal?"

"For one thing, we'll let our people know that we would never actually go ahead with that part of the arrangement; we're sure the aliens will honor the arrangement anyway, once they have what they really want, which is the derelict. The people don't need to know what we really intend to do."

"That brings us to the question of who to use for that part of the arrangement," Harrington said with an unpleasant look.

"You have someone in mind." It wasn't a question.

"I know who I'd like to use, but I don't think he's the best choice," she explained.

"Good to know you're being realistic," Flynn said. "It would be hard to get close enough to Austin anyway. He's demonstrated in the past that he's a hard man to kill, and he's on his home turf."

A feral look flashed through her gaze as she said, "It isn't the problem with getting close enough to capture him that's the issue. He's already shown he's willing to sacrifice himself for a noble cause, so giving him another noble cause to die for wouldn't mean anything. I want him to suffer in worst way possible, and he suffers the most when people who are important to him suffer."

"There are plenty of people to choose from. We could start with people on Earth," Flynn suggested.

Harrington shook her head. "I've received word from my lawyers that my case may finally be showing signs of life again. The problem is that it isn't moving in the direction I wanted, so I'm going to have to disappear. That means I can't move against people on Earth; the disappearance or death of anyone with a connection to me will naturally draw unwanted attention if it happens at the same as I disappear. It'll take time to go where we're going, and the last thing we want is for people to start looking for me where we don't want them to look. If I just vanish without a trace and life seems to go on for everyone else, people will assume that I've found a really good hiding place somewhere in the neighborhood and keep looking for me here.

"Too bad," she mused. "I'd really love to stick it to that old fox J. W. Preacher. He's made more than one speech vilifying me, and it appears the courts are finally starting to listen to him. However, there are others close to Austin that will do nicely." Her face brightened at the thought. She walked over to the display and brought up a familiar image. "Considering where we're going and what we want to do, it's time to bring her out of retirement. I assume you know where to find her."

"Yes." Flynn nodded. "She's been enjoying a quiet life since her last assignment and thinks no one knows where she is. She may not want to become active again," he warned.

Harrington scoffed. "She'll become active again, or she'll find her quiet life a thing of the past. I have access to files that she wouldn't want made public, including some interesting information concerning her part in trying to take out Austin. If I release those files, there will be plenty of people wanting a piece of her, including Austin; she'll never have another moment's peace."

"She's set up multiple false identities, and there are rumors she's changed her appearance," Flynn said, "so telling people about her past might not work for us. There are no images of her since her 'retirement.'"

"That can change. Money talks, as you've pointed out more than once," she noted. "However, I'm willing to give her a chance to come around on her own. She may even decide she has a personal reason for joining with us. But make sure she comes aboard," she warned. "We have far too much at stake for her to think she has any choice in the matter."

Flynn's expression never changed as he nodded and left.

CHAPTER FOURTEEN

R affles wasn't surprised to find Porter in a quiet corner in the lab; he often went there when he wanted to take a break from his work. They'd all been excited by the initial news that contact with the aliens had been successful and a dialogue had been established. However, as more information about the dialogue circulated, Porter found his excitement had begun to be replaced by something else.

"Hi, Gerry," Raffles said. "I thought I'd find you here. What do you think about the latest news about the aliens? They're finally talking to us."

"Yes," Porter said without much enthusiasm. "We have their attention because there's something they want."

"Isn't that a good thing? They want something, and there're things we want. Maybe we can make a deal that will finally give us lasting peace."

"Maybe, but what about what they want? For starters, they want the derelict! They've already killed plenty of people trying to get it. Aren't those lives worth anything?"

"Sure, but that has more to do with Citadel than with us," Raffles replied casually. "They never attacked us directly to get it."

"That's probably only because the derelict wasn't here," Porter said sharply. "Besides, they nearly destroyed Earth after their initial contact with Citadel. That didn't have anything to do with us, but they went ahead and did it. Even before attacking us, they nearly destroyed Mars, and Mars didn't have anything to do with it either. Austin and Citadel are the only reasons we're still around; we owe them something for that."

"I get it, Gerry," she said soothingly. "However, we don't know anything about the derelict. For all we know, that ship belongs to them, or at least their ancestors, anyway. That would give them the right to it."

Porter shook his head. "Citadel doesn't think so. They think it came from another race, which makes sense. If that ship really belonged to the aliens, then they would already know how it works and how to build more of them. They don't seem to know anything about it."

"Perhaps the ship has some special significance for them," Raffles suggested, "such as a religious one, which makes it a crime for someone else to even be near it. Some humans can be pretty touchy when it comes to religious relics."

"Perhaps," Porter admitted grudgingly. "However, they haven't explained it in those terms."

"They might not want to discuss their religion with us."

"That's possible, but that seems to be a pretty dangerous prize to consider giving up, all things considered.

Besides, we don't seem to be pushing them very hard to get the best deal possible. Instead, we're willing to play along with them about giving them humans. How can we possibly consider doing that?" Porter asked in an alarmed tone.

"We're still not sure what they really mean by their request to examine humans," Raffles said. "We're just guessing that the word is 'examine,' and not something more like 'interview' or 'comprehend.' For all we know, they may have a more effective means of communications that only works at close distance."

"For all we know, they may just regard us as low level creatures to be studied and dissected," Porter shot back. "I'm not sure the problem has always been one of interpretation; it may be that there are some things they understand that they don't want us to understand."

"Regardless of the reason, Flynn has assured us that we won't actually make any people available." She shrugged. "While it is somewhat dishonest, we'll just tell them the people will be turned over last, and we'll start with the exchange of the derelict for the new technology. When that is completed, we won't go any further."

"What do we do if they insist on our honoring the agreement by threatening a new attack if we don't comply? What then? Would we ask for volunteers or just have everyone draw lots?"

Raffles didn't want to worry about such things. "The ship is the main thing, and they'll just have to accept that when they're getting something that's truly priceless, they don't need anything more."

"Funny you should say it that way," Porter said. "I get it that their warp-field-generator technology would be amazing to have, but it kind of pales in comparison to having the derelict. It seems to me that we could get a much better deal if we wanted. If I didn't know better, I'd say we were looking to make a deal so that we can get something valuable, rather than so we can ensure a lasting peace. What I don't understand is why that's so important."

"Look on the bright side, Gerry," Raffles said in one of her calculated sincere tones. "Whatever happens, it will be something that won't affect us. It might not even take place in our solar system, except in the form of the technology delivered to us. The hard part will probably take place far from here, and that will be Flynn's problem to deal with."

CHAPTER FIFTEEN

The view of the ocean was stunning. The waves seemed to pound the sand with irresistible force, only to peter out at the last moment and fall back into the ocean with foamy streaks of green containing pieces of driftwood. The cliffs too were magnificent, with dark granite ramparts bursting out of the sand, reaching over two hundred feet toward the deep-blue sky. The walls of the cliffs had visitors, mostly birds whose nests were nearly invisible among the many fissures that creased the surface.

The beach was popular with visitors who were ready to embrace the sun and the warm rays that toasted the sand, which was tempered by a gentle, cool breeze. Most people stretched out on the sand at a distance from the cliffs that allowed them to appreciate the rugged beauty of the outcroppings when they weren't focusing on the ocean. Each instant saw a change to the sunlight dancing along the ocean's surface, interrupted at times by birds drifting lazily through the sky.

One woman chose to be different, having stretched out on a reclining beach chair practically touching the base of the cliffs. Other than a wide-brimmed hat and dark sunglasses, she wore nothing. The lack of clothes wasn't remarkable, as most people never bothered with a swimsuit at the beach. What was more remarkable was the fact that her smooth, pale skin seemed not to be affected by the sun's rays.

The woman had a perfect view of the beach, although it was hard to tell if she was even awake. Eventually, she showed signs of life as a man walked toward her in a slow, easy stride. Like the rest of the beachgoers, he was carrying a beach bag and wore nothing. Her head titled slightly as if to acknowledge the man's approach. When the man was still thirty feet away, she reached into her beach bag and spoke calmly. "Drop your beach bag and come up here, where we can talk without being disturbed."

Without a word, the man dropped his bag and continued on toward the woman. His body language indicated that he was somewhat ill at ease.

The woman had a sardonic twist to her mouth as she said, "I wouldn't have thought you to be concerned about modesty, Flynn." She took off her sunglasses, and she did a quick assessment that made it clear that any concerns were unfounded.

Flynn shrugged. "It isn't modesty that concerns me, Powers. I never travel anywhere without a weapon nearby."

"Interesting to know that's what makes you feel naked." She waved around with one hand as she continued. "Anyway, I don't like to take unnecessary chances.

This location allows me to keep track of everyone from a long way off. The dress code makes it a lot harder for someone to bring a weapon, or anything else, around."

Flynn looked up and said, "Also, the cliff has a nice overhang that makes it damned near impossible for anyone to see you from above, let alone make a move on you. I assume that having me leave my bag back there means you're the only one with easy access to a weapon, should any problems arise."

A look of approval crossed his features as he paused and looked at her. "The change to your face is amazing, Powers. I know it's you since I know what to look for, but anyone else would have walked right past you without a second glance." He gave the rest of her body a professional scan as he continued. "I believe you've had a few things done elsewhere as well."

Powers nodded. "You've done your homework. The fact that you even found me is impressive. Tell me why we're here."

"First of all, we need someone with special skills when it comes to infiltrating operations and capturing people, someone who isn't squeamish when it comes to nasty situations."

"I'm not the only one with those skills," she replied.

"No, you're not," Flynn agreed. "However, I know your reputation, and you might find this opportunity interesting."

"Money is the most interesting thing about any assignment," she noted. "After money, the next most interesting thing is whether I believe I can pull it off and survive in one piece."

Flynn scanned her again as he replied, "From what I can see, you've managed to keep everything in one piece just fine."

She ignored the comment. "Someone else can worry about vengeance or becoming a martyr, but I have enough money to stay comfortable for quite a while. Why are you interested in me for this?"

"You're one of the few people in this solar system outside of the Citadel Group who has detailed knowledge of the operations of a Keith Thomas–class transport. We need someone to help us take one on a journey."

"Having detailed knowledge of a ship's operations isn't the same as being able to run it, especially by myself," she warned. "You'd still need a captain and a crew."

"You could help us round them up and then watch them, to make sure they don't do anything we don't want them to do."

"I'm not going anywhere near a Citadel ship," Powers scoffed. "Unlike some people, Sam Austin isn't shy about stretching the necks of the people who cross him. My name is probably near the top of his list for that honor."

"Probably right below Harrington's name, I'd guess," Flynn replied in agreement. "You're one of the few people from Harrington's War to have eluded him. You've done even better than Harrington in that regard, since she's under house arrest and Austin doesn't know where you are."

"That better not change," she warned, "or I'll save him the trouble of going after certain people."

He ignored the threat. "You still haven't heard the best part." He paused for a moment, but Powers only allowed a faint look of interest to show on her face. He shrugged and continued. "In addition to your usual fee, one of the people you get to capture is Liz Austin. Another is Sara Albretti."

Powers's eyes finally gleamed with interest.

"The value of Liz Austin is obvious," he said. "In addition, as I recall, Captain Albretti managed to disrupt your efforts to work with Roetter and kill Austin. She was the first one to figure out that Major Roetter's accomplice was a woman."

The look on Powers's face turned lethal as she replied, "That bitch pointed out Roetter to her husband, who gutted him like a fish."

"Don't tell me you actually had feelings for your lover," Flynn said with a hint of sarcasm.

"He wasn't my lover, and I didn't give a damn about him," she practically hissed. "He was just a means to an end. Unfortunately, because of his carelessness, I had to haul ass out of there when she spotted that hair on his clothes. I was damned lucky to get to Mars without being caught. Of course, once I got to Mars, getting off had nothing to do with luck and everything to do with my own resources," she concluded smugly. The woman gave a cold smile as she said, "OK, Flynn, you've got me interested. Write down the right number, and we'll talk again."

As he picked up a stick and scratched a figure in the sand, he said, "I'm not going to insult you by haggling, Powers."

She nodded when she saw the figure and said, "That's the right number." She finally pulled her hand out of her bag as she rose. "We'll talk again once my bank account has been increased accordingly."

After a few swift, efficient moves, she had covered herself with a dress and was walking away from the beach, bag in hand. Flynn watched her for a while as he blotted out the figure in the sand with his foot. He put on a pair of shorts and a shirt from his bag and walked away from the beach in a different direction, his weapon once again close to him.

Powers never looked back.

CHAPTER SIXTEEN

In the years since Austin had first arrived on Citadel, he'd made various improvements to the buildings on his property, including expanding his house to accommodate his family. Yabuno and Turner found themselves appreciating Austin's expansion plans, which included his study where the three of them were currently. They were sitting in comfortable chairs, discussing the latest results from their efforts to translate the derelict symbol into another step forward with their technology.

Austin brought the main display online. "As I recall, you were challenged by trying to keep the warp-field bubbles stabilized enough that the ship inside wouldn't 'bounce' around in multiple directions. We hadn't yet conducted any trials at the higher energy levels that would be needed to maintain control." He grinned. "Since I haven't heard cries of 'eureka' bouncing off the mountains, I don't expect that all of the problems have been solved. It wouldn't surprise me if the journey to date has been entertaining though."

They turned to the display. Austin noted that the usual deep blackness of space was interrupted by spectacular swaths of color, with countless stars mottling the overall effect. From these images, he knew that they were watching a nebula, evidence of the death throes of a distant star; they also told him that a different location just outside their star system had been selected for these tests.

It was impossible to get a feel for the size of the vessel, as the image lacked anything to use for comparison. They only knew it was large because it was another cargo ship. For safety reasons, no one was aboard; everything was preprogrammed.

The by-now-familiar images of a distorted vessel were a signal that the generators had come online. Unlike previous tests, where the ship looked like it was being pulled in several directions, the image appeared stable.

Austin spoke. "I take it you've worked out how to keep things stable when the warp bubble is only of limited usefulness?"

"That's right." Yabuno nodded. "Of course, eliminating the instability at this level means we can't actually see into the warp bubble, so the images are a composite of the readings from the sensors that were placed within as well as outside it." He checked out a chronometer. "We'll be getting to where we attempted to power it up to a full-blown warp bubble in another few seconds."

Images of the ship began to flicker into and out of view, becoming increasingly distorted as the seconds passed. The ship no longer appeared to be stable and looked as if it were almost tumbling around inside its cocoon. The bubble seemed to be fighting to stabilize itself, although it became clearer as they kept watching that it was a losing battle. At the appropriate time, the programming sought to end the trial by collapsing the bubble in a controlled manner. Instead, they had a brief glimpse of the bubble's edge rushing wildly toward the ship before everything vanished. A moment later, the ship came into view in normal space-time. The damage to the structure was plain. It was as if a giant fist had tried to crush one side of the ship and been partially successful.

"I'm not certain if I'd call it entertaining, but it wasn't dull," Austin noted with a chuckle. "It started out fine. Tell me what happened."

"The new approach worked at first," Yabuno replied. "Going to a full-blown warp bubble is when everything began to fall apart, with space-time being warped around the ship in an erratic fashion. It was actually space-time that was experiencing the movement, rather than the ship. In fact, someone on board the ship wouldn't have had any sensation of motion."

"There would have been quite a sensation of something at the end though," Austin said pointedly.

"What we saw at the end was what happens when an unstable warp bubble collapses. The distortions in the bubble affect the way the collapse takes place. There was a significant inward deformation in the bubble in one location that came into contact with the ship, crushing it slightly before the collapse was complete."

The concern was plain on Austin's face. "What would have happened if it had taken slightly longer for it to collapse?"

Yabuno sighed. "That side of the ship would have been crushed completely. There wouldn't have been any point to searching for bodies."

Austin's tone was somber. "At the risk of oversimplifying things, there are two major, related problems. The first is that the warp-field bubble isn't stable enough to allow for either staying in a fixed position or moving around in a controlled manner. The second is that collapsing the warp bubble is risky, possibly fatal, for anyone on board."

His expression brightened slightly. "The good news is that this trial shows that we're continuing to improve the technology, even though it isn't usable yet. For one thing, the damage to the vessel can be repaired fairly quickly, probably before any more testing takes place."

"You agree that it's worth doing more testing?" Turner asked.

"Of course I do," Austin replied. "As frustrating as this must be for you, you're still well ahead of where we were in the timeline of developing the original generators that got the first ships here. I suggest that you focus next on improving the process of collapsing the bubble from its full-power mode. Nothing else matters if we can't ensure that people will survive returning to normal space-time."

"As you mentioned, the two problems are related, Sam," Yabuno pointed out. "We may not be able to solve one without solving the other."

"That may be true," Austin admitted, "but there's also some different stuff in play when collapsing a bubble. My take, from what I saw today, is that you may be able to solve those issues even if you haven't solved the underlying issues of how to function within the bubble itself. One of the benefits of the instability is that we have information regarding what was happening inside the bubble. Let's put that information to good use."

He grinned. "I guess this means I'll have to tell Curly you're not done breaking things."

CHAPTER SEVENTEEN

It was very unusual for the entire scientific team to be together in one place, with no one participating remotely. Some of the people had never met each other in person, and greetings were exchanged. What made things even more unusual was the fact that their meeting place was in the same orbiting lab that held the alien artifact, rather than a place on Earth. Most people held on to the rails that were arranged around the room, to avoid floating aimlessly.

Strong emotional undercurrents ran through the room. For some of the people present, the undercurrent was one of excitement. For others, it was more like tension. For nearly everyone, there was a measure of uncertainty—the last was because no one had been told just why the meeting was necessary or why everyone needed to be present.

As they waited for something to happen, Raffles gravitated toward Porter. She hadn't made many connections with the rest of the team; her lack of technical skills combined with her personality and the fact that she wasn't being protected by a senior executive meant that the other team members had little use for her.

"I don't know why I needed to be here in person," she complained. "They're probably going to announce that they've made the breakthrough they wanted and are going to thank us for our contributions. I could listen to that just as well back home."

"I don't see why I need to be here either," Porter agreed. "My work's been done for some time, although I don't mind being able to stay here and use their labs for my follow-up analysis. It made having to return the data less painful, knowing I'd still have access to it here." Porter had a sly look on his face. "They don't know that I've been working on my paper to publish my findings and that I'm ready to forward a copy to a scientific journal for review. This is my last day here at the lab, and I'll be forwarding the data to another location after this meeting, so I'll have the support I'll need for my paper."

He chuckled. "Although there's something to be said for being thanked in person and being the first to know about anything major that they plan on doing next, that won't be of any concern to me. It's time for me to get back to my life." In spite of himself, he laughed. "For once, Lillian, one of your promises to me has come true. I can see a Nobel Prize in my future." He didn't notice the worried look on Raffles's face.

The people were surprised to see a large display come to life next to the vacant podium in the room. They relaxed a bit as they saw Flynn's familiar image appear.

"Good morning, everyone," he began in a positive tone. "Please forgive the fact that it isn't feasible for me to be there in person. As you know, we've spent the past months trying to do something that no one has ever done before—communicate with an alien race. During those months, we've explored areas of common interest in order to determine whether we can come to an understanding that will lead to peace between humans and aliens. I'm pleased to announce that we have, in fact, reached a deal.

"In return for the derelict, the aliens will give us their warp-field-generator technology, to be installed in all of our ships. It will even be compatible with ships that weren't designed with warp-field generators originally. Once the aliens have the derelict, they won't have any further interest in humans. So long as they stay away from us, we don't really care what they want to do with that ship. Space is vast enough that we need never meet again."

"What about their demand for humans to examine?" Porter asked. "Do they understand that isn't part of the deal?"

"First, I think the actual word is still in question. For all we know, they really just mean that they want to understand us better and can only do that in a face-to-face encounter."

Porter persisted. "Regardless of what word they meant, Mr. Flynn, we can't be willing to make a bargain with human lives."

A new feeling rippled through the room—unease.

Flynn, however, adopted a tone designed specifically to defuse the situation. "That's quite right, Dr. Porter, which is why we have no intention of making any people available directly. We will, instead, wait until after the initial exchange has taken place and offer to do a remote conference with both humans and aliens present."

"What if they don't agree? What happens then?"

"We'll leave. Given the choice between further arguments or being left with something as priceless as the derelict, we're confident they'll be satisfied with the thing they've wanted forever."

As Porter mulled over the man's words, Flynn continued.

"That brings us to the next step. While I'm sure some of you are assuming that your individual roles with this project may be at an end, you couldn't be more wrong."

An image of the ancient ship appeared alongside Flynn as he continued. "As we know, even the aliens can't transport the ship while using their warp-field generators. That means the derelict has to be handed over to them from someplace in or near the Citadel star system. Since the exchange of the derelict for their technology has to take place at the same time, we must be in that system as well."

"What does that have to do with us?" asked Dr. Spatcher. "This team wasn't put together with any particular expertise in warp-field technology. How could it, when most of the top knowledge in that field lies within the Citadel Group? There are a couple of us who have studied their original warp-field-generator technology, but that turned out to be a dead end, for them as well as us."

"While we hope those people will have a chance to evaluate the technology we receive from the aliens, we need the rest of you for something else. We need you to keep doing what you've already been doing but to do it from the Citadel system," Flynn explained.

The mood became a confusing combination of emotions; some people grinned at the prospect of a voyage, and others became very anxious at the thought. The noise quieted down as Flynn's voice drowned out all dissenting chatter. "The majority of you have been involved in the communication side, and there's no reason to believe that more challenges won't arise after we get to Citadel that will require your expertise again. We can't possibly try to close the agreement with delays of two or more months at a time. As for the rest of you, we have to be prepared to address problems that may arise requiring your expertise. Once again, long delays will be unacceptable."

Porter was curious. "How would we get there? The only ships that can make the trip are Citadel ships. Are they providing a ship?"

Flynn nodded. "Yes, we'll be traveling on a Citadel ship, although the arrangements will be somewhat unusual. We've explained before the need for extreme secrecy; Citadel can't acknowledge any of this activity openly until after the agreement has been completed. That means even the crew of the Citadel transport won't know anything about the project."

"What are we going to do?" someone asked sarcastically. "Are we going to stow away aboard in crates marked 'imported sausage'?"

Porter noted uneasily that Flynn seemed slightly amused by the comment. "That's not a bad idea, although we plan on refining it somewhat. Everyone on the project, me included, will be put in stasis and placed into a specialized container that will be loaded onto the transport. The container will have life support to keep us safe and healthy for the duration of the trip."

"How do we wake up if we're all in stasis?" Porter asked. "For that matter, what happens if something goes wrong during the trip?"

"A member of the crew will know all about us and will supervise our being loaded onto the transport and off-loaded at the other side. This person will also keep tabs on us during the trip and knows how to initiate our revival once we arrive in the Citadel system, awaiting entry to Citadel itself. After that happens, we can take the next steps needed to bring the agreement to conclusion."

"What if we don't want to go?" Porter asked, voicing the question that was on the minds of more than a few of them. "There are some people who have already given a lot of their time to this project and need to take a break. Others may not want to submit to stasis, even if you tell us it will be safe."

All traces of amusement faded from Flynn's expression. "When we started this project, we made clear that it wasn't a short-term commitment and that the extreme security needs associated with it meant you may need to be sequestered from your regular lives for a significant time. None of you objected, especially when faced with the prospect of doing something extraordinary and being paid very well to do it."

The room was deathly still.

"We never limited that sequestration requirement to activities in this solar system. You need to get used to the fact that we're all going on this journey and the decision is final. The sooner we get started, the sooner we can be done and return to this solar system."

"We need to say good-bye to our families," someone protested. "We can't just disappear without explanation."

"While we'd like to be able to accommodate your request, there is too much of a chance that someone will want to let a loved one or outside colleague know what is happening, derailing this project and its objectives. You all set up your explanations some time ago, including the notion that this project may require your being unavailable suddenly for over six months. We've already sent out your notifications to that effect on your behalf."

"Isn't this kidnapping?" Porter asked weakly.

"Is it?" Flynn replied. "We aren't on Earth, and you all agreed to whatever travel might be needed in connection with this project. We're just enforcing that agreement." His gaze brightened. "Relax. This isn't a one-way trip, and you'll all receive a hell of a bonus for the travel, plus the chance to stay on the ground floor of something amazing. I'm going along as well, and I sure as hell am planning on coming back. I'll make sure you do as well."

Although he wasn't in the room, he nodded toward several doorways. "Let's get going. The next transport is due to depart in short order, and there's some special cargo that needs to be on board."

Porter backed off, hating himself for his weakness in not standing his ground and refusing to be a further part of the project. He knew it was immoral to allow the aliens to think humans could be bargained away, even if the humans weren't going to go through with it. The right thing to do was to refuse to do a deal until the aliens understood humans properly. Unfortunately, no one had the courage to challenge Flynn. Although the feeling of uncertainty hadn't departed, the people began to drift toward the doorways and their new destinations. Porter went along with them.

Harrington had an approving look on her face as Flynn ended the transmission. "Well done, Mr. Flynn. Nice to be reminded how easy it is to manipulate people who claim to be smart. It wouldn't have been any harder to herd sheep."

Flynn allowed a smile to cross his face. "While the reasons for wanting them to join us in Citadel's solar system are valid, they don't realize that we want to make sure that no one stays behind who might figure out what we're really doing or have a change of heart for some other reason, and try to save his skin by telling the authorities about it."

"What are you planning on telling them if they figure it out after we arrive?"

Flynn's smile turned cynical. "It won't matter by then. At that point, they'll be just as committed to the plan as the rest of us, whether they like it or not. If they fight us, they can face the gallows on Citadel."

CHAPTER EIGHTEEN

President Lee sat in the Oval Office, facing his attorney general and his chief of staff. The two people squirmed in their seats as they faced a look of shocked disbelief from the president.

"How the hell did Courtney Harrington escape from house arrest, and where is she now?"

"We're still looking into it. Mr. President," the attorney general began. A hint of self-preservation crept into her voice. "As you know, she's never been under any direct physical restraints pending the outcome of her court cases. While I advised she at least be fitted with some form of monitoring device, you determined it wouldn't be appropriate under the circumstances and directed us not to take those steps. Our monitoring was, therefore, from a discreet distance, which isn't impossible to defeat."

Grant Steffel, the chief of staff, leaped out of his chair. "Don't you dare try to pin the blame for this debacle on the president, Woodville! All federal prisoners are ultimately *your* responsibility."

Woodville, who was six feet tall, stood and faced down the much shorter Steffel. "Save your posturing for someone who cares about it, Steffel." She turned back to the president. "Mr. President, to your great credit, you allowed my people a free hand when it came to going after all of the wrongdoers from the Harrison administration. Unfortunately, this office tied my hands when it came to pursuing the former president herself. While I accept that we have been in uncharted waters legally, you have repeatedly refused to accept the legal opinions prepared by my people and to allow them to act against Ms. Harrington as vigorously as we were entitled. Considering her lack of remorse and unwillingness to accept the consequences of her actions, the results were predictable. However, I believe in accountability, so you may have my resignation, effective immediately."

To Steffel's disappointment, Lee motioned for Woodville to remain. "Sit down, Elizabeth. I have no intention of accepting your resignation." He sighed. "You've only said the truth, and that shouldn't be a crime in this town. The fact is we need to track and capture Harrington, and you're the best person to lead that effort. This time, for what it's worth, you will have the same freedom to act that you did with respect to her fellow war criminals."

"What if she's hiding somewhere else in the solar system?" Woodville asked. "Our writ doesn't run that far."

Lee nodded toward another man in the room, who had observed everything in silence. "General Buck, I need you and the rest of Space Command to work with the attorney general to find Harrington. While I doubt she's off planet, because it would cramp her style, we need to be thorough in our search. If she's anywhere off planet, I want you to bring her back here."

Buck stood at attention as he said, "Yes, Mr. President."

Lee turned back to Woodville. "Put together whatever presidential findings and executive orders are needed for you and General Buck to carry out my instructions, and get them to me for signature right away. I'd imagine your people have already been working on them in anticipation of the outcome of the court cases or in case I came to my senses," he added dryly. Woodville's face colored slightly, but she didn't respond.

"There's one thing we haven't discussed, Mr. President," Buck said.

"What is it, General?"

"What about Citadel?"

"What about Citadel?" Lee replied in puzzlement.

"Shouldn't the United States notify Citadel about these events?"

"Why should we?" Steffel asked. "It isn't as if Harrington would ever set foot anywhere near Citadel, and the rest of this is a law-enforcement matter. While it's a high-profile one, it's still something to be handled internally."

"It is of huge importance to Citadel," Buck insisted. "It's been frustrating that she's been able to postpone her punishment."

"We all get it, General," Steffel said. "To them, Harrington is a war criminal who has been duly tried and convicted."

"*We* consider Harrington a war criminal too, Steffel," Woodville reminded him pointedly.

"Yes," Steffel agreed, "but what purpose would be served by notifying Citadel that Harrington is in hiding? We're much better off waiting to tell them about Harrington until after we've captured her. It would also be better for you domestically, Mr. President."

"Isn't maintaining the goodwill of a key ally a good reason for notifying them about the situation, Mr. President?" Buck asked.

"Which conversation would you rather have, Mr. President?" Steffel asked cynically. "Do you want to tell Austin there's a problem, or do you want to tell him there *was* a problem that's been solved?"

Although Lee had doubts about either approach, he decided to take the path of political expediency. "We'll treat it as an internal matter for now and inform Citadel when we have it under control."

Woodville tried one last time. "I believe that approach is a mistake, Mr. President, and will lead to more damage to our relationship with Citadel."

"Perhaps, but I've made my decision. Please carry out your instructions."

Steffel was careful to keep the others from seeing the triumphant look on his face as he left.

CHAPTER NINETEEN

Powers's tension was masked by a calm facade. She'd created several false identities and backgrounds, one of which had gotten her aboard a Keith Thomas transport bound for Citadel several years earlier as a crew member. Although it had been harder to do than when she'd last done it, she'd managed to use another false identity to insert herself into the crew of a sister ship to carry out her new assignment. The Citadel Group's security had improved since the last time she'd been vetted, but her fake identity survived the scrutiny.

Flynn had provided her with the information she needed to select a transport where she wouldn't run into any of her crew mates from her previous assignment. She was surprised at Flynn's success in obtaining the information. Although she'd been unable to avoid encountering a couple of people who had known her previously, there had been no unusual reactions to her presence. She'd been pleased by the confirmation that her appearance had changed enough that no one made the connection to her.

She'd spent the last three months aboard the transport with little to do except pretend to be just another member of the crew. She'd been careful to deflect all efforts at establishing a relationship with any of the crew members, although she'd stayed on cordial terms with a number of the women. She wasn't about to create a situation where she'd have to explain her plans to people after they arrived in Citadel or, even worse, spend time with anyone. She'd learned her lesson from having to share her quarters with Roetter during her last voyage.

The reason for her current tension was the fact that they'd finally arrived at the entrance to the safe path through the radiation field that surrounded Citadel's solar system. They were at a critical stage. She thought back on the grumblings from the people they were smuggling into the system. Harrington in particular was unhappy over the news regarding how they had to prepare for the trip and expressed her unhappiness in a private meeting with Powers and Flynn.

Powers wasn't sure whether Harrington's face was flushed from anger or embarrassment as she declared, "I thought this just applied to everyone else. I thought I'd be awake during the voyage. I'm not going to strip off my clothes and lie down with a bunch of other naked people! This isn't like a day at the beach, after all."

"You don't have a choice," Powers replied firmly. "Before any cargo is taken aboard for the trip to Citadel, the container is scanned. We need for the scanners to report that the contents of this container read as the carcasses of livestock that they need to import; the scanners can't tell the difference between a carcass in a preservative environment and a body in stasis. However, clothing, jewelry, and other personal items are a different matter and impossible to explain away. When we arrive at the entrance to the radiation field, the ship's holds will be scanned again, and the results had better match."

"Aren't you some kind of genius when it comes to manipulating systems?" Harrington challenged. "Why can't you just reprogram everything to report what we want reported and leave us to travel in comfort?"

Powers sighed mentally. "It doesn't work that way. The kind of access that you're describing won't happen until after we've arrived in Citadel. That means I won't be able to do anything about the initial scan of the container, which also means everything blows up if the initial scan indicates everyone is awake. Besides, there's no way to provide enough resources to sustain all of you for the trip."

"Why can't we come aboard in stasis but be revived after departure?"

This time the sigh was audible. "Same problem as before: the scan results taken during the voyage won't match the initial scan, and there won't be any resources to support you. Also, you would all be placed back into stasis just before arriving at Citadel and then revived again after the scans have been completed, and there would still be anomalies, since an environment where people have been living, breathing, eating, and doing all the other things that people do will read differently from undisturbed carcasses. There is also the fact that there is some risk associated with placing someone into stasis and bringing him back out quickly." She shook her head. "You have to face the fact that everyone will need to be in stasis for the entire trip."

"That raises another point. I thought stasis had to be maintained in individual units, where life signs can be monitored properly."

"That's how the stasis will be set up, but individual units aren't used for carcasses that are being shipped and would attract attention we don't want. Instead, we've taken a cargo hold container that is compatible with the containers that the Keith Thomas transports use and adapted it to allow for maintaining stasis throughout the container once everyone has been stabilized individually. While it won't be as reliable as individual units, it should work. The system will appear to be a sophisticated environmental control setup when scanned." Powers shrugged. "As I've already stated, we don't have any other choice."

Harrington was incredulous. "You mean we will be loaded together like naked carcasses once we've been placed in stasis, and we'll be expected to stay that way for three months? What happens if there's a problem?" She shuddered. "What happens if one of us wakes up? How do we let you know, and what will you do about it?"

"First of all, you'll be on special racks rather than touching each other physically; these types of carcasses need a bit of breathing room. Also, it's very unlikely that a problem would arise, but if it does, we've arranged for a discreet alarm to reach me."

"What happens then?" Harrington demanded. "You aren't in charge of the cargo, so you can't just waltz into that area and bring us help." Her eyes narrowed as she continued. "I want to know you won't just stay quiet and let us rot if things go wrong."

Powers was silent for twenty seconds before answering. "I'll make allowances for the fact that you're nervous about stasis, but that's the last time you will ever question my reliability. I stepped in when that fool Roetter bungled his assignment. I broke him out of prison and hid him aboard my ship and gave him another shot at Austin. He screwed up again and nearly compromised me in the process."

Harrington tried another approach. "All right, everyone else can go aboard as carcasses but Powers can smuggle me aboard the transport and find a hiding place for me. You've undoubtedly learned some lessons from your experience with Roetter."

Powers gave off a cold laugh. "The lessons I learned were never to do it again unless I had a death wish." She stared hard at Harrington. "Your approach carries risks I'm not going to accept. You can find another way to get to Citadel if you're determined to place the mission and everyone else in jeopardy as an accommodation to your vanity.

Harrington was furious over being reprimanded by someone she regarded as hired help and turned toward Flynn. "Mr. Flynn, perhaps you'd better give Powers a reminder of who is in charge here." The tension in the room shot up as Powers and Flynn eyed each other warily.

Powers spoke in a calm voice. "Unlike you, Ms. Harrington, Flynn is fully aware that I'm no more one of your lackeys than he is. He's also not stupid enough to try to take me on, as it would probably cost two lives, neither of which would be mine."

"She's right, Ms. Harrington. She's armed, for one thing."

Harrington was shocked to hear Flynn's reaction. "So are you!"

"Powers was in a better position to use her weapon when you challenged her, and she still holds that advantage. I'd just hasten my own demise if I were to try anything." Very slowly, Flynn moved his arms away from any hidden weapons of his own as he continued. "Besides, we need her. There's no one else who can do what she can. Also, everything she's been telling us about the stasis is correct. Her way is the best way for us to achieve our objectives." Flynn's tone stayed calm. "Don't forget, *I'm* going to trust that this plan works too, since *I'll* be in that damned container. I don't take these risks lightly either." Flynn's tone brought the tension down, although no one felt completely comfortable at that moment. Powers didn't say anything as she looked at Harrington expectantly. Harrington disappointed her by leaving without another word.

Powers turned to Flynn and said, "One thing I know about you is that your word is good, Flynn. I want your word that there won't be any efforts to take me out once the mission has been completed." She gave him a hard stare. "Otherwise, you can kiss your ass good-bye if a problem pops up while you're all frozen hunks of meat."

Flynn chose his words carefully. "You have my word that no one on the team will try to take you out, Powers." Flynn's look turned hard as granite. "You understand, of course, that all bets are off if you turn on us. If that happens, I'll cut your throat myself."

Powers knew that trusting Flynn completely would be unwise, but she believed Flynn himself wouldn't try to take her out. She had no similar trust in Harrington, however, so she knew she'd need to be on her guard. She mused over how easy it would be to find a way to "discover" the bodies in the hold and turn them over to Austin. That wasn't really the answer, of course, since Harrington would rat her out, and she'd have no way to get back to Earth's solar system and safety. *It would be better to simply ensure that the environmental controls failed,* she thought. Her cohorts would enter into something a lot more permanent than sleep, and Harrington's plans would go with her to whatever hell awaited her. There would be no way to tie Powers to the specialized container, and she would be free to go back to Earth and disappear again.

Unfortunately, Powers would have to give up any hope of capturing Liz Austin and Sara Albretti if she sent Harrington to an early death. Although taking Austin's wife prisoner would be quite a coup, Powers's professional ego was still smarting from Albretti. Albretti had spotted Roetter entering the engineering section aboard *KT-7* to assassinate Austin, had noticed the strand of Powers's hair on Roetter's body, and clued her colleagues to search for a woman.

Powers's interest in capturing Austin and Albretti, her belief in Flynn's promise, plus the desire for the remainder of her substantial fee upon completion of the mission kept her from doing anything when the holds were scanned. She'd managed to be nearby as the chief engineer relayed the local authorities' findings to the captain.

"I have the report from the inspectors, Captain," she began. "Everything scans as it should."

"Thanks, Chief," the captain replied in a light tone. "I take it none of the perishables is past its expiration date?"

The chief chuckled. "No, Captain. Everything is of a safe vintage and should still be that way when we arrive at Citadel."

CHAPTER TWENTY

Austin always looked forward to any messages from J. W. Preacher. The man had been a good friend for years and was always a keen observer of human events. Just as importantly, as Citadel's ambassador to the Allied Nations, he was their eyes and ears back on Earth.

"Greetings, Sam," Preacher's message began warmly. "I trust everything is well with you since we last exchanged messages. I've just received word that I am once again a great-grandpa, so that adds to Preachers I have the privilege of spoiling.

"I spoke with Amelia Gordon the other day, and Madame President of Mars sends her regards. We talked about the status of things on her planet, and you'd never know the aliens had ever attacked them. Not only has all of the damage been repaired, but they've also expanded the size of some of their settlements." His smile dimmed slightly as he continued. "Frankly, they've done a better job than Earth has of preparing to defend themselves in case the aliens ever return.

"I've attached to this report several files with details on the treaties we discussed over the last several messages. As you will see when you take a look at them, everything is as we anticipated, so I'm sure you'll be OK with ratifying them."

Preacher's expression took on a look of concern. "No report would be complete without a comment on the status of our least-favorite individual. The good news is that Harrington's case is finally moving along, no thanks to President Lee. The Supreme Court held oral arguments recently, and my reading of the judicial tea leaves tells me that the court is likely to clear the way for Harrington to be extradited to Citadel. This could have happened some time ago if President Lee had lent more support."

Preacher shrugged. "Lee is a fine man on a personal level and might have been an adequate president in other times, but he seems out of his depth over what to do about Harrington. His continued dithering over the matter hasn't done the relationship with Citadel any favors, which I've reminded him on more than one occasion."

Preacher's expression darkened. "All of this should be good news, except there are rumors that Harrington has disappeared. As you know, she's been under the equivalent of house arrest for a long time now, instead of prison, where she should have been." Preacher shook his head. "While I understand this was a gesture of courtesy toward a former president, allowing her a certain amount of leeway regarding her movements was the wrong thing to do. Lee doesn't want to come to terms with the fact that the former president was impeached, convicted by Congress of war crimes and crimes against humanity, and doesn't deserve any courtesies.

"Although his office hasn't said anything officially, he's been made to look a fool, as his people are looking everywhere for Harrington. This escape must have been planned well in advance, as she was obviously ready to move once she got the same news I did about the Supreme Court. Since she doesn't usually maintain a low profile, something will probably trip her up.

"Before you say it, I'll watch my back," he said. "Fortunately, the security around the embassy is better than it was when Harrington's goons invaded the place. I've already passed the word to the rest of the Citadel Group team to be careful as well.

"While we're on that subject, you'd best watch your back too, Sam," he said in a concerned tone. "While her sense of self-preservation means she isn't likely to show up in your neck of the woods, it wouldn't be out of character for her to try to send some mischief your way now that she's facing extradition. Lee will probably want to send you a message about the situation."

Preacher chuckled. "Knowing how that weasel of a chief advisor Steffel thinks, he's probably advised Lee not to talk to me until he can report Harrington's been recaptured. I assume that Lee's been keeping sufficient tabs on her activities such that he'd let us know if there were any special reason for us to be concerned about her disappearance. That means it's probably OK to let him stew for a while before I make a show of demanding that he give us an update on what he's doing to find her.

"Feel free to send me a reply with your thoughts on the matter. I'll wait a few days after I get your reply, in case Lee sends a message to me after this one goes out and you need to be more specific in your response. Hopefully, it will all have been resolved by the time your message arrives." The amusement faded from his gaze. "Of course, you may want to send a message to Lee directly that tells him what you think about his letting Harrington get away."

CHAPTER TWENTY-ONE

Harrington's focus was blurred, both mentally and physically. She heard noises around her without understanding them at first. As the fog faded away, she became aware that she was staring at the naked body of one of her team members. As that fact sunk in, she finally thought to look down and was reminded that she was in the same condition. She wanted to move someplace where no one could see her, but she didn't yet have enough coordination to get to her feet and keep herself covered at the same time. She decided to work on getting to her feet and then worry about protecting her modesty.

She struggled to look around and saw others in various stages of dress as they came back to full awareness. No one paid her any attention. She was still on her knees when she looked over to see Flynn already up and starting to get dressed in the clothes Powers had provided. She flushed as Flynn saw her, his face revealing that he was still too foggy to keep fully under control. Harrington cursed silently as she felt heat ripple across her face and elsewhere.

The numbness was replaced by a fury that splashed across her face as she struggled to stand. Harrington planned on chewing out Powers for having placed her deep within the group of sleepers, instead of near the entrance, where she could be revived first and dressed properly ahead of the others.

She felt a hand on her arm, steadying her as a voice said, "Don't try to get up until the numbness has worn off completely. It isn't worth taking a fall just to protect your modesty." Harrington's head managed to jerk in the direction of the voice and looked into Powers's face.

"I wouldn't have to worry about my modesty if you had arranged for me to be revived first, as I instructed, Powers!" Harrington snapped.

Harrington felt the warning from a slight increase in pressure on her arm as Powers replied, "You were, in fact, placed where you could be among the first to be revived. Unfortunately, one of the tricky aspects of maintaining stasis in this environment is that we can't always be sure who will revive first. In spite of everything I tried, you stayed in a deep sleep while others began to revive."

Powers gestured in a way that took in the entire compartment as she said, "There's you and your people, and just one of me, and I can't stay with one person as her nursemaid while others need help getting up." Powers rolled her eyes as she continued. "Besides, I don't know why you're looking so embarrassed; everyone is in the same boat. There isn't anything remotely sexy about seeing a bunch of naked people wake up from stasis."

Another hand supported Harrington under her other arm, and she was able to stand finally. She looked at

Flynn, whose expression had returned to its usual neutral look, as he handed her clothes to her. He turned away without a word and helped someone else stand.

Later, as the entire group was dressed and fully recovered from stasis, they went over their plans.

"We'll only have a limited window to take over this ship," Powers said. "We have to act before this container is transferred from this hold to a space-bound storage facility, but we can't do anything before the passengers have left." There was a weary look on her face for a moment. "For what it's worth, being in stasis means you weren't bored for three months with no place to go. Everyone else, passengers and crew, is even more sick of the sight of these walls than you are, so they won't stay aboard for any longer than necessary."

She pointed to a display. "I was able to arrange for this container to be the last one to be off-loaded, so that should be enough time for the passengers to leave. It's a good thing for us that off-loading is now automated; there won't be any prying eyes to watch us as we leave the container."

"What about environmental controls?" Harrington asked. "Walking outside won't do much good if there's nothing but vacuum waiting for us."

Powers zoomed in on an image as she replied, "For safety and security, there are bulkheads in these holds to isolate potential problems. I've arranged for our section to maintain a suitable environment while the outer sections are being off-loaded."

"Talk us through what happens next," Flynn said.

Powers brought up an image of the interior layout of the ship and pointed to a storage area. Her finger traced a path as she spoke. "Everyone will be waiting in this area while Flynn and I make our way to the captain. He'll be in his cabin, where he can receive any messages about the progress of the off-loading or anything else." Powers let out a chuckle as she continued. "We're in luck because his girlfriend will be tied up for an extra day before they can get together, so he's staying on the ship. Most of the rest of the crew is clearing out as fast as they can, so there won't be more than a skeleton crew on board shortly."

"Will they be enough to run the ship?" Flynn asked.

"Yes." She nodded. "We won't be using the warp-field generators, and I've worked out programming to automate much of the rest of what needs to be done. Fortunately, the ship always has an ample supply of food and other supplies to sustain a crew in case of a mishap far away from home, so there won't be any need to draw attention to ourselves by arranging for anything to be brought on board. We can't keep this up indefinitely, but with the help of the crew, we should be able to make it work until we're done."

Harrington asked, "Won't someone notice that our old container is empty now?"

Powers shook her head. "It was scanned when we were checked out at the entrance to the radiation field. While I haven't been able to change the readings from the scanners, I've altered the programming so it looks like the seals haven't been broken. By the time they realize they've stored an empty container, we'll be long gone."

Several heads turned at noises erupting from the back of the room. Porter was at the head of a group of scientists as they moved to front. Flynn and Powers shifted subtly, and Flynn gave an imperceptible nod to several of his people as they waited. Porter pointed at the display as he said, "This isn't what we were led to believe would happen!"

"What do you mean, Dr. Porter?" Flynn asked calmly.

"We thought we were embarking on a mission of historic proportions, that we were helping to find a peaceful solution to the conflict between the aliens and the human race. We accepted that the nature of this mission was such that we were willing to undergo stasis in order to avoid revealing what we were doing. We expected to work with the people of Citadel." Porter gestured angrily at the display. "Instead, we've been listening to you discuss this ship like we're a bunch of pirates. The people on Citadel don't even know about us, do they?"

Harrington stepped forward. Up until that moment, none of the scientists had taken particular notice of the woman who had awoken with the rest of them and was dressed casually. They hadn't made the connection to the former president of the United States, who had always been dressed and coiffed immaculately. Several of the scientists gasped.

"I think you can guess why we couldn't take a chance on notifying anyone in Citadel about our plans," she said. "Before anyone starts hyperventilating and calling me the personification of evil, the objective is exactly what Mr. Flynn has portrayed it to be—we want to communicate with the aliens in order to resolve our conflict peacefully.

Some of you know that this effort was underway while I was still in office, so this is something I've felt strongly about for a long time."

Spatcher stepped forward and locked his gaze on Harrington's eyes. "You're a war criminal and at this point probably a fugitive from justice."

Harrington walked over to a display and brought up images of destruction on Mars and Earth. She jabbed at the images as she said, "That's what happened the last time the aliens visited our solar system. How many of you want to see it happen again? How many of you want to face families back home after another attack and tell them we might have been able to stop the killings but weren't willing to take extraordinary steps to make it happen?"

As expected, Harrington's words blunted the force of the protest. The destruction, especially on Mars, was too awful to contemplate its repetition. After watching the images, Spatcher looked away, rather than try to regain contact with Harrington's face. Harrington turned toward Porter. "What about you, Dr. Porter? Are you ready to throw away an opportunity that may never come along again?"

Porter's gaze was steady as he replied, "What about *you*, Ms. Harrington? It seems to me that you can show your intentions best by placing yourself at the mercy of Sam Austin and letting this mission speak for itself. He's an amazing man; perhaps he'll set aside your death sentence if he believes you're sincere about what we're doing. As I recall, he once traveled to Earth without escort ships to demonstrate his peaceful intentions. Isn't it time for you to do the same?"

"Sam will be even more willing to agree that mercy is the right approach if he sees something even better than our good intentions," Harrington replied. "If we can show him results, then I'll gladly leave it to him to decide whether it is worth my life."

"What about the capture of this ship? That's what you're planning, isn't it?"

Harrington clasped her hands in a sign of earnestness. "We don't have a choice in light of how Austin feels about me. However, I give you my word that we'll do everything possible to make sure no one is hurt."

Porter's face revealed the struggle between skepticism and belief. Although the skepticism didn't win, it didn't leave his face entirely either. "All right, Ms. Harrington," he said at last. "I'm willing to stay with the mission and try for lasting peace with the aliens." The skepticism flared for an instant. "Don't make me regret that decision. If you do, I reserve the right to notify Sam. Since I'm working with you, I'll be judged by him too, but one thing I won't do is contribute toward more hard feelings between our two solar systems."

"Fair enough, Dr. Porter," Harrington said. She looked around and asked, "What about the rest of you?"

None of the other scientists met her eyes, and she smiled.

Flynn and Powers made their way through the passageways quietly. As a precaution, Flynn wore the same type of crew clothes as Powers, making them unremarkable to anyone who might see them. As it turned out,

Powers's predictions about the passengers and crew had been correct; the passageways were deserted, making the crew clothes unnecessary. Each of them carried a standard travel bag, their weapons within easy reach.

Captain Benitez was in his quarters, working on his reports while keeping half an eye on the secondary display that listed the status of the crew, passengers, and cargo. One reason for burying himself in report writing was to take his mind off the fact that his girlfriend wasn't able to meet up with him for another day.

She was part of the crew on another Keith Thomas–class transport. While her ship had arrived a day before his, she'd decided to visit some friends on one of the mining operations among the asteroids. Her transportation off the asteroid had been delayed, so she'd sent him a message telling him she missed him. Considering her lack of attire while recording the message, it was clear she had the same thing in mind as he did for when they finally got together. After all, it had been three months.

Earlier, as he'd settled down in front of his main display, he'd mused about how much the place felt like a ghost town. Once the ship was in port, people rarely bothered to wander through the ship to his quarters to talk when a quick call to his link would do just as well. For that reason, he hadn't bothered keeping the hatch to his quarters closed.

With a start, he realized he wasn't alone. At first, all he took in was the familiar sight of people in crew suits. The smile of recognition upon seeing Powers faded as he saw her expression and the man next to her. He began to move toward his display but was stopped by a brief flash of movement. A moment later, his struggles ceased as everything faded into blackness.

The light in his quarters fought with the darkness in his mind as it struggled back toward consciousness. Benitez had no idea how long it had taken to come all the way back into focus. Something was wrong, he noted, as he tried, without success, to move. The light won out over the darkness, and he found himself tied securely to a chair. His expression was one of puzzled recognition as he saw Powers.

"Morrison," he said, using the name she had selected for her alter ego aboard his ship. "What's going on?" He nodded toward the man as he continued. "Who the hell are you, and what are you and Morrison doing here?" He tested his restraints. "For that matter, why am I tied up?"

Powers nodded toward Flynn as well as she replied, "Captain, you need to listen to this man very carefully. There's some information he wants from you, and for your sake, you'd better give it to him." She shook her head slowly. "Trust me, you don't want to give him a reason to be unpleasant."

Benitez was still tied to the chair, motionless and slumped over. His skin, normally a rich brown color, was unnaturally pale. As Flynn and Powers stood in front of Benitez's display, Flynn glanced back at their captive and said, "For his sake, those command codes he finally gave up had better be genuine. If they aren't, I won't be as gentle with him a second time." He turned back to Powers as she entered the codes.

Powers barely seemed to hear Flynn as she concentrated on her task. She looked up from the display as she said, "The codes he entered are genuine, and we now have command control over this ship." Her body relaxed slightly as she faced her colleague. "While we can't operate the ship fully without some help, we can make sure no one else can run it without our OK. We shouldn't have any problems once we explain things to the crew." Her expression darkened. "After I take care of some settings, including how to deal with any messages that the captain receives, I have an old friend to visit."

"Just make sure your friend is still alive and in one piece when you bring her here, along with Austin's wife; Harrington has plans for them," Flynn reminded his colleague pointedly. "While I meant what I said about not going after you, don't put me in a situation where I have to change things because you wouldn't follow the rules. That reminds me—you need to release the command codes to me as well."

"Why?" Powers asked in a slightly unsettled tone. "You couldn't take the ship through its mission without me anyway."

"That's true," Flynn acknowledged. "However, if the unthinkable happens and you don't come back, we'll all be in a jam if we don't have access to those codes. I'll be damned if I'm going to let myself be stuck here without a way out. At least we'd have some leverage with the crew."

"Fine," Powers replied. "I'll release the codes to you before I leave." She nodded at Benitez. "What do you want to do about him?"

Flynn's expression remained neutral. "Do we need him for anything else?"

Powers shook her head. "No. Key things that still need to happen include piloting the ship and any engineering issues, and the captain isn't needed for either of those. Wash is the pilot, and the chief handles everything in engineering."

"Good. I'll dispose of Benitez permanently and bring the rest of our people back. We can take over the rest of the ship while you do your work. Just make sure you take care of the master codes."

She moved toward a display, entered several commands, and pointed at it. "OK, there's your confirmation that you have the codes as well. If anything happens to me, at least you'll have control of the ship, for all the good it'll do you," she added. She made a motion of pushing him away as she continued. "Now, leave me alone while I'm working. I don't need the distraction."

CHAPTER TWENTY-TWO

Albretti continued to admire his wife's naked body as he pushed her to the other side of their bed with a reluctant hand. "No fair, Sara," he said, grinning. "You know I can't stay any longer right now, since Sam asked me to fill in for *Pathfinder*'s captain today. That means they can't start the tests on the updated warp-field generators without my being there. He's sending a shuttle down to pick me up."

She grinned with equal admiration at her husband as he got out of bed. "That's too bad, lover. It was wonderful to have the place to ourselves last night after dropping Gina off with Mark and Karen. I really enjoyed the way we woke up this morning and was looking forward to our inspecting the south fields today, just the two of us," she said mischievously. "I guess I'll have to go by myself. You can think about me while you're in space. You can also think about the fact that Gina will be back with us tonight, and the lost opportunity that represents," she concluded with an amused look.

He got up and headed toward the bathroom to get ready. "This test had better be worth it," he grumbled as he looked back over his shoulder and saw his wife stretched out on the bed once again, with her delightful curves in full view.

"Alan and Bret seem to think so," she called through the doorway.

Albretti laughed. "That's true, but we haven't quite gotten there yet." His expression turned serious. "I don't want to sound like I don't have any faith in them though. Their progress has been amazing, even though things don't always work out the way we think they will."

Suddenly, Sara was through the doorway, her own expression serious. "I don't care about whether they succeed. I just care about you. What worries me is the fact that those experiments sometimes don't work out; space-time can be pretty nasty when it distorts nearby and reaches for you. Promise me you won't be anywhere near the place, after *Pathfinder* has done its job."

In an instant, she was in her husband's arms in a tight embrace, and her gaze turned mischievous again. "Maybe we'll think of some way to celebrate later anyway," she said

CHAPTER TWENTY-THREE

P owers headed toward a shuttle, her steps containing a slight spring of anticipation. Once aboard the shuttle, she brought images of the planet online with a few quick gestures. Although the proportion of land and ocean was around the same as on Earth, the three main continents of Citadel would never be mistaken for the ones back home. She took note of the mountain ranges that thrust high into the skies on the continent that the settlers had chosen to call home. Although the peaks would be dwarfed by the Himalayan range, they were proof that the planet was alive, tectonically speaking. Even though the color palette differed from that of Earth's in places, the overall view was still one that felt familiar to humans looking down from space, with a predominance of blue and other colors that "muddied" things up.

None of these facts mattered to Powers. Instead, she worked to break remotely from her shuttle into the communications array for the planet and confirm the locations of Liz Austin and Sara Albretti. She was on a tight schedule and needed to find her targets quickly.

Powers turned her skills toward the greatest prey of all, Liz Austin. With the capture of Austin's wife, anything was possible. Powers's calm demeanor showed increasing strain with the passing of each minute. She cursed the fact that, for many decades, Austin had managed to stay ahead of everyone when it came to maintaining unbreakable encryption for his personal communications. While communications arrays normally included the ability to track people linked into them, he'd clearly implemented an extra layer of technology over this one, so that no matter what steps others took, he and his family couldn't be tracked without his permission.

Powers finally had to concede defeat. She'd have to be satisfied with capturing Sara Albretti. She enjoyed a moment of satisfaction as she broke through the security and located her quarry. She could hardly believe her good fortune, as her target was out by herself on the land she shared with her husband. *She's probably inspecting something boring, like a crop*, Powers mused.

As her shuttle began its descent, she performed some additional electronic magic.

CHAPTER TWENTY-FOUR

Cheaters were the most lethal animals yet encountered on Citadel, after humans. Although their faces would never be mistaken for those of the great cats on Earth, they had a lot in common with their fellow predators. They walked on four limbs, and their bodies revealed a superb combination of flexibility and brute strength, backed up by terrifying claws and fangs. Their fur was short and mottled in a pattern somewhat like that of cheetahs, with vaguely similar markings around the eyes. However, they were larger than cheetahs and much tougher and stronger, suggesting something at least as large and deadly as a leopard or jaguar.

Like leopards, they were excellent climbers and famed for their patience when waiting for prey and for attacking without warning. Unlike leopards or jaguars, they weren't shy about attacking humans, which the first explorers learned the hard way. They considered these skills to be developed almost to an unfair advantage, practically cheating. It seemed natural to call them cheaters.

Although many cheaters had been persuaded, one way or another, to avoid the areas where the humans had carved out their homes, not all of them had been willing to move into the territories of their fellow cheaters and engage in deadly fights for survival against their brethren. They were solitary creatures and continued to hunt the animals that their ancestors had been hunting for thousands of years. Their patience meant that the human intruders sometimes became prey too.

Powers analyzed the information from Sara's link to learn when she would be alone. Although Powers had a lot of confidence in her own abilities, she'd watched Joe Albretti in action when he'd stopped Roetter's attempt to kill Austin. He'd saved Austin's life by killing the would-be assassin with efficient, lethal moves. Trying to move against Sara while Albretti was around would make things riskier than they needed to be. The better approach was to be sure he was nowhere near when Powers moved against his wife. Powers considered it a good sign to learn that Sara was in a remote part of their holdings on Citadel, while Albretti was off planet, on *Pathfinder*.

Sara's transport was nearby, and she felt secure from threats like cheaters due to her vehicle's ability to detect and alert her to the presence of the deadly animals. She'd been looking at one of their crops, a hardy, native plant that was akin to an Earth grain; its shades of magenta and violet moved slightly in the gentle breeze.

After having completed her survey of the crop, she took the time to appreciate the stunning views around her. The edge of the plantings bordered upon a forest, with thick canopies of branches and leaves that had never been disturbed by humans. Farther into the distance, beyond their lands, was a range of mountains, the sides painted with blues, grays, greens, and browns, plus some exotic colors from unique native growths with no Earth counterparts. The caps were frosted with powdery snow. The mountain range rippled through many of the settlers' holdings, reaching all the way to the Austin acreage and beyond. Thin wisps of clouds drifted lazily around the mountain caps, disturbing an otherwise brilliant blue sky.

A distracted cheater didn't realize that another hunter was observing it from some distance away, through means the animal could not understand. The predator was instead focused on one of those humans that had first appeared when the cheater was little older than a cub. Humans were nothing like anything else the cheater had known, being a strange combination of predator and prey.

The animal had first become aware of the intruder when the wind shifted, bringing with it the unmistakable scent of humans. With the wind as a guide, the cheater soon spotted the prey. With terrible patience, the lithe stalker seemed to blend and melt its way through the forest canopy toward the creature. It was now at the edge of the forest, practically within striking range. Strangely, this human moved in an irregular pattern, showing no signs that it was aware of the clawed death poised nearby. None of the cheater's other prey would have been so careless.

Powers took in the scene through her scope, understanding why Sara was clueless about the danger. Prior to moving into a low orbit, Powers had managed a remote break-in to the systems that kept track of ships entering and leaving Citadel space and blocked them from seeing her vessel. She then did the same thing with the systems that controlled Sara's home and security, allowing Powers's descent from space to Sara's lands to go unnoticed. The beauty of the untamed world had made no impression on her as she'd nudged her craft over unfamiliar terrain toward her landing spot. Powers had managed to touch down so quietly that not even the cheater had been aware of her presence.

She frowned slightly as she took note of the animal's movements. Under other circumstances, she would have been glad to leave the hunter to complete its objective, but Harrington wanted Sara alive and unharmed. With an inaudible sigh, Powers trained her scope on the cheater and waited.

Sara had wandered gradually toward the edge of the planted fields. The day had started out overcast and cool, but the weather was changing rapidly, and the sun's rays beat down with increasing heat. She'd unzipped her jacket and wanted to take advantage of the shade offered by the extensive canopy. Before she reached the forest, she stopped, smiled, closed her eyes, and raised her face to take in the warmth of the sun. She started as she heard sounds she knew very well. She lunged to one side as a familiar shape burst from the forest in her direction and heard the sound of a gun from a different direction.

The shape seemed to flinch, and something was missing from what would have been a perfectly fluid movement of muscle, claws, and fangs. Sara had drawn her weapon by the time the cheater reached the ground and dispatched it with several shots to the head.

She approached the body with wary steps, her thoughts slightly off-balance. *Where the hell did that thing come from, and why didn't I get any warning?* She also wondered where the shot had come from. She knew she'd probably have been dead without the distraction of that shot.

She fought the urge to whirl around as a voice called out calmly, "Don't move, Albretti, if you want to avoid what the cheater got. Drop your gun, knife, pack, and belt, and then put your arms up where I can see them." After Sara complied, the voice continued. "All right, now step away from your gear. Stop at ten paces, and then you can turn around. If you stop at nine paces, I'll shoot you."

Sara was puzzled to see an unfamiliar woman facing her, although she had a vague sense that she should know her. "Who are you, and why are you following me?"

"Aren't you going to thank me for saving your life?" Powers answered sardonically.

"Thanks," Sara said. "Why go to the trouble of saving my life to hold a weapon on me?"

"I've been wondering the same thing, but someone wants to meet you and prefers that you be alive at the time."

"Who is that person?"

"You'll find out at the right time." Powers tossed a pair of restraints, which landed at Sara's feet. "Put these on, hands behind you."

Sara's gaze was cold. "I don't think so," she replied. "I'm not going to truss myself up and walk for miles through rough terrain to whatever ground transport you have stashed somewhere."

"Don't worry," Powers said. "We only have about a mile to go."

Sara was confused. "There's nothing in the way of a settlement for miles, and I know there isn't a shuttle any-where around here; the alarms would have alerted me."

"You mean the same alarms that should have alerted you to the cheater?" Powers asked tauntingly.

"So much for saving my life after all," Sara replied sarcastically. "I wouldn't have been in any danger if you hadn't screwed with my security in the first place." She thought about the implications. "There aren't many peo-ple who could do that," she said slowly. "I'm sure there isn't anyone on Citadel who would do it, so that means you aren't from around here." Her eyes widened as rec-ognition flashed across her face. "Powers! I knew there was something about you that bothered me."

Powers nodded slightly. "I'm impressed, Albretti." She motioned toward her face with one hand while keep-ing her weapon trained on Sara. "You're the first person to recognize me since I took on the new me."

"You must be crazy to come to Citadel, Powers," Sara said incredulously. "The only thing that's saved your neck from a noose so far is the distance between our two systems. I'm sure Sam will thank you for saving him the trouble of tracking you down and hanging you. You can rot in hell with your lover, Roetter!"

Powers's calm expression faded for a moment. "Roetter wasn't my lover!"

"That's not what one of your colleagues said," Sara retorted. "You answered the hatch stark-naked after he caught the two of you in the sack together. Can't say much about your taste in men," she said with disdain.

Powers glared at Sara. "That was just for show, and it worked. Anyway, Roetter had too high an opinion of his abilities for his own good. He should have been able to carry out his mission. He would have, except Austin got lucky." Her expression turned feral as she continued. "Believe me, if I'd been the one with the mission, Austin would be dead."

Now it was Sara's turn to do some taunting. "No, it just means that *you* would have been the one I spotted instead of Roetter. You wouldn't have been any less dead than Roetter after Joe got through with you."

Powers decided that the conversation had gone on long enough. "We're getting off point. Put the restraints on."

Sara didn't move, so Powers kept her gaze focused on her prey's face as she pulled a different weapon from a holster. Sara lunged to one side as a round went off, missing her by a few millimeters. In an instant, she had pulled on a low-hanging branch, and it whipped back into the path of the next round, deflecting it. She melted into the thick growth, dodging through the uneven terrain as fast as her legs would take her. Powers cursed under her breath as she dashed after her would-be prisoner.

The lack of any trails worked to Sara's advantage, as Powers couldn't anticipate where her quarry would be and aim another shot accordingly. With plenty of plants and trees forming a natural maze, there was no way for Powers to take a shortcut to capture her prey. She had little choice but to keep after Sara and trust that her own link's special technology would help Powers keep track of Sara's movements.

She knew she was still on the right track as she saw Sara's jacket, crumpled and thrust into a bush, as if removed in great haste. She frowned as she realized it meant she could no longer count on following the jacket's bright color.

A hasty glance at her link told her Sara was nearby, although still moving away. She smiled as she noted the direction her quarry had taken while marveling at her sense of direction in the tangled wilderness. Sara was obviously counting on the surrounding growth providing cover long enough for her to make her way back to her surface transport and to safety. She would already have tried to send a call for help, only to find that Powers had overridden the communications system, blocking any messages from being sent. Sara was no fool; she knew about Powers's technological skills and must have known that Powers would be able to track her with her link. Sara would have already switched off her own link to avoid being tracked through it.

Unfortunately for Sara, her pursuer's own link was sophisticated enough to continue to track her quarry even with Sara's link shut off. Powers began to make her way toward Sara's transport as well, although with slightly less of a sense of urgency than her quarry undoubtedly had.

Sara's transport was parked near the edge of a clearing. She stopped as she stood next to a grove of trees, leery of stepping into the open. She saw no sign of Powers and decided to make a quick run for the transport.

Almost immediately, she found herself on the ground, crawling back behind the protection of the trees, as the transport's defenses targeted her as an unwelcome intruder. She stared at her link, which should have identified her to the vehicle as a friendly figure, even if it was shut off. She paused for a moment in shock, then anger as she realized that Powers had anticipated the move and ensured that she wouldn't be able to get near the vehicle.

She heard a sound behind her and dived to one side just as a round slammed into the tree near where she'd been crouching. She twisted as she moved and saw Powers approaching carefully, blocking Sara's retreat. Powers fired another round as Sara shifted in a different direction, followed by another miss. She couldn't keep it up though; Powers had planned her position well. She was too far away for Sara to reach her with a sudden move but close enough that there wasn't anyplace for Sara to use for cover. Finally, a round struck her, and she crumpled to the ground.

Fortunately for Sara, Powers had taken her orders seriously and used a tranquilizing projectile. Although she should have been in a good mood over having subdued her quarry, she surveyed the situation with a sour expression. She'd downplayed the distance to the shuttle to keep her captive guessing, and it hadn't helped that they'd ended up even farther away as Sara sought escape. The hidden craft was now over two miles away. Leaving Sara there while she walked to the shuttle wasn't an option. There'd be hell to pay if she returned and found Sara wounded or worse by the local predators. She replaced the tranquilizer rounds in her weapon with lethal ones, since tranquilizers didn't have much effect on cheaters. She stifled a curse as she picked up her limp captive and started toward the shuttle.

Although she considered using Sara's transport, she'd been surprised to learn that she couldn't just override the security features on the vehicle. She'd found herself having to step back within the safety of the forest as Sara had done, to avoid being targeted. She needed the biometric codes contained within Sara's link, which was on the ground nearby. Powers realized that Sara must have found a moment to wipe the codes. Since Sara wasn't waking up anytime soon, there was no way to get the codes to reactivate the link's security features. Powers scanned the area, her concern increasing. The longer they stayed on the planet, the more likely her plan would fall apart.

With each step, Powers was reminded that the distance itself wasn't the only problem. She was traveling over land that had never known a paved road or even enough repeat traffic to create a trail. Hers was an intricate dance that required her to dodge roots, rocks, and holes constantly, while balancing an awkward load. A twisted or broken ankle could be deadly, as there was no one she could call for help.

At least I won't have to worry about cheaters paying a visit much longer, she thought with some satisfaction. She'd made certain her shuttle was equipped with a detection system. It had a limited range, so Powers and Sara were still unprotected. Soon, however, the human hunter would be able to receive warnings through her link if there were sign of any clawed death lurking nearby.

She continued to pick her way through a tangled web of roots and undergrowth, cursing the fact that she couldn't take her eyes off the ground for more than a few seconds at a time. Suddenly, she heard a sound overhead and sought out the source. At the same moment she took her eyes off the ground, the sole of her boot slipped along the edge of a root, and her awkward load sent her hurtling to the side. Sara dropped limply to the ground.

Powers was lucky to have slipped when she did, as the cheater was startled by the change in position. She wasn't completely unscathed; a claw had scratched a path across her thigh. She was a predator in her own right, and her weapon was already drawn and seeking its target before the animal even reached the ground. In an instant, several rounds entered the attacker's oddly shaped skull. The animal slumped to the ground as the life drained rapidly from its golden eyes.

Powers took a look at her leg and was relieved to find that the scratch wasn't deep enough to prevent her from placing weight on it. She needed a bandage that would last until she reached her shuttle, however, so she tore a strip from her shirt and bound the leg well enough to stay in place for a while.

She looked back toward her captive and checked for any injuries from dropping her to the ground. Her expression was anything but friendly as she picked up her awkward burden again and headed toward her shuttle.

After stumbling over seemingly endless tangles of terrain, they finally reached the shuttle. Several more times during the trek, she'd nearly tripped while carrying her still-unconscious load, worrying if she'd be able to shed the extra weight in time to avoid being taken out by another cheater. The heat of the day, plus carrying Sara's dead weight and fending off the cheater, had left her brow and the front of her jumpsuit covered in sweat.

Without ceremony, she dumped her unmoving cargo on the deck near the rear of the shuttle. After checking to make sure Sara was still out, she pulled her prisoner's arms behind her and fastened the restraints. She then used another set of restraints to tie the first set to a cargo tie-down.

For the first time in what seemed like hours, Powers was finally able to exhale in relief. She pulled off her jumpsuit so she could take a closer look at her leg. She'd been lucky; the tough material had taken most of the blow. She reached for a first aid kit to clean her wound properly. She reveled in the fact that she felt cool for the first time since touching down on the planet. She had her prey, and it was time to return to the ship before anyone figured out what was happening. She wasn't ready to relax, however, since she still had some tricky maneuvers ahead.

Powers finally started to relax as her shuttle was on its final approach to *KT-2*. A glance behind her confirmed that Sara was still out and restrained. After receiving a brief signal from the shuttle, the exterior hatch to the shuttle bay opened, admitting the craft. In an earlier time, images from the interior of the bay would have reflected off the main window, but they'd long since moved toward getting their images from displays, which filtered out distractions. Moments later, the bay was sealed and pressurizing. While she waited for the bay to become habitable, she worked at a display to take the final steps to cover her tracks. An innocuous message to the *KT-2* communications system sent everything back to its previous status, with no trail leading back to her. She was relieved to note that there were even a few minutes to spare before the Citadel system blackout ended. Their mission was still secret.

Flynn greeted her at the airlock as she pulled her prisoner aboard the ship. His eyes widened as he took note of the fact that her jumpsuit was soaked with sweat and zipped down far enough to see that most of her shirt was missing. From the tear in the leg of her jumpsuit, he guessed the shirt was serving as a bandage.

He reached over to help carry Sara, but Powers pushed him away. "I can take care of her, Flynn," she said, clearly pissed over the trouble she'd experienced but determined to finish the job. Flynn watched as Powers walked away with her prisoner.

CHAPTER TWENTY-FIVE

Powers had cleaned up and was meeting with Harrington and Flynn. The former president was having trouble seeing the bright side of things as Powers reported on her results. "While I admit that capturing Captain Albretti is important for us, you let the most important target all get away," she complained.

"Even I have limits when it comes to Austin and his special privacy technology," Powers retorted. "He's had over a hundred years of staying ahead of practically everyone else when it comes to preventing people from monitoring his activities. Even the US government has been burned in the past when caught trying to snoop on him."

"His security hasn't always been foolproof. Nearly anyone can be corrupted, and someone once found the right person," Harrington replied maliciously. "That precious house of his in California didn't do so well that time."

"Let's keep in mind the rest of that story," Powers said, frowning. "It wasn't one of Austin's people who sold him out but someone within the government. That was back when the government still had key information about his security measures, left over from when he was president of the United States. He's never allowed that kind of information to be shared since then. He obviously doesn't even share it with the rest of Citadel," she said ruefully.

"All right, I see your point," Harrington conceded. "Are you sure you covered all your tracks? Is there any way they could trace that shuttle back here?"

Powers shook her head. "Not a chance. Even Bret Yabuno couldn't find us, and he's at least as good as I am," she acknowledged.

"She's starting to wake up," Flynn said, as he kept watch on a display.

Harrington was looking forward to meeting an old adversary. "Let's not keep her waiting."

Sara awoke in an unfamiliar cabin, slightly groggy but otherwise unharmed. She moved off the bunk easily, noting that there weren't any restraints. As her head swung around, she came to a sudden stop. There were three people in the compartment with her. She wasn't surprised to see Powers, considering that Powers had kidnapped her. There was also a man she didn't recognize. However, thoughts of those two vanished and a shocked look rippled across her face.

"Harrington!" she gasped. "What the hell are you doing here?"

"Nice to see you too, Captain Albretti," Harrington replied without warmth. "I've been looking forward to this moment for quite some time.

"What could possibly bring you to Citadel, knowing that you've already been found guilty of war crimes and crimes against humanity? Have you decided to make things easier all around and surrender?" she asked sarcastically.

"I've no intention of ever making things easier for Sam Austin," Harrington replied with a smile that added no warmth to her expression.

Sara looked around. "Where are we? I can tell we're on one of our transports."

For the first time, the man spoke. "My name is Flynn, Captain. This isn't just any transport; it's your former command, *KT-2*. Welcome home," he said.

Sara's gaze grew suspicious. "If this is *KT-2*, then Captain Benitez is in command. Where is he?"

"Captain Benitez had trouble understanding the need for cooperation on his part and forced us to take extreme measures to obtain certain information."

Sara fought back shocked tears. "You killed him— probably to get his command codes for running this ship! What good would those codes do you, anyway? There can't be more than a skeleton crew left on board." She looked at Powers dismissively. "You may be smart, but even you can't run one of these things."

Flynn drew her attention back to him. "For now, all you need to know is that there is a specific assignment for you to carry out. If you do as you're told, you'll get out of this situation in one piece."

"Cross us," Harrington said, "and you'll wish you could walk out an airlock without a suit rather than face your friends on Citadel and tell them their loved ones are dead because of you."

"If my friends die, it will be because *you* killed them, Harrington, not me," Sara said defiantly.

"That won't make them any less dead, Captain," Harrington warned.

CHAPTER TWENTY-SIX

Austin was aboard *Pathfinder* as the scout ship pre-pared to escort another cargo ship through the radiation field. It was time for another test, and Austin wanted to get a better view of the festivities. He had bor-rowed Joe Albretti to serve as *Pathfinder's* captain for the mission, since the regular captain was unavailable and Albretti understood *Pathfinder* as well as anyone.

"The test rat is being towed into position behind us, Sam," Albretti said with a grin. Austin looked at a display and saw the cargo ship fall into line behind them as they headed toward the planet-side entrance to the radiation field.

Albretti's grin changed to a frown as the communica-tions specialist gave him a message. "Something strange is happening back home," he explained to Austin.

"What is it, Joe?" Austin asked with a quizzical look.

"Sara is overdue to pick up Gina. Mark and Karen can't raise her on her link. She was out inspecting one of our fields today."

"Where is she? Is she still out there or somewhere else? What does the system say?"

"That's just the problem," Albretti said with increasing concern. "She isn't showing up anywhere. She's completely off the grid."

"Bring *Pathfinder* and the test ship to a halt, so we can focus on finding Sara," Austin ordered. "We can worry about the test another time."

"That's not necessary," Albretti protested. "It probably isn't anything more than a glitch somewhere and shouldn't inconvenience everyone else. I can take a shuttle back to Citadel to sort things out. You're just as good a captain of *Pathfinder* as I am."

"Whether I can serve as *Pathfinder*'s captain isn't the point," Austin replied. "While it might just be a technical failure on the part of her link or a glitch in the system, it might be that Sara is in trouble and needs our help. We don't abandon our people, Joe, so bring this ship to a stop, and have the other one do so as well."

Austin looked at another display as he said to the communications specialist, "Get Melody Lambert online right away. I also want satellite images of where Sara went today. Joe will give you the location and the time. Pass it along to Melody as well. Find Sara's ground transport and scour the area around it for any signs of her."

Moments later, Lambert's face showed up on another display. "What's up, Sam?" she asked.

"Sara Albretti has gone missing," Austin replied. "She was supposed to be on her land on Citadel. Check whether there are any problems with the system, and try to locate her through her link or anything else you can think of."

"We have a problem, Sam," the communications specialist called out. "There aren't any satellite images from that location during the time Sara was there."

"You hear that?" Austin asked Lambert as he linked their communications together. After she nodded, he said, "You should have the data on Sara's location by now. Are we missing satellite images from that area for the entire day or just from when Sara was there?"

A look of intense concentration flashed across her face as she consulted other displays. "This isn't right. We have satellite images for most of the day, but there's a gap."

"Is there any reason for the gap? Resource reallocation, maintenance, glitch, sunspots?"

Lambert shook her head. "Nothing."

"Are there any images from that area that show Sara arriving?"

"Yes." Lambert nodded. "She definitely arrived while using her ground transport. I also have images of her as she moved around the fields."

"What about her link?" Austin asked. "Do we have data from it from the same time as the satellite images?"

"Yes. The images and the data cease at about the same time. Come to think of it, I can get access to her ground transport's logs and see what they have to say about any data from its security system." Lambert frowned. "That data was cut off at the same time. That doesn't look like a coincidence."

"Not likely," he agreed, his expression darkening. "How long does the blackout on the satellite images last? Is it long enough for someone to take a shuttle down, wander around a bit, and then take a shuttle back up?"

Lambert was startled. "How did you know?"

"That would be a reason for cutting off the data—someone didn't want to be seen while visiting that area."

"And kidnapping Sara?" Albretti asked. "Why?"

"It doesn't make sense," Austin said. He turned back toward the display. "Melody, we have other satellites and sensors. Check to see if there are any other images of the area or of any shuttle in the area around that time. Maybe we'll get lucky. Also, I want to confirm the status of every shuttle in this system. If a shuttle was out somewhere, I want to know where, with a visual confirmation. If a shuttle is supposed to be in its bay, I want a visual confirmation. Check with every transport and see if any shuttles are missing."

"I'm working on it."

Austin brought Liz up on his link. "Liz, I know you're in the middle of coordinating the off-loading of the new settlers from *KT-2*, but Sara Albretti has gone missing while inspecting her fields. We can't locate her through her link or anything else. We need to be thorough and rule out any possibility that she's still there and needs our help. I want you to organize a search party and scour the area. I'm sending the coordinates and the time she arrived. Make sure Mark and Karen know.

"Her ground transport is still there, so she can't have gotten far on foot. Double the distance she might have traveled on foot, and check out everything within that area. Use everything you have to check for any thermals or other signs that she's still there.

Liz looked at him in alarm. "What aren't you telling me? You sound like you don't think she's there at all, which doesn't make sense. She can't just vanish from a planet."

"She couldn't without some help, and we're assuming that any help was unwanted. We're also checking out every place off planet we can think of."

Lambert came back online as Liz signed off. "I have some preliminary news, Sam. There isn't a single view of that terrain from any other location during the time in question, even using magnification from extreme distances away." She shook her head. "There's no way that all of those locations would come up blank."

"What about any images of a shuttle that left Citadel? It had to go somewhere, and even if the images were deleted, the path of those deletions might tell us where to look."

"I'm still checking on it, but it doesn't look like we have images of shuttles anywhere for an extended period."

Austin's expression became harder. "How long?"

"Long enough for a shuttle to reach just about anyplace within this solar system and park itself."

Albretti was incredulous. "You mean someone shut down key sensors throughout this system and no one noticed?"

"Take it easy, Joe," Austin said in a lower voice. "We'll deal with what we have for now and worry about other things later."

"We're still checking on the status of every shuttle in this system, but the operation of some shuttles is automated, so we might not have direct confirmation regarding the activities of each of them. Also, people don't always log in when boarding a shuttle, so we may not be able to match a shuttle's activities with people we can interview. In some cases, we may be limited to getting a visual confirmation that a shuttle has been parked in its bay."

"What about things like individual ships? While they can be networked into the system, it would be next to impossible to shut down their sensors without raising a lot of alarms. Maybe one of them detected something that was blocked elsewhere."

Lambert nodded. "We're checking on it, Sam, and collecting everything that they have, but so far, we haven't seen any images where a shuttle would have traveled."

Austin's gaze showed his frustration. "OK, I understand, Melody. Let me know when you have more information." Austin turned away from the displays. "Is there anything that's happened recently that seems out of the ordinary in any way, Joe?"

Albretti shook his head. "Nothing. Sara's been checking out our fields over the last week; it hasn't been anything unusual."

"Who knew about her location?"

"Not many people." He shrugged. "While it hasn't been a big secret, only Mark, Karen, and I knew the specific place she would be visiting today." He stared at Austin. "How the hell did whoever took her know where to look?"

"Exactly." Austin nodded. He contacted Yabuno on his link. Moments later, Yabuno's image appeared on a display. "Melody filled me in on what's been happening. Joe, you know we'll do whatever is necessary to find Sara. Sam, what can I do to help?"

"You know our systems better than just about anyone. See if you can find out whether someone tried to use the system to get Sara's location. Maybe you can backtrack and learn something about the person. Come to think of it, check to see if anyone else has been the subject of a location inquiry today, and then let's eliminate all legitimate inquiries. Most of the time, someone just contacts the other person directly instead of using the system, so it shouldn't take long. The other thing I want is for you to figure out how someone got access to our systems in the first place and to make sure no one can do it again."

After Yabuno signed off, Austin spoke to the communications specialist. "It may be a case of closing the barn door after the horse has escaped, but until further notice, I want all shuttles to get clearance before departing for anyplace within the system. Before clearance is granted, there needs to be a physical inspection, including scanning for life signs. Also, everyone needs to log in to board a shuttle."

Yabuno came back online. His features showed a level of concern that hadn't been there before. "First, I have confirmation that someone wanted to know Sara's location. Since Sara lives with Joe, the system very politely added that Joe is off world, on *Pathfinder*. However, there's more bad news; someone wanted to know where Liz was today."

In spite of the concern over Sara's absence, Austin spoke with a touch of grim humor. "I have a feeling you're going to tell me my extra security protocols kept the person from learning anything."

Yabuno gave a humorless snort. "Yes, you'll remind me this is another reason why you've been so stubborn over the years about taking extra steps to protect yourself, and you'd be right. If it had been a legitimate inquiry, we'd know the identity of the person making the request. This person was good enough to break off the inquiry before giving away anything.

"While I haven't yet worked out every place with this person's fingerprints in our systems, I've made some temporary changes to ensure that sensors and other monitoring systems can't be locked out without my OK. If someone plans on moving around this system again, we'll have a record."

"There's something about the inquiry and associated skills needed to pull this off that feels familiar," Yabuno said, deep in thought. "Not just anyone could do what this person did."

"Check out all of Melody's people that have the skills to do it. For that matter, check out anyone within Citadel whom you believe may have the skills. I hope to God we don't have a rotten apple, but if we do, we'd better find it quickly. What else?"

Yabuno brought up a familiar image. "*KT-2* arrived earlier today, with a lot of settlers who have already been off-loaded and are in the process of getting to their lands." He pointed to images of multiple shuttles heading to Citadel.

Austin closed his eyes for a moment, as thoughts of treachery from years ago came back to him. "Heaven help us if there's another saboteur among us after all this time. Check their backgrounds to see if any of them has the skills needed to pull this off. Also, confirm all of their locations, and see if anyone has been near Sara's location today. Liz can help you with the information."

Yabuno's gaze grew harder. "Let's get back to the main point. While going after anyone is a bad sign, it gets much worse if we know someone is after Liz, because that means someone is really after you. I've already notified the rest of the team to let us know if anyone else is missing, but I'm guessing that there won't be anyone else, because there weren't any other inquiries."

"Why go after just Sara and Liz, then? With the sensors compromised, this person, or group of persons, could have gone after others without our knowing it."

"Maybe there was a limited window of time available and only one or two targets could be fit within that window. Once Liz was eliminated because she couldn't be located, the person went to the next target."

"Sara," Albretti said. "That might be why there weren't any other inquiries; once the person knew Sara was available and I wasn't nearby, there wouldn't have been any need to check on anyone else. Sara might have just been a form of leverage to get at Sam specifically or Citadel generally, not that it makes me feel any better," he added.

"Another possibility is that you or Sara were really the target, Joe," Yabuno said. "If that's the case, we need to figure out who the hell hates Sara or you enough to go to all this trouble."

"I'm not sure there's anyone like that, not with the means of making it happen. It makes more sense that Sara was just the next one on the list after Liz wasn't available."

"Her Majesty hates everyone at Citadel enough to try to strike at us," Yabuno said pointedly.

"Yes, but Harrington's under house arrest, in another star system," Albretti replied. "The only way she could act against us is by sending someone here on one of our transports, and she doesn't have the power of the US government behind her anymore to make it happen."

"I hope that means her wings really are clipped enough not to be able to do any more mischief," Austin said. "If that's true, we still need to figure out who's responsible, and for what purpose."

"That's strange," Albretti said, gazing at a display.

"What's strange?" Austin asked.

"*KT-2* just arrived and off-loaded its passengers and cargo, right?"

"We know that. What's the problem?"

"The ship is heading away from the yard. If they stay on course, they'll end up back at the entrance to the radiation field on this side."

"Without getting checked out in the yard or taking on cargo for the return trip?" Yabuno asked in surprise. "Hell, they can't have more than a skeleton crew aboard right now; the rest of the crew must be scattered all over the system, after having been cooped up for three months. There's no way they could be planning on heading back to Earth with that setup."

"Perhaps they're just retracing their steps to check on something they noticed on the way in," Albretti suggested.

"Jose Benitez is her captain right now, isn't he?" Austin asked.

"That's right." Albretti nodded. "He took over after Sara stepped down as her captain. He's a good man, knows what he's doing."

"While I normally don't want to micromanage a captain running his ship, we sure as hell don't need a distraction like this while we're worried about Sara," Austin said in a clipped tone. "Contact Benitez and advise him of what's been happening. Find out why he isn't taking his ship over to the yard for its scheduled maintenance and inspection. If there's something he wants to check out near the radiation field, tell him we'll send a probe later.

"While you're at it, ask him if he has data on any shuttles that may have been operating in his area. I know Melody may have already gotten to him with her request for data, but he's shorthanded right now. Offer to send someone over to look at the data."

As Yabuno went back to working with Lambert to analyze the data from the other ships, Austin contacted Liz. "How's the search coming along?"

"We have a team heading over to the site right now. Tell Joe it wasn't hard to get people to help, especially when they knew it was Sara who is missing," she answered, clearly pleased. "Mark is helping, and Karen is still looking after Gina. We'll have some good portable detection equipment on site. Hopefully, we'll be able to spot something that can't be seen from orbit." Her smile faded. "You realize that finding Sara may not be good news."

"Yes," Austin replied tersely. "She could be dead and buried somewhere on their land, with her link and other personal gear destroyed to avoid tracking. However, a recently buried body is just about impossible to hide with the equipment we have. Freshly disturbed ground will show up, as will thermal signatures. There would be other anomalies as well.

"Now, as important as it is to find Sara, I want you to stay behind locked doors, and let no one in until I say it's OK. Have Mark take charge on site."

"This is worse than Sara getting lost, isn't it?" she asked uneasily. "What else is going on?"

"I already mentioned that we have reason to believe that Sara was abducted. The person who did it was good enough to defeat every form of surveillance that's part of the system and hide the approach and escape, probably in a shuttle. We're not sure where Sara is right now, although she must still be in the star system.

"What's changed since we last talked is that the system shows that someone tried to find out *your* location in addition to locating Sara. We believe you were the first target, and Sara was targeted only because the extra security measures I incorporated into our systems couldn't be compromised."

Her eyes widened in alarm as she asked, "In that case, shouldn't Matt, Luke, and I be around people we know and trust, instead of alone?"

Austin shook his head. "No, for two reasons. The first is that in a group, you need to be absolutely certain about every one of them for it to be a secure environment. There is always the chance of other people showing up. Those people would need to be monitored, which may not work if people have to split up to conduct a search. All it takes is a moment for an accident to happen that isn't really an accident, and you're either dead or missing.

"The second reason is that the security at our place is the best around. Since the main system couldn't get past our measures, our system will detect anyone approaching who isn't supposed to be there. I'm going to modify the system remotely to respond lethally to anyone who isn't authorized by me. Also, is the ground transport within the compound?"

"Yes."

"Good. I'm also going to instruct the ground transport to use its weapons to deal with any kind of attack, especially one that might come from a shuttle." There was a dangerous glint in Austin's gaze. "We don't need to talk about other security measures that haven't been made public.

"Other than staying on *Pathfinder*, there isn't anyplace else in this system where you might be as secure, and there's a hell of a lot more room for you to stretch your legs in our compound than along the decks here. The view's much nicer too," Austin said with a bit of grim humor.

"All right, Sam, I'll stay here with the boys. Mark probably needs to feel that he's doing extra anyway, since it's his family too."

As Liz signed off, Albretti spoke with Austin. "Benitez is tied up with his engineering people, so I spoke with someone on his bridge named Morrison. She said they detected some unusual readings at the outer entrance to the radiation field before coming in. Benitez didn't think it was important enough to hold things up, with everyone being stir-crazy from a three-month voyage, so he took care of that and off-loading his cargo before going back.

"Everyone who plans on being off during the lay-over has already left, so checking it out now won't be an inconvenience for anyone else." In spite of the moment, Albretti made a small noise. "She rolled her eyes and said that the more important reason is that his girlfriend has been held up for a day out by the mines, and he needs to stay occupied until they can get together."

"All right," Austin said reluctantly. "I guess we'll cut him a little slack. No reason why he can't be doing something useful while they have the time. What were these readings?" Austin asked.

"She said she didn't know any details; the captain and the engineers were looking into it."

"We have more important things to handle, so don't worry about it now, but when you have a moment, check out the readings from our regular sensors around that entrance. I'll be interested in hearing about them. The issue had better not be completely bogus, because his staff should be able to take a break during the layover, even if they're stuck aboard ship."

CHAPTER TWENTY-SEVEN

Powers and Flynn were on the bridge. The vessel was underway, heading toward the radiation field and a perverse kind of safety. They had a new problem to deal with.

"Where is Captain Benitez?" demanded the transport's pilot, who was known throughout the transport community as "Wash."

"That's not your concern right now, Mr. Washington," Flynn said. "Your only concern is getting this ship through the radiation field safely."

Wash crossed his arms as he replied, "You can pilot this ship yourself if you want, but I'm not doing anything until you tell me what's happened to Captain Benitez." He threw a disgusted look at Powers as he continued. "I don't know why you sold us out, Morrison, but good luck trying to get us through on your own."

Flynn's expression didn't change as he nodded to Powers, who brought a new image up on a display. Several people gasped and turned away quickly. The glazed eyes of Benitez looked out at them vacantly, confirming that they were looking at a corpse.

"You bastards," Wash said furiously. "You can go fuck yourselves before I'll help you."

"Careful, Wash," Powers replied calmly as she walked over to another member of the bridge crew. In a move that was so smooth it seemed almost casual, she drew her weapon and aimed it at the crew member. The terrified man could only stare at the barrel as it pointed between his eyes. "The fact that Captain Benitez is dead should show you that we're quite serious," she continued. "Do you really want another example?"

Wash glared at Powers but knew he couldn't sacrifice another life. "All right, Morrison, you win. I'll pilot us through the radiation field, for all the good it'll do you. Don't plan on any help if you want to use the warp-field generators," he warned. "Since you didn't wait to have them inspected, we have no idea whether they're in any kind of shape to be used."

With the same deceptively casual movement, Powers pulled her weapon away from her target's head. "Just get us through the radiation field, Wash, and we'll take it from there," she answered. "Remember, I can always take out someone if you try to play any games with us. If I do, it'll be one of your friends." The bridge was silent as she walked back to her station.

Flynn pulled her aside. "Where do we stand as far as Austin is concerned?" he asked in a low voice.

"Thanks to Morrison," she replied, "Austin has no idea there's anything wrong on board. By the time he figures it out, we'll be through the radiation field. After that, we'll want his full attention anyway."

"Why the stall tactics? Couldn't we have sent some doctored data to them?"

"Not a good idea," she replied, shaking her head. "They'll be scrutinizing every bit of data they have to locate the shuttle. While I could, given enough time, do a top-rate job of manipulating the data, nothing we could send them now would pass muster, especially if Yabuno looks at it. Also, we have to assume that Austin himself may look at some of the data, and he has an amazing eye for detail, especially if something isn't quite right."

CHAPTER TWENTY-EIGHT

Hours later, Austin and the others were no closer to finding Sara. During a lull in the activity aboard *Pathfinder*, he took a call from Liz.

"How are things going out there?" she asked.

He couldn't keep the frustration from his voice. "We aren't having any luck. Sara has vanished. The only thing we know is she can't have left this star system. What's been happening with the search planet side?"

"I just spoke with Mark, and the only good news is that there isn't any sign of a body."

"What's the bad news?"

Her anxiety was plain as she brought up some images. "They found the body of a cheater near a set of tracks that probably came from Sara. They also found most of her gear on the ground nearby."

"How did the cheater die?"

"Someone shot it."

"Sara?"

She shook her head. "No, the angle suggests the cheater would have been attacking Sara and was shot from a different direction. They found a second set of tracks and believe that whoever took her first saved her life."

"That's interesting," Austin said hopefully. "It means that whoever wanted her wanted her alive, at least for now. What else did they find?"

Liz brought up another image. "They found tracks leading away from the cheater. Sara's jacket was nearby."

Austin nodded. "She kept her head and knew the jacket would call attention to her, so she dumped it."

"They could tell from the tracks that someone followed Sara and caught up with her before she could get to her transport. There was only one set of tracks leading away."

"That's not so good," Austin replied. "Sara would have either been dead or unconscious and was carried by whomever captured her."

"They found several rounds from a weapon in that area, including one embedded in a tree. It was a tranquilizing round."

"That confirms that her captor wanted her alive. Where did the tracks lead?"

Liz brought up another image. Austin took one look, and his expression hardened. "Those impressions in the ground could have come from a shuttle, which pretty much confirms what we've assumed about how she got off the planet. While I doubt whomever took Sara is still around, I don't want to take any chances, so stay at the house for now." His gaze was puzzled for a moment. "It just occurred to me. Why didn't they use Sara's transport to get to the shuttle?"

Liz brought up a familiar image. "Sara's link had been wiped."

"Where did you find it?"

"It was near where Sara probably fell. Bret has checked it out remotely. He thinks it was blocked from sending out messages, and Sara switched it off so she couldn't be tracked by it. She must have seen her pursuer as she was about to approach her transport and wiped the codes then."

Austin's brow was furrowed as he gazed at the display. "Why didn't she just approach her transport anyway?"

"Probably for the same reason our people didn't," Liz replied with an anxious look. "Several people started to approach the transport, only they were targeted as intruders." She knew the question Austin was about to ask. "Don't worry, no one was hurt. Bret has gotten remote access to the transport and returned it to its proper settings. At least we can be thankful that Sara's kidnapper had to work hard to capture her."

"Yes, but it looks like the outcome was what he or she wanted," Austin said pessimistically.

After Liz signed off, Austin turned back to the activities aboard *Pathfinder*.

"We have pretty good information from our people on the surface that a shuttle was used to take Sara off planet," he informed the group. "At this point, that isn't really news. Where do we stand with our search out here?"

Lambert was using a display to show the images from the various transports and other vessels in the star system. "We've gone over every image that was recorded by anyone, and nothing shows up anywhere."

"What about transponders?" Austin asked, his voice revealing his fight with fatigue. "Can we account for every shuttle by reviewing their transponder signals?"

"No," she replied with a shake of her head. "Unlike a transport, for example, a shuttle transponder is only active when the craft is powered on for use."

"The shuttle might have had to blend in with the rest of the traffic at some point, which would have meant bringing the transponder back online. Are there any transponder signals that appeared suddenly, as if from nowhere?"

"No. The most likely scenario is that the shuttle traveled to wherever it is docked with the transponder off the whole time. That way, there wouldn't be the giveaway you just mentioned."

"Wouldn't the transponder have to have been activated to allow the shuttle access to its docking bay?"

"Yes," she admitted, "but bays aren't high-security areas. It isn't hard to get in manually and then wipe the record that the shuttle entered."

Austin thought about something else. "Bret, you pointed out that a lot of *KT-2* shuttles were active earlier today."

Yabuno shrugged. "Sure, but they were full of passengers and crew members heading out."

"What about the return trips?" Austin persisted. "Aren't all of the shuttles back on the ship?"

"Yes, but they all would have had their regular pilots at the controls. Off the top of my head, none of them has the skills needed to do what was done to our system."

Austin moved to a new thought. "Don't our protocols require that all activities outside a transport be monitored remotely while loading or unloading takes place? A feed goes to the captain and is recorded for further review as needed. Do we have that data from *KT-2*?"

Lambert scanned her files and said, "No, we never received anything from them after I asked for their data. Their captain was occupied with some problem, so I spoke with someone on their bridge named Morrison. She said she'd pass the request on to the captain. It's a long shot anyway, Sam," she warned.

"Did anyone from *KT-2* ever get back to you, Joe?" Austin asked.

Albretti shook his head. "I haven't heard a word, but I wasn't expecting anything back, because Morrison said she'd pass what they had to Melody."

Austin's expression was impatient. "Things may be somewhat relaxed over there because they're technically on layover, but we don't have the luxury of overlooking anything that might be of help. Either Benitez or this Morrison person isn't getting the job done. Get ahold of *KT-2* and tell them I want to speak with Benitez personally, and I don't give a damn if he's putting the final touches on a grand unified theory of everything!"

"They entered the radiation field a little while ago. Things are somewhat hairy in there right now, so communications may be lousy at best."

"Try them anyway."

"No response." Albretti looked at a display with a puzzled expression.

"What's the matter, Joe?" Austin asked.

"Benitez is better than that at navigation. Take a look."

They watch in silence as the transport seemed to struggle through a tight series of maneuvers.

"No experienced pilot would maneuver like that," Austin agreed. "Who's their pilot?"

"Wash is their pilot. He should be able to do this practically blindfolded."

"Right now, it looks like he's flying blind," Austin observed. "Bret, what are the readings on *KT-2*? Are they having a problem from too much exposure to radiation?"

Yabuno glanced at another display. "Although they're moving their ship around like a bunch of trainees, they haven't veered off the safe path yet, so there shouldn't be any problems with radiation."

"What about the ship itself? Are there any signs of damage or readings showing any other problems?"

"It's hard to tell from this distance, considering the interference from the radiation field, but I can't see anything wrong." He shook his head. "I don't understand it. Even a skeleton crew shouldn't have any problems getting through the field, considering the veterans they have on board."

"Send a priority message to the communications array at the entrance on the other side, telling them to stand down the moment they get out of the field." Austin looked at the others with a hard gaze. "Something's wrong with this setup. Benitez is far too good a captain to be doing this without a good reason, which makes me wonder whether he's really behind it. For starters, as far as we know, no one has spoken with Benitez directly for hours. I want to know who the hell Morrison is. I don't know that name."

The image Yabuno brought up on the display was of a woman they didn't recognize. "She's usually on the bridge, monitoring any of several stations as a systems specialist. She has a background in troubleshooting system problems."

"Does she have the skills to break into our systems and cover her tracks?"

Yabuno's eyes widened at the question. "Her background doesn't say so, but it might not be showing everything she can do."

The fatigue was gone from Austin's face. "Get *Pathfinder* there as fast as she'll go, Joe."

"On it, Sam. They have quite a head start," Albretti warned. "Although we were already heading there for the tests when all hell broke loose, we're still at least an hour away. Do you think Sara's aboard?"

"We're sure as hell going to find out. Line up a boarding party; we're going to check out every inch of that ship. Is Morrison a pilot, Bret?"

"No," Yabuno replied, shaking his head. "There isn't anything to suggest she has any experience in actually running a ship, certainly nothing like a transport. Only someone from the Citadel Group would have that background, and she first joined *KT-2*'s crew at the start of the trip that just ended."

"Assuming for the moment there isn't an innocent explanation for their actions, why wouldn't they have simply sent Melody the files to divert attention?" Albretti asked.

"They had two choices if they were going to send their files," Yabuno replied. "The first would be to send the files without any edits. I'm going to guess that there's something in those files that they wouldn't want us to see. Perhaps there's a departure or arrival of a shuttle that they don't want to explain.

"The second is to edit the files before sending them. The problem is that it can be tricky to do it well enough to avoid detection by someone as sharp as Melody."

"It would be even harder to get anything past *you*," Austin noted dryly.

Yabuno grinned as he continued. "We've been going over all of everyone's files in great detail, trying to find evidence of a shuttle. Anything that looks odd in any way has gotten a lot of close scrutiny. I think they just decided it would be better to hope we wouldn't notice."

"They couldn't have believed we'd *never* notice," Austin said. "The question is whether they've been able to gain enough time for whatever they have in mind."

"What do they gain by being outside the radiation field, anyway?" Yabuno asked, waving at a display. "They can't be planning on returning to Earth; we can get a message to the Citadel Group back there to intercept them long before they can complete the trip. Besides, the warp-field generators haven't been checked out. Turning around and using them again, especially with a skeleton crew, would be pretty stupid. Stupid is the one thing they haven't been so far."

"I don't know what they have in mind," Austin said as he brought up an image of the area beyond the radiation field. There's nothing out there, and *Pathfinder* can catch them before they get far anyway."

"I still don't get why they're doing such a lousy job of piloting the ship," Albretti said.

"I think I get it," Austin said with a nod at the display. "Whoever Morrison is, she isn't a pilot, so she has to rely on Wash to do it. Wash is pretty sharp, so he's doing everything he can to call attention to his ship without endangering anyone. While a fellow pilot like Joe would know something's wrong, whoever's calling the shots might not."

CHAPTER TWENTY-NINE

A display in the compartment came to life with an image of Powers. "They're onto us," she warned. "Austin is telling *KT-2* to stand down, and it isn't a request anymore."

"Have we responded?" Flynn asked.

Powers gestured over her shoulder to an image of the radiation field on the main display. "No, but it isn't a surprise that we wouldn't respond to them at this point. We've now entered the radiation field, and it often screws up communications between ships."

"Why doesn't that apply to communications from Citadel out to the array?"

Powers brought up new images on their display. "They've set up relay stations that are hardened, to deal with the radiation. They replace them regularly, so they rarely have a problem with those communications. It isn't as effective with transports, although I've heard they're working on improvements."

Powers hesitated for a moment and then brought up another image. No one could fail to recognize *Pathfinder*.

The other occupant in the compartment spoke. "What do the graphic readouts say?"

"They say *Pathfinder* is heading toward us at top speed, Ms. Harrington."

"Should we worry?"

"Maybe, maybe not," Powers replied. "We're already in the radiation field, and they could never overtake us before we exit it. Whether we need to worry after that depends on the arrangements we've made. If we've been hung out to dry by our 'friends,' then the game is over," she replied matter-of-factly.

"No one said there wouldn't be any risks, and they certainly aren't our friends. However, we've given them a pretty good reason not to sell us out," Harrington said.

Everyone on board *Pathfinder* watched the display intently. They saw *KT-2* complete another maneuver to avoid the invisible danger that could extinguish life with even a short time of exposure. "How long before they're out of the field?" Austin asked, his eyes never straying from the display.

"Their final turn is coming up in less than a minute, and then they're out of danger," Yabuno replied.

"Wash seems to have gone back to proper maneuvering," Albretti noted. "That last move was a normal one."

Austin spoke. "They must know we're in pursuit, so there isn't any reason for Wash to take more chances." He looked over toward Yabuno. "Any word from Melody on the data she's been reviewing?"

Yabuno shook his head. "Nothing. If anyone had any independent eyes or scanners on *KT-2*, we can't find anything."

"They're out of the radiation field," Albretti called out. As the transport continued on a new course, he half muttered, "What the hell are they doing now?"

They watched as the transport traveled farther from the entrance to the radiation field. To add to the mystery, *KT-2* wasn't setting itself up into position for a warp-field movement. There continued to be no communications from the vessel.

Austin looked at Yabuno, his brow wrinkled in confusion. "Where the hell could they be heading?"

"The good news is it doesn't appear that they've gone insane and are trying to make a warp bubble for long-distance travel," Yabuno replied.

"Yes," Austin agreed, "but there isn't anything in that direction that would be of any use to them." He looked back at a display. "Now that they're outside the radiation field, they should be able to read us without any problems. Link me into them directly through the communications array."

"Go ahead, Sam."

Austin faced the large display. "*KT-2*, this is Sam Austin. Captain Benitez, if you can read me, you are instructed to stand down until *Pathfinder* can reach you. Do not continue to travel toward deep space. If you can communicate, do so immediately, and advise us of any damage or dangerous situation aboard your transport. Morrison, if you are standing in for Captain

Benitez for any reason, the same goes for you and for anyone else aboard *KT-2* who can see or hear this message."

Austin looked at Albretti, who shook his head. "We're still ten minutes away from the entrance to this side, Sam. If they don't stand down, they'll have a hell of a lead on us by the time we get free of the radiation."

"Fat lot of good that lead will do them, once we use our own warp-field generators," Yabuno noted. Suddenly, his eyes became impossibly wide as he pointed toward a display. They turned and found themselves looking at a familiar sight. An enormous spaceship from their all-too-familiar enemy materialized from its own warp bubble and proceeded straight toward the transport. To their further shock, the much smaller ship didn't veer off course.

Austin gestured quickly and faced the display again. "*KT-2*, whatever's the problem, get out of there at once! You're heading straight for an alien ship!" Austin whirled back to Yabuno as he demanded, "Can we give them any cover from the big rail guns?"

Yabuno hesitated for a moment as he consulted another display. "The angle is wrong," he said with a shrug. "Damn it, we might have been in a better position to help them if they hadn't headed out there and had waited near the entrance instead. As it is, anything we launch is just as likely to hit them as the alien ship. It's almost as if they want *KT-2* to serve as a shield for the other ship." He shook his head. "They're coming within range of the aliens, and there isn't a damned thing we can do about it."

"Bring the rail guns online and prepare to launch a series of rocks at them the moment *KT-2* has shifted out of the way or, if it comes to it, after the aliens have finished with *KT-2*," Austin said, his expression darkening. "Have the guns keep reloading and launching until there isn't any alien ship left."

"Well, it didn't take them very long," Albretti said.

"What do you mean?" Austin replied.

"Their EMP contraption is online." Albretti gestured at the display. They saw the dreaded weapon deployed and ready.

"Could they be responsible for what's happening to *KT-2*?" Austin asked. "If so, we have a hell of a new problem on our hands."

"Look!" Albretti cried out as the transport reduced speed and came to a halt well within range of the much larger ship's main weapon. "She's just sitting there. Why haven't they blasted her to pieces?"

Yabuno gave a sharp intake of breath. "Sam, I think *KT-2* is transmitting to the aliens."

"Can you understand it?"

He shook his head. "I can't make out anything at all." He manipulated a display and looked at Turner. "Alan, it looks like a series of symbols, which I've forwarded to you. Please tell us they mean something to you."

After what seemed like an eternity, Turner looked up from his display. "I can't understand any of this, and no, it doesn't look like the symbols from the race that created the derelict. The only thing that comes to mind is that these symbols might be a simpler form of communication than the derelict's symbols. I think I see suggestions of mathematical concepts here and there. If I'm not completely full of crap, I might even be able to understand them, given some time." He stiffened slightly and continued. "It looks like the aliens are now responding to *KT-2* using the same types of symbols."

"Who the hell are the aliens talking to onboard our ship?" Austin wondered. "We've been assuming that there are only humans on board. What if Benitez has some unwanted visitors and isn't in control?"

"We haven't come up with any better guesses so far," Yabuno agreed, "although it doesn't explain why Sara has vanished, or why they needed to pull a transport out of our system. It would have made more sense for them to have ordered the transport to wreak as much damage on the inner-system side of the radiation field as possible." He nearly winced as he said, "Imagine what they could do to Citadel with a rail gun."

"I'd rather not," Austin replied. He looked back at the image of their transport and said, "We're still just guessing at this point. Bret, send them another message telling them we want to talk. Maybe now that they've chatted, they're ready to let us in on the secret."

"The message has been sent." Yabuno had a surprised look. "They've already sent us a message saying they want to talk. That's strange, because they couldn't have had a chance to react to what we just sent."

"Let's get some answers, then. Put it on the main display."

Moments later, they found themselves staring at the scene arranged on the bridge of *KT-2*; there wasn't an alien in sight. There were several people whom they could identify as members of the crew, but the scene veered toward surreal when they saw that all of the visible crew members were flanked by armed strangers. Only when they took in the face of the person sitting in the captain's chair, however, did they know they were watching something that should have been impossible. Courtney Harrington was staring back at them, looking very much at home.

CHAPTER THIRTY

Austin stared at the display, a shocked look on his face.

"What the hell are you doing aboard *KT-2*, Courtney, and where is Captain Benitez?" he demanded.

"I decided it was time for a change of scenery, and this ship seemed the right place to find it."

The look of shock on Austin's face dissolved into disgust. "In other words, once it became clear that your case was about to blow up in the courts, you decided to run instead of face your punishment."

"Don't tell me you wouldn't have done the same, Sam."

"There isn't much that I would do the same way as you. How the hell did you get aboard *KT-2*, and why are you here?"

"There have always been people willing to help me. Some of them were clever enough to get me aboard this ship. Your security isn't as good as you think, since we were able to take over your ship without any difficulty once we arrived," she taunted.

"How many of these people of yours would lift a finger to help you without being paid?" Austin countered. "You still haven't answered why you are here and what has happened to Captain Benitez."

Harrington's expression dismissed the man before she replied, "He wouldn't cooperate with us, so he was made an example for the rest of the crew. The example was quite effective," she added.

"He's dead, then?"

Harrington stared back but didn't deny it. "That's another murder to be added to your ledger," Austin said grimly. He brought up an image of the alien vessel and asked, "Why haven't they blasted you to ashes?"

"You seem to think that I have no choice but to deal with you, Sam, but you're wrong."

Austin was aghast. "What the hell have you gotten yourself into, Courtney?"

Harrington had lived for the moment when she would finally be one up on Austin. The smile on her face was anything but friendly. "It's not what I've gotten myself into, Sam, but what I've gotten myself out of."

The shock changed to puzzlement as Austin asked, "What do you mean?"

"Not that long ago, you acted as if you had my fate in your hands. You acted as if my very life was something for you to take away."

"It wasn't *my* doing, Courtney," Austin replied, his features darkening. "*I'm* not the one who decided that her personal ambitions justified committing war crimes and murdering people. *I'm* not the one who sought to wage war against another nation to satisfy her ego."

Austin continued more quietly. "*I'm* not the one who has, apparently, decided to go to war against her own people by allying herself with a race that has tried to exterminate ours and will likely try again."

Harrington had a dismissive look as she countered, "I'm not at war with humans, Sam. I just don't see any reason why our security should be jeopardized by another race that wants something we don't need or really want. What I've done is ensure that the security of two star systems is guaranteed at a nominal cost to us."

Austin shook his head. "What is this 'nominal cost,' Courtney?"

"You know full well what it is, Sam. It's the same thing that led to tension between Earth and Citadel."

"You know that's bullshit. The 'tension' was something you manufactured to try to get your sorry ass reelected."

"The tension was real, Sam. If you'd been willing to set aside your own pride and share the derelict with us, none of what happened needed to take place."

Austin's eyes turned to an icy shade as he said, "Don't bother trying to play the part of the innocent statesman, Courtney. Your cover was blown on that crap a long time ago."

Harrington made a motion of waving away Austin's comment. "It doesn't really matter anyway, since you're going to give me what I want."

A look of derision flashed across Austin's face. "Why do you think so?"

"Not only do I have the crew and passengers of this transport, but I have someone else as well. Look!"

A man Austin didn't recognize came into view, but he was more focused on the woman he pushed before him. Sara fell hard against a deck rail.

She got to her feet and said, "Mara Powers is also on board, Sam, although she now calls herself Pamela Morrison. Her hair is dark, and she's had her features altered, but she's still recognizable. I can't say it's much of an improvement though."

Sara's next words were cut off as the man slapped her hard across the mouth. Her husband started to rush toward the image before Austin stopped him with a hand on his chest.

Harrington watched with amusement. "I see that I have your attention. Captain Sara Albretti isn't someone whom I view kindly. She interfered with Major Roetter when he sought to capture the derelict, and she interfered again when he tried to remove you from the picture."

"You mean she prevented him from carrying out an assassination that you ordered," Austin said.

"Presidents have given similar orders for close to two centuries, perhaps longer."

"Once again, don't waste our time on that claim," Austin scoffed. "Your orders constituted war crimes. Captain Albretti's actions prevented a full-blown war from breaking out."

"Whatever, Sam. Do you believe me when I say that it would give me great pleasure to have Captain Albretti executed right in front of everyone?"

"Yes, I believe you," Austin replied.

"That's good, because if you don't do what I say, I'll start having people on this ship executed, starting with Captain Albretti."

"What do you want?"

"You will attach remote thrusters to the derelict and send it out here, safely past the radiation field. You and the rest of your people will stay in your system."

"What else?"

"You will transmit to me everything you have learned about the derelict."

"We still don't know how it works, Courtney!"

For the first time, the man standing on *KT-2*'s bridge spoke. "That's OK, Austin, because we have people who would be more than happy to review your data and take it from there. After all, we were smart enough to take your data on the alien ship that you destroyed in our system and figure out where to find a piece of the debris," he pointed out.

Austin shifted his attention to the man. "Who are you?"

"My name, for what it's worth, is Flynn."

"I take it you learned enough from that debris to communicate with the aliens."

Flynn looked smug as he replied, "That's right. We'll probably be able to do something similar with the data on the derelict."

"Do you really think so?"

The smug look vanished from Flynn's face, which paled slightly as he said, "We probably won't do any worse than your people have done."

"You have other things to worry about than the success of interpreting that data, Flynn," Austin warned. "Do you recall what happened to the last person who hijacked one of our transports?"

"Roetter was an arrogant fool," Flynn replied. "I won't make the same mistakes."

A dangerous glint appeared in Austin's eyes as he replied, "You've already made them, Flynn. The only thing that would make your situation even worse is if you've killed any of our people. You'd better not have the blood of Captain Benitez on your hands. However, there's a price you'll pay for your conduct toward Captain Albretti."

Flynn almost smirked again. "I'm not worried about her husband, Austin."

"What makes you think I'm talking about him?" Austin said. "I once told Roetter that he and I would have a very unpleasant conversation. I can confirm that it was everything I promised it would be. I'll have an unpleasant conversation with you as well, unless you surrender *KT-2* to us."

"I'm not worried about you either, Austin," Flynn said dismissively. "Are you going to tell me that I can't hide in this star system and that you'll track me down in my own star system no matter where I hide?"

"*You* said it," Austin replied. "Your biggest mistake was identifying yourself to me. You should have stayed hidden in the shadows like the coward you are."

"If you two are done with your pissing contest," Harrington interrupted, "I'll tell you about the rest of what will happen. The aliens will leave their ship here, to make sure none of you tries to leave this system. You have a series of weapons arranged out here that you will take offline, including the rail guns. I'm sure it won't come as a surprise to learn that they'll be destroyed. For reasons you know all too well, the aliens really hate those things." Harrington's smile became a bit more malicious as she continued. "I suppose you could try to pass through the radiation field directly to challenge the aliens, but we all know how that would turn out."

"Anything else?"

"Yes. Since you will want your people to be able to return to Citadel once the deal has been completed, we will need another one of your transports to accompany us on this trip. We'll keep one of the ships for our use and send your people home in the other one."

"You can't even operate *KT-2* by yourselves," Austin said sarcastically. "How would you operate another transport?"

"I'm not an expert, but my scientific advisor will arrange for all commands on *KT-2* to be mirrored on the other transport, while keeping them a safe distance from each other. The new technology we will receive from the aliens is so easy to operate, we won't have any problem returning to our own star system without your help. Our people will have plenty of time to learn more about your ship once it arrives back home. I'm sure people would like to get their hands on that technology as well!" she said gleefully.

A warning look flashed across her face. "You're clever when it comes to special codes that can override the command codes for your ships. To be on the safe side, we won't decide which transport will receive the new technology until we arrive at the base. If you try to insert any special codes or booby traps into either ship, we'll know about it. That will lead to some executions, beginning with Captain Albretti. Do you understand?"

"I understand, Courtney."

"Do you agree to these terms?"

Austin shook his head. "Not until I know when the hostages will be released."

"They'll be released once the derelict has been turned over to the aliens."

"When will that happen?"

"I'll let you know."

Austin's face turned to stone as he said, "That's not good enough. I'm not going to agree to an open-ended arrangement where you can continue to string us along."

Harrington's eyes narrowed. "You'll agree, or I'll order some people to die right now. I understand you well enough to know you'll never let it go that far."

"Go ahead, then."

Harrington's face paled as she replied, "What do you mean?"

"I mean what I said. You haven't given me any reason to believe that there's any end game for my people other than their deaths. I therefore have no reason to give you what you want. You can't reenter this system, and your new friends are still stuck out there. If you kill any of my people, I'll find a way to hunt you down and kill you, no matter what you do or where you hide. I'll also bet that without the derelict, the aliens won't have any reason to continue to work with you." Austin's gaze was hard as he continued. "You asked me a moment ago whether I believed your threat against Captain Albright. Now, it's your turn. Do you believe me?"

Harrington searched Austin's face and realized that there were still some lines she wasn't ready to cross yet. "Yes, I believe you," she said. "All right, your people will be released in thirty-three days."

"Why thirty-three days?"

"That's how long it will take us to reach the aliens' home."

"There aren't any planets within thirty-three days' travel, except perhaps using the warp-field generators," Austin scoffed. "I'm sure as hell not going to agree to our people being stranded somewhere that would take many years of travel to get back here using normal propulsion."

"It won't require using the warp-field generators," Harrington countered. "I'm talking about thirty-three days' travel time using normal propulsion."

"With normal propulsion, you can't even get to a *star* in thirty-three days, let alone one with a planet that could sustain life as we understand it."

"I'm not talking about a planet, Sam."

Austin was puzzled. "I don't understand. What kind of home takes thirty-three days to reach but isn't a planet or near a star?"

"As best as we can understand their communications," Flynn replied, "they aren't from this part of the galaxy at all. They've established a forward base that happens to be within thirty-three days' travel of this system. We're not sure how many of their ships are at their base, but it is a place of operations that lets them do a couple of things. One is to search for the derelict. The other is to search for areas to colonize."

"So you're prepared to give them both of those things," Austin said.

"No, we're not," Harrington countered. "We all know they can't colonize the Citadel system, since their ships are too large to get through the radiation field using the safe path, and you've already demonstrated you can take care of their smaller scout ships if they enter your system. Also, it doesn't take a genius to see that you've improved your security since then."

"What about your own system?" Austin asked pointedly.

"They've given us their word that they'll leave our system alone once they have the derelict."

Austin didn't hide his revulsion as he asked, "You're either the stupidest or most cynical person I've seen get to a high office in a hundred years. Is what you're doing worth selling out humanity?"

"First, I'm not selling out anyone!" Harrington replied with some heat. "We're simply making a deal that works for everyone. In exchange for the derelict, the aliens will give us some of their technology. While it won't be as advanced as what they'll get from the derelict, it will be more advanced than anyone has seen in either of our star systems."

Harrington's eyes glittered with a triumphant look as she said, "I'll be able to name my price for this technology, which will include a full pardon and promise not to extradite me to Citadel." She looked around the bridge and added, "That deal will apply to the people who have helped me too."

"You're a fool to believe you can deal with these creatures," Austin said vehemently. "They've made it clear that they don't regard humans as much more than garden pests. You don't make deals with pests. You just build traps to kill them. Whatever arrangement you've made with the aliens will be discarded the moment they have what they want."

"You don't know that, Sam," Harrington snapped. "You just want everyone to believe it, so you can effectively be in charge of two star systems, by raising the specter of danger from aliens whenever you want something."

"I sure as hell already have plenty to worry about regarding the security of *this* star system," Austin said with a snort. "I don't need the headache of worrying about what happens in yours. Unfortunately, I don't have much choice, thanks to the messes you created."

"You can stop worrying once our system has the aliens' technology." Her tone was sarcastic as she continued, "We'll probably be able to teach *you* some things—if your pride will allow it and you're willing to pay the price for it."

"Speaking of prices, you're kidding yourself if you believe that President Lee will agree to what you want in exchange for the aliens' technology, even if they were to give it to you," Austin said.

"Lee is a weak man who wouldn't have gotten into office without your interference," Harrington said with contempt. "Besides, he won't have any choice. Once the people on Earth know the aliens have the derelict, they'll have to make a deal to get the next best thing. After all, even if you were willing to give Citadel's technology to Earth, it won't be as advanced as what I'll have to offer. Which do you think they'll want to protect them?"

"We've destroyed four alien ships with our technology."

"In one engagement, you lost nine ships against one of their ships."

"Don't go there, Courtney," Austin warned. "We lost a lot of lives because your pirates were morons who wouldn't yield control of those ships to our people. We went after the alien ship in question with our own people and took it out. We then did the same with another one."

"You lost more ships that time as well. Besides, what you used to do it won't be enough once the aliens have the derelict, Sam. Face it; if you don't upgrade to version 2.0, which is what I have to offer, even *your* advantages may not be enough to save your hides the next time around. It sure as hell won't be enough for Earth or Mars, which don't have radiation fields to protect them."

Sara broke away from Flynn and blurted, "Don't do it, Sam! You know you can't trust these people! They'll sell out anyone to get what they want!" A moment later, she was restrained and silenced, although Flynn did not strike her again.

Harrington ignored the outburst. Her face had an expectant look as she asked, "What is your answer, Sam? Do you agree to my terms?"

Austin's face revealed none of the turmoil he had to be feeling as he answered, "Yes, I agree, provided you allow my people to send messages back regularly to confirm that they are still unharmed. By regularly, I mean at least once every twenty-four hours. Our communications network extends out quite a ways, so we should be able to receive reports for a large part of the trip. When you encounter the end of the network, you will deploy additional sensors, so you are never out of contact with us.

"You'll use the system aboard *KT-2* for making log entries, so we can confirm that the messages are being made when they're supposed to be. Captain Albretti will provide the messages. The thrusters on the derelict will all contain high explosives, which will detonate if our people are harmed. Whether they would be able to destroy the derelict is open to question, but I can guarantee you don't want to be anywhere near it if those thrusters detonate."

Austin's eyes turned a cold blue as he continued. "That's the only way I'll agree to hand over everything up front. That means, among other things, that Captain Albretti is now your best friend, because no excuse you make will work if she's harmed in any way. I won't buy any notion of an accident, so don't even think about it.

"In addition, the thrusters will have a hell of a sensitive tripwire, so I wouldn't advise trying to disable them. *KT-2* will stay within close range of the derelict, to keep the tripwire active. If you try to move her out of range, the tripwire will be triggered, and there won't be anything to show to the aliens. In addition, the files with our data will be encrypted. You'll get the keys to unlock those files, as well as the codes to release the thrusters, when my people are released. If my people are harmed or not released to me in thirty-three days for any reason, the deal is off, so you'd better keep them in good health."

The look of expectation turned to a look of triumph as Harrington replied, "The same goes for you, Sam. If you don't honor your part of the deal, your people will die, and the fault will be yours."

"We understand each other, Courtney. When do you leave?"

"We will leave as soon as the derelict and the second transport have been transferred out here and the weapons have been taken offline and surrendered for destruction."

Austin turned his focus to Sara and said, "Captain Albretti, I understand your concerns about this arrangement; it feels like a witches' brew, but we don't always have the options we'd like to have. I want you to remember that you are a former captain of *KT-2* and to act accordingly. You need to set an example for others to follow. Can I count on you to do that?"

Sara shrugged Flynn's hand away from her mouth as she replied, "Yes, Sam, I understand. You can count on me to do what I need to do."

A brief look of condescension showed on Harrington's face before it vanished and the display went blank.

The room was silent for a moment as the enormity of Harrington's demands began to sink in.

Yabuno turned to Austin. "How much of what Harrington wants are we going to give her?"

Austin's expression was melancholy as he answered, "We're going to give her everything we said we'd give, Bret."

"The derelict is our best leverage!" Albretti practically shouted. "If we hand it over, she might kill our people anyway, including Sara!"

Austin shook his head. "While that may be her ultimate intention, she wants them for some reason for now, something other than just as hostages. Besides, she figures that so long as we receive regular updates from our people, we'll have an incentive to stay in our system quietly."

Liz spoke. "I don't like the thought of our people being brought along for some reason other than just as hostages, Sam."

"I don't like it either, Liz," Austin replied. "One thing that Courtney doesn't quite appreciate is that her arrangement also means that we have thirty-three days to work out how to get our people back."

"How the hell are we going to do that once we surrender our weapons?" Yabuno asked.

"Citadel has long been full of surprises," Austin replied with grim humor. "Let's put our heads together and come up with something."

CHAPTER THIRTY-ONE

The mood among the team was somber as they tried to come up with another surprise. Yabuno gestured toward a display as he said, "It was hard to watch as our forward rail guns were turned over to those bastards. One by one, they were in the line of fire from that damned EMP weapon."

"It was kind of shocking to see how quickly they were reduced to nothing more than space debris," Turner mused sadly.

"I couldn't watch," Liz said. "Without those weapons, we may not have survived retrieving the derelict from the aliens. We're naked before them in a way that we haven't been for a long time." She glanced over at Austin with a humorless look. "You looked positively grim as you watched the display. I don't think you took your eyes off them the entire time."

Austin's eyes had a determined expression in them as he answered, "I wasn't going to waste an opportunity."

The other faces in the room had puzzled looks as Yabuno asked, "What opportunity? We've seen them take out our equipment before."

"That's true, but we're missing something." Austin walked over to a large display and asked, "This image is in real time. What's wrong with it?"

"What's wrong is that we're looking at an alien ship that we can't blast to pieces because we gave them our weapons," Yabuno said sourly.

"We'll talk about our weapons shortly, but what's wrong with this picture?"

Albretti spoke. "The communications array is still intact. They didn't trash it when they trashed our weapons."

"Why leave it alone and take the chance we might be able to use it to our advantage somehow?" Austin asked. "That's precisely the kind of thing Courtney was worried about, us throwing something at them they hadn't anticipated."

"There's a simple reason why the array is still intact, Sam," Lambert said. "We both need for it to be working, to allow our people to send back reports on their continuing good health, etc. If Harrington had destroyed it, then she wouldn't be able to keep her part of the bargain and we would try to destroy the derelict."

"That makes sense," Austin admitted, "but Courtney couldn't have known in advance that I'd insist on that condition. In fact, she seemed shocked that I insisted on that. That tells me that she should have expected to leave here with everything destroyed, including the array. However, she only insisted on destroying our weapons."

"You think she wanted to keep the array functioning?" Lambert asked.

Yabuno's eyes showed increasing interest as he asked, "Why?"

Austin brought up an image from the destruction of the original alien ship in Earth's system. He gestured toward it as he asked, "Haven't you wondered how the hell they were able to contact the aliens?"

"Flynn said they recovered a useful piece of debris," Lambert said. "It's hard to believe, but I guess it might have been functional enough to allow them to make contact."

Austin's eyes shifted toward Yabuno, who snorted, "There's no way any debris still could have been working after what we did to their ship! For starters, we pounded it with plenty of EM pulses of our own. What wasn't already fried by then would have been fried when their ship became a miniature sun."

Yabuno walked over to the display as he brought up another image and continued. "As you can see from these readings, there were massive EM pulses ripping out their innards just before they were consumed by all that energy. While we now know that at least one component survived, it shouldn't have been usable, especially without a power source."

"What does that mean?" Albretti asked.

Lambert spoke up. "It means that whatever that component was able to do, it wouldn't have been able to make contact with the aliens, especially over the vast distances involved."

"What good was it, then?"

Turner traced a finger along the images as he mused aloud, "Perhaps it was used to decipher enough of the aliens' language for them to communicate."

"What good would that do Harrington if they couldn't send and receive messages?" Albretti countered.

"How sure are we that her people didn't have a way to send messages to points outside our solar system?"

"With what, Alan?" Albretti asked. "Even though they disabled our main beacon during Harrington's War, they couldn't do anything with it."

Lambert's face took on a sly look as she looked at Turner. "You're thinking of the alternative beacon, aren't you?"

"It fits, Melody."

"How could they get access to the alternative beacon?" Albretti asked. "Didn't we retrieve it after they stole it from our embassy?"

"Yes," Lambert replied, "and we made sure they hadn't broken the encryption, so they couldn't send messages to and from Citadel."

"What about sending messages elsewhere?" Turner asked.

Albretti was puzzled. "What do you mean? Where else could they have sent messages?"

Lambert walked over to the display, and a moment later they saw an image of the communications array. "We'd know, of course, that any messages sent to Citadel through the alternate beacon without being encrypted were phonies." Her features darkened with understanding as she continued. "However, we have a complex communications network that extends well beyond Citadel.

Why couldn't they have used it to send messages to the aliens?"

"How? It wasn't like we gave them the keys to the thing."

"No," Lambert replied, "but the alternate beacon wasn't up and running initially; it needed to be brought online. When they did that, they might have learned enough to post messages that didn't need to be verified."

"Son of a bitch!" Albretti swore. "They've been using our own network against us!"

"As you figured, Sam, that's why they didn't destroy the array," Turner concluded. "They need it to communicate with the aliens."

Austin nodded and looked at Lambert. "Melody, can we keep track of their communications over the network without their knowing that we're doing it?"

Lambert glanced over at a display for a few moments before answering. "Sure. I'll bet Powers thinks she can keep track of everything from her end, but even she doesn't know all there is to know about the network; the way it relays everything around lets us pick up the traffic."

"Good. Track and record it. Forward everything to Alan and Bret for analysis."

"Aren't we kind of late in the game for translations, Sam?" Albretti asked. "They've probably had months, perhaps longer, to understand that stuff. The best we'd get right now is just a snippet of what they have. How can we make any sense of it?"

Turner chuckled without humor as he answered. "We should be able to benefit from those months of effort, Joe. Their communications with the aliens will have been formatted within certain protocols to facilitate under-standing. While we won't have the answers all at once, we won't be starting from scratch either."

"That's good news, Alan," Austin said, but a question was plain on his face as he looked at Yabuno.

Yabuno nodded. "Yes, it's still there. We *definitely* won't be starting from scratch."

It was now Lambert's turn to be puzzled. "What are you talking about, Bret?"

"Remember how we figured out your predecessor was a snake, Melody? I inserted a mirroring protocol that captured our communications traffic back in the day, which we used to confirm that Brittel had sold us out by sending files on the old settler ships to Captain Card's masters. I never took it down, so all of Harrington's com-munications with the aliens should be tucked away some-where. I'd give long odds that we'll find some very help-ful information once we look hard enough. Knowing the protocols they're using will be a big help."

"Won't that traffic be encrypted?"

"Some of the internal communications might be," Turner said, "but not the ones with the aliens. Encryption would just get in the way of an already difficult transla-tion task. Besides, we may find that it won't be as diffi-cult to decipher human encryption as it is to read alien symbols."

"There's a vast amount of data to check out, even if we have a basic idea of the time frame," Austin said. "The question is whether we'll have enough time for the data to make a difference."

CHAPTER THIRTY-TWO

"How certain are we that Austin hasn't done something to this ship that will blow up in our faces at some point?" Harrington asked Powers.

"With Austin, it's hard to be certain about anything," Powers replied, "but we've been monitoring all communications traffic since before we first made contact with them, and no extra pieces of code, no matter how innocent they might seem, have shown up. Now that we've departed from their system, all we have to worry about is anything getting to us through their network." She nodded toward a display. "The only time we allow any access to the network is when we communicate with the aliens or when Albretti sends a report on the status of her people."

"That's the perfect time to try something tricky," Harrington said.

"That's why Powers is the one who monitors everything Albretti does, Ms. Harrington," Flynn responded.

"Are they still monitoring our progress?" Harrington asked.

"Yes," Powers replied. "They know exactly where we are. Fortunately, it works both ways. We can keep track of their movements beyond their system. Everything's been quiet, and we have enough of a lead at this point that they couldn't possibly catch up to us with their conventional propulsion."

"I still worry about what happens if they get out of their system. They can catch us in no time with their warp-field generators."

"We don't stay in touch with the aliens just because we're good friends," Flynn said in a dry tone. "In addition to our keeping them informed about our progress, they'll let us know immediately if anyone from Citadel tries to get out. Even if Austin tries but fails, we'll know to be extra cautious."

"Besides," Powers added, "nothing has changed with respect to their warp-field generators; they still can't get out of their system with them. Austin may be willing to take risks to get what he wants, but he isn't about to sacrifice several of their ships and their crews just to try to rescue another crew."

"If the people aren't important to him, what about the derelict?" Harrington asked. "He was willing to sacrifice his ships and people to recover that ship once before. Why not try it a second time?" A look of desire flashed across her face as she continued. "I know *I* would for something that valuable."

"Same answer," Powers replied. "Regardless of whether he's a saint or just human, he's bottled up in that system. So long as he keeps receiving his messages, he'll stay there."

Flynn looked at Powers. "Speaking of messages, it's about time for Albretti to make another report."

"Keep everything calm, Albretti, and you'll live to see another day," Powers reminded Sara.

Sara didn't bother to respond as she brought the log online. While she waited for the signal, she thought back to the previous day, which had been the first day of transmission.

"I'll set everything up, Albretti," Powers had said, "and you'll start talking when I tell you. You'll say what I tell you and stop talking when I tell you."

"No," she'd replied. "That's not how it's going to happen." Before Powers could cut her off, she'd continued, "I'm going to set things up in a way that will make it clear that this is a real transmission, not a fake."

"There's no way I'm going to let you do that, Albretti," Powers had said emphatically. "I need to be able to vet whatever you say, to make sure that you aren't playing games with us."

Sara had shaken her head slightly. "You have it backward, Powers. *You're* the ones that need me to do it this way. If Sam thinks they aren't real log entries and real broadcasts through the log system, he won't believe I'm still alive. If he doesn't believe I'm still alive, then you just screwed yourselves, because he won't release the derelict or the files to you. If I'm just reading and doing what you want me to read, he'll know it."

"She's right, Powers, at least partly," a voice had said from the hatchway. The women had whirled to face Flynn, who had appeared without a sound. An expression of approval had appeared on his face. "In fact, she should let Austin know about our progress, since it will show our good intentions."

Flynn had given Sara a hard look as he'd continued. "However, Powers, not you, will set things up and always keep an eye on you. Don't count on Austin's demands protecting you. If you try to sneak additional information to him to undermine our mission or work with anything that he tries to sneak through, Powers will shoot you and make sure Austin sees it. We're willing to take the chance of finding out whether Austin is interested in saving any other lives." Flynn had left without another word.

Flynn entered Harrington's cabin and said, "Powers is setting things up for Albretti's next message. Now that we've put some distance between this ship and Citadel, don't you think it's time you explained what you really have in mind?"

Harrington had a slightly amused expression as she replied. "You mean, why am I willing to do a deal that isn't as good as we might get, considering what the derelict is worth?"

"Yes, something like that," he agreed.

"It's really simple. On the one hand, I want to get something that is truly valuable and better than anything Citadel can offer. The warp-field-generator technology is perfect, since it will let all of humanity travel anywhere Austin's people can travel and more efficiently. Even better, it won't require anything from Citadel to implement.

"On the other hand, I don't want us to get too much in the deal, as strange as that may seem. I want everyone to be nervous over the fact that the aliens might be even stronger after they get a hold of the derelict. Once that happens, people will agree to any deal that will get them something. If nothing else, having advanced-warp-field-generator technology will make it easier for the elites to abandon Earth's solar system in the event of another attack."

"What about the rest of the people?"

She shrugged. "It doesn't matter. There isn't anything that would make a difference for the vast majority of the people back home if the aliens decide to attack, so there isn't much point in worrying about them."

Flynn was still puzzled about something. "Wouldn't people be just as willing to negotiate if you had *more* technologies available from a deal with the aliens?"

The former president's gaze was brutal. "From what our people have reported, other alien technology may be complicated enough that we'd need to get the cooperation of Citadel to make it work, which means that Citadel would have a say in the matter. We know that Citadel would never agree to a deal that would work for me. I want a deal that is good enough to place me in the driver's seat but isn't so good that I have to share that seat with others who want to bury me. What makes this really interesting is the fact that their desire for some humans as part of the deal is nonnegotiable—no humans, no deal."

"What do you think the chances are of Earth agreeing to a deal with you if anything happens to those humans?" Flynn asked skeptically.

"We can always claim that we never understood the aliens to have any bad intentions where humans were concerned." Harrington pulled some images up on a display. "Even our own people aren't entirely sure why the aliens want our people, and we've contributed to that confusion by emphasizing harmless motives."

"Austin will claim you planned on sacrificing those people all along in order to get your deal," he warned.

"Austin can claim whatever he wants," she said disdainfully. "I've never made any public statement to the effect that I believe those people will be harmed. I've taken the position that we have to be willing to take some risks in the pursuit of peace, and that means Citadel has to be willing to put aside its own issues as well.

"As far as taking the hostages is concerned, that was the only way we'd be able to take the derelict, plus a couple of transports, to a safe place where the exchange could be made. In a sense, we're taking tough measures to avoid another fight between Citadel and the aliens. We'll claim that once we met, the aliens demanded we turn over the hostages or face destruction. We took the course best calculated to save lives in two solar systems."

A feral look returned to her face. "If it doesn't end well for Captain Albretti and her colleagues, then that can work out well for us too. People will be reminded why it's important to do a deal to get the warp-field technology, and Austin will know that I've won. Now do you understand?"

"Yes, I get it." Flynn nodded. "What I don't know is whether the aliens will really leave us alone once they have that ship."

"I doubt we'll ever see them again once they have it," she replied dismissively. "Face it—we can't use it anyway, and we just won't be important enough for them to worry about once they have something that valuable."

Sara faced the display. "This is Sara Albretti, making my report at 1430 hours on the third day following our departure," she began. "Just before I came here to make this report, I made my rounds of the Citadel personnel on board this vessel and confirmed that they were all unharmed." Sara sent a hostile look toward Powers. "I'm excluding, of course, Captain Benitez from this report, as we already know what's happened to him. As you know, the time and date displayed in this log report are a direct feed from the ship's chronometer and, therefore, cannot be altered." She gestured toward another display with split images. "As you can see, the log has captured exterior images from multiple directions, and they show that the stars around me match the timing of this report."

She looked back toward the display. "Harrington said it will take us thirty-three days to reach the aliens, and then it'll be over. I don't mind saying that that day can't arrive too soon for me." She looked over toward Powers as she said, "I don't like looking at traitors."

Sara ended the transmission, and Powers escorted her back to her quarters. Not for the first time, Sara tried to get through to her captor. "Powers, haven't you figured out yet that something isn't right about this deal? What is it Harrington isn't telling us?"

Powers sighed. "I don't know why I bother to answer you, Albretti," she replied. "This is the same conversation we've already had. I've said it before; you are hostages, nothing more. Once we reach our destination, you will send your final transmission to Austin, who will release the derelict and its files to our control. We will release the derelict to the aliens and receive technology from them, and you can then head back to Citadel unharmed."

"Here's one thing that doesn't make sense," Sara pressed. "While I get that you need a ship to use for your escape, I still don't understand why you asked Sam for another ship for your people. You have plenty of trouble as it is running this one. It can't be any easier with the other one in tow."

"You're right that we don't have the skills to operate one of your transports for an extended time," Powers admitted. "While I have the skills to keep things working for this trip, we don't yet have the experience needed to be able to use warp-field generators and take a transport back to our solar system.

"Our top priority will be to get out of town," Powers said bluntly, "since it won't be healthy for any of us to stay in this system. Austin has probably already picked out a bull's eye for each of us. The aliens have assured us that the technology they share will be more than sufficient to enable us to improve upon and even simplify your warp-field generators, so that we can get back to our own solar system in one of your ships."

Sara shuddered. "Why would you be willing to trust them? They've never demonstrated anything but contempt for human life before. For all you know, they'll take the derelict and leave you to your fates."

Powers gave Sara a mocking look. "Austin thought he was being clever by attaching high explosives to the derelict to obtain our cooperation. We'd have done it ourselves anyway! Those explosives mean that the aliens won't get the derelict until we get their technology. They'll have to show that it really is as simple as they claim." She shrugged. "Besides, they know we won't stiff them on delivery, since we can't haul the derelict with us; even *they* can't use their warp-field generators to do that."

"What if a problem arises with the generators during the trip back to Earth? You don't know the first thing about how they work, so you'd be stranded many years away from any help."

"We can still send distress signals," Powers reminded her. "It might take a while for a signal to reach the nearest communications beacon, but it'll get through, thanks to your mini warp bubbles. Austin would like that anyway, since it would probably mean he could rescue us and bring us back to Citadel for hanging."

"What if you end up nowhere near a communications beacon? Your only option would be deciding whether to die quickly or slowly."

"You face that potential issue anytime you take one of your transports from one system to the other," Powers pointed out. "It's a risk we're prepared to accept."

"The risk won't end there. What makes you think it'll be any safer for you back in Earth's solar system? I didn't have much trouble recognizing you," Sara reminded Powers pointedly. "You should have stayed hidden; at least you might have stayed alive longer."

Her captor allowed a faint smile to appear briefly on her face. "You were lucky; if it hadn't been for the unique circumstances, even you wouldn't have recognized me. In addition, I don't take things for granted, so my appearance will probably change more extensively after I return to Earth. That means there won't be much point in trying to remember my features; I'll blend back into the scenery, and no one will find me who I don't want to.

"Besides, President Lee won't have any choice about agreeing to Harrington's terms, not with the knowledge that we have alien technology and the ability to communicate with the aliens directly." The smile faded as she said, "I learned a long time ago that people will do almost anything to protect their asses, even if it means selling out someone with a higher moral compass, like Austin. Lee won't allow Austin to make trouble in Earth's solar system if it means that he might have to deal with the aliens alone. Lee controls the Space Command, which means he controls the defense of the solar system. Since Mars isn't strong enough to go it alone to defend itself against a sustained attack, their president won't have any choice but to fall in line behind Lee. Division within the ranks would mean their certain defeat in the event of an attack."

They stopped in front of Sara's quarters. As she stepped inside, Powers said, "Although I'm always armed, I don't worry about whether you will try to do something stupid when going to or from making your log reports.

Captain Benitez served as an example of what would happen if you cross us. Although you'd probably think of it as being noble where the well-being of the Citadel crew is concerned, your moral compass is just another sign of your weakness that we can exploit."

Sara turned to Powers and said, "I hope that one of these days your lack of faith in humanity will prove misplaced, to your great horror."

"I've stayed alive for a long time by assuming that people will put their self-preservation ahead of everything else," Powers said. "Things like honor and duty always fall farther down the list, if they make it all." The door closed, and Sara was once again locked inside.

Flynn was in his cabin, finishing a call about the security arrangements for the crew members. After satisfying himself that everything was in order, he decided to get some rest when he heard a noise at the hatch. In an instant, he was at the hatch with a knife in his hand, the result of years of experience that had kept him alive.

He relaxed slightly when he heard Powers's voice. She saw the weapon as she entered. "I see you still aren't taking any chances, Flynn."

He laughed as he lowered the knife to his side. "No reason to change my habits now. It's those habits that have kept me alive far longer than most in our line of work."

"Albretti completed her call," Powers reported. She rolled her eyes. "She's sure she can get me to come over to her side if I will only listen to reason. As she sees it, Harrington hasn't been honest with us and probably has something horrible in mind."

"What do you think Harrington has in mind?" Flynn asked.

"She plans on screwing over Albretti and the rest of the crew, of course," she answered. "I don't believe for a moment that she won't sell out all of them to make the deal with the aliens. Hell, considering the trouble she's already caused me, I might have gotten rid of Albretti already if it weren't for the fact that she and the rest of them have to be alive to be turned over to the aliens."

"That doesn't bother you?"

"No"—she shrugged—"as long as it doesn't get in the way of my own survival. Speaking of survival, how are we going to make sure that Harrington doesn't get rid of us once she doesn't need us anymore?" As Flynn frowned, she added, "Don't get me wrong. I'm not talking about turning on anyone. I'm just not convinced Harrington wouldn't try something to eliminate any unwanted problems—including *both* of us," she emphasized.

"She's gone to the trouble to demand a pardon and safe conduct for us," Flynn reminded her. "Why would she bother if she wanted to eliminate anyone?"

"That's something she's said to Austin. Don't forget, neither of us is a scientist. She'll have the technology and everything she needs from us before she'll get around to demanding anything from the people back on Earth. Who knows what the final deal will be by that point?"

"What are you saying?"

"I'm saying that we should honor our commitment to help obtain the alien technology but be prepared to look after our own interests when the time comes. I don't believe in relying on anyone's goodwill after she already has everything she needs from us."

"'Us'?" Flynn asked quizzically.

Powers moved closer to Flynn. "We've been dancing around this attraction for months now. It was on my mind a lot while you were in stasis. It's time we did something about it."

Flynn reached for the zipper on her jumpsuit, and soon her outfit was on the deck in a pile. She was wearing only a bra and panties. He still had the knife and moved the blade toward her slowly. Her eyes widened slightly, but she didn't react otherwise. With an easy motion, one strap and then the other were cut cleanly. With another motion, the front was opened, leaving her breasts fully exposed. As the bra fell to the floor, she shivered slightly from the contact with the blade. Her smooth skin showed no traces of any scratches. He put the knife away.

He pointed toward the fresh bandage on her leg. "That looks a lot less dramatic than what you were wearing before."

She smiled. "It doesn't hurt, since modern medicine has already taken care of a lot of the healing. In fact, it's time for the bandage to come off anyway." With a quick motion, the bandage was on the deck. All that remained from her attack were several small lines, which would fade and vanish completely within another few days. "Go ahead and touch it if you want."

As he traced his hand along the thin lines, he mused, "That was some job you did, the other day, Powers, bringing in Albretti. I'm not impressed very easily, but I don't know many people who would have been able to pull it off. You had to fight off a couple of cheaters and hike through lousy terrain while carrying a dead weight. You then covered your tracks perfectly, so that Austin had no idea where you were. Then, you showed you didn't need any help getting Albretti to her compartment, and here we are."

"This is an odd time to tell me this," she said with a slight smile. "I'd have thought you wanted to talk about other things."

"You mean, like how the view is even more interesting now than when you showed up with half your shirt missing?" As they moved over to the bed, he said, "It's actually related, Powers. It's a way of saying that I hope you've been straight with me because I respect you enough that I'd really hate to have to cut this lovely throat."

"You've already had your chance at that," she murmured.

CHAPTER THIRTY-THREE

Austin and Liz were alone in their stateroom aboard *Pathfinder*, trying to get a few hours' rest as everyone worked desperately against Harrington's deadline. He gave Liz a rueful look. "In view of how big of a challenge it's been to coordinate everything before our time runs out, you probably wish you'd told me to get lost when I asked you to do it."

In spite of the fatigue, she smiled back at him. "This isn't the first time I've coordinated something big, Sam. I've handled the off-loading of what seems like countless waves of colonists, as well as a lot of the original work on getting the first groups of people over here. Once you've coordinated all the work needed to have hundreds of settlers build their homes at the same time, doing what we've been doing doesn't seem quite so daunting."

Austin brushed a strand of her hair away from her face. "Still, it hasn't been easy for either of us to be here instead of with Matt and Luke. I can't begin to say how much of a godsend Donna has been, looking after them while looking after her own kids."

"It helps her deal with the fact that Bret has been just as much stranded out here as anyone else," she said. "For now, her kids and ours all think everything is a great adventure. She told me the other day that it helps just hearing a lot of laughter around her house, especially the laughter of children."

Her expression turned melancholy. "I wish there were a way to make things easier for Joe. While Gina couldn't be in better hands with Mark and Karen looking after her, I know it's tearing him apart, worrying about Sara. The darkest part for him is wondering how he would tell Gina her mommy won't be coming back. Do you think he'll be in any shape to be in charge of *Pathfinder* if we have a breakthrough?"

Austin shrugged. "That's hard to say, but Joe's pretty tough. Flynn obviously thinks *he's* tough, and he probably is, but I've been reading people since before his grandfather was born. I wouldn't take any bets on his survival if Joe ever gets his hands on him."

"I wouldn't take any bets if *you* get a hold of him either," she said dryly.

Austin chuckled. "I once told Pete Lee that sheep don't last long on a frontier." His expression turned serious. "I've never been a sheep, and I've had to do things over the years to ensure that I can deal with people like Flynn. As far as I'm concerned, he's earned whatever happens to him. If I happen to be the one to help him get what he's earned, I can live with it."

"Speaking of Lee, do you think he'd actually consider doing a deal with Harrington?"

Austin tried to wipe the fatigue from his eyes, an acknowledgment that the question had weighed upon him heavily. "I wish I knew him well enough to be certain he wouldn't give Harrington the time of day, but he's already shown an indecisiveness that can be deadly for a US president. I don't buy into the notion that a person is more responsible for the murder of someone than the actual murderer. However, Lee needs to answer for allowing that murderer to avoid facing punishment for her crimes. It's bad enough that we've already lost Benitez; I just hope we won't have to add the lives of the hostages to that ledger.

"Ultimately, even if Lee were to agree to a deal with Harrington, Citadel would never recognize it. We've waited too long already, and we won't be put off any longer."

"What if the United States were to guarantee her safety?"

Austin frowned. "I've already sent a message to Lee on the subject. You can probably guess what I told him about any guarantees of safety."

"It sounds like we're at a turning point with the United States, or at least with Lee."

"That's about it." He nodded. "As the president of Citadel, I've never ordered any direct action against the United States, not even when we had ample cause during Harrington's War. It seems somewhat ironic that the final straw has come after she's been forced out of office. In a sense, I don't much care how things turn out. If Harrington somehow manages to make her way back to Earth, I will order the Citadel Group forces to capture her and bring her back here, regardless of where she is hiding and who is protecting her. If someone ends up being outraged by events, I'd rather it not be the people of Citadel for a change, especially if justice finally prevailed."

The frown dissolved as Liz reached over and caressed his face. "We're supposed to be getting some rest," she said, changing the subject. A mischievous look crept into her gaze as she sat up in bed. The covers fell away, leaving her naked. As Austin returned her look with an appreciative one of his own, she said, "I don't think either of us is any good at sleeping right now. Fortunately, rest doesn't always mean sleep, my love."

"You're so right," Austin said gently as he pulled her toward him.

CHAPTER THIRTY-FOUR

President Pete Lee rose to greet J. W. Preacher with genuine warmth as Citadel's ambassador entered the Oval Office. "This is a pleasant surprise, Ambassador," he began. "It's been too long since we last spoke face to face, J. W."

At a gesture from the president, Preacher settled himself into one of the comfortable chairs in the room, and Lee came around to sit nearby in another chair.

"Thank you, Mr. President," Preacher replied. "But I'm afraid this isn't just a social visit." He pulled out his link and gestured at a large display. "With your permission, Mr. President, I'd like to play you a message from Sam Austin."

Lee nodded, and moments later, Austin's image appeared.

There was none of the usual friendly demeanor in Austin's features as he began. "Hello, Pete. While I'd like to say that I wanted to chat because we are overdue for a conversation, that isn't the reason for this message. Earlier today, we received a visit from someone I never expected to see except within our custody. With the help of the same operative who tried to kill me the last time I visited Earth, Courtney Harrington managed to smuggle herself and some of her armed thugs onto one of our transports and take it over after it reached our star system. She then had her operative kidnap Sara Albretti from her home on Citadel and take her back to the transport, to join the rest of the crew as prisoners and hostages. Harrington then killed the captain of the transport and forced the pilot to take the ship back through the radiation field, to wait for her new best friend."

The image of a familiar enemy appeared as he continued. "Everything she's done has been because she's gotten into bed with the devil. Somehow, even though she was supposed to be under house arrest, with her activities monitored, it escaped the notice of everyone on Earth that she was continuing to fund efforts to communicate with the aliens. She even had someone search for debris from the ship we destroyed near the asteroid belt and was able to use the debris they found to learn to communicate with the aliens. I'll let her speak for herself as to what she wants."

The image of the former president appeared, and Lee listened in silence as she outlined her demands. His complexion paled slightly as she mentioned her opinion of him.

After Harrington's message ended, Austin spoke. "It wouldn't do any good to talk about my anger and frustration over your failure to carry out your duty as president, including providing for the general welfare of US citizens. That will happen later, and there will be a reckoning over the loss of Captain Benitez, who was a good man. If the lives of any more of our people are lost, the account to be settled will be even greater."

Austin shook his head in disappointment. "I've waited for you to become the leader you need to be, but I'm through being patient with you. Thanks to the freedom you allowed Harrington, we're facing a situation where even desperate measures may not be sufficient to rescue the hostages. Even if, by some miracle, we manage to save our people, we face even tougher odds of being able to recover the derelict a second time. If we fail, it means that the aliens will be even more dangerous than they are already, assuming that they'll have more success than we've had in understanding the derelict's technology." Although the message was recorded, Austin seemed to stare hard at Lee directly. "That danger will apply to your people as well as mine."

Austin's look changed to the kind of sadness that sometimes exists between people who should be friends. "I wish you had told me directly about Harrington's escape from captivity, Pete, including what you should have known about what she'd been doing. If you had, then we'd have known to be on the lookout for her. We might have even been able to stop her efforts completely, since she used our communications network without our knowledge to establish contact with the aliens.

"While there isn't really anything you can do at this point to redeem yourself, at least you can be prepared to finally be a leader and fulfill your oath. If Harrington succeeds in getting her hands on the promised alien technology, you must see that she won't profit from her crimes by getting you to agree to a deal that overlooks her crimes. You need to ensure that she is finally treated as the pariah in your star system that she already is in ours and that the law in your system has already declared her to be." Austin's gaze turned even colder. "I can assure you that Citadel will not recognize the validity of any agreement that claims to provide sanctuary to Harrington and her people.

"I have given further instructions to J. W., which he will discuss with you. I hope we will survive the next thirty-three days." The image faded abruptly.

The room was silent for a moment, as Lee tried to take in everything. "J. W.," he began, "what does Sam plan on doing with this information?"

"What you're really asking is whether Sam plans on releasing this information to the public, putting you in a highly unflattering light," the crafty man said. "At this point, Sam has instructed me not to release any information about Harrington's activities. While he still has plenty of respect for the office he once held, he isn't doing this to save face for you. He wants to avoid any panic that may drive people to clamor for you to do something stupid."

His gaze turned hard. "Make no mistake about whether there will be consequences down the road, Mr. President; as Sam has already pointed out, all of what's happened could have been avoided with the proper leadership on your part."

"Who are you to tell me about leadership?" Lee asked. "This has been uncharted water ever since Harrington was impeached. I've had to balance the demands of Citadel with my responsibilities as president, and there isn't any instruction manual for what to do. I have to ensure the office isn't weakened, so that future presidents would be unable to perform their jobs effectively. I hadn't planned on spending so much time focusing on Harrington and Citadel; I thought it would be over by now."

Preacher's reply was devastating. "While I haven't had the privilege of holding the office you hold, I have had the privilege over the years of observing and advising someone who has. Sam Austin didn't plan on dealing with the Bio War during his tenure, but he did anyway. He didn't plan on dealing with rogue elements on Mars who nearly succeeded in their efforts to destroy much of life in the United States, but he did."

"You may feel sorry for yourself about the fact that you knew when you were the president-elect that you'd have to deal with Harrington's crimes. Of course, that meant you had two months to prepare for the job following your election. Sam didn't have that luxury when he first became president. He'd barely been sworn in as vice president when assassins destroyed the building where President Thomson was attending the funeral of a dear friend. Once he was sworn in as president, he didn't rest until the murderers were brought to justice."

Preacher rose to leave. "Knowing Sam as I do, he'll be in the vanguard of the people trying to rescue the hostages. That means the message I received may be the last time I ever hear from him. If that's the case, don't make his sacrifice a waste."

Lee was silent as Preacher left.

CHAPTER THIRTY-FIVE

No one from Citadel needed to be reminded that time was short. The fact that nearly all of their engineering and design people were meeting in the engine room of a transport, and not in a conference room, was acknowledgment of the increasing desperation of the situation.

"I hope Harrington hasn't been blowing smoke at us," Austin said, "because we're screwed if they've already arrived at their rendezvous with the aliens." He looked around the room and gestured toward the unfamiliar configurations. "Please tell me that this collection of stuff is as good as it is insane looking. I doubt I understand even half of it."

Yabuno walked to a display, rubbing without thought at the dark smudges under his eyes. He brought up images that were by now numbingly familiar. "Our simulations tell us that we're nearly there, Sam. They match the readings from the new configurations." He pushed the images away in frustration. "There's something about the math that we're just not figuring out yet though."

Austin looked at Turner, whose eyes were even heavier with fatigue than Yabuno's. Turner brought the images back that Yabuno had pushed away and said, "That's been the challenge in trying to understand the symbols from the derelict. I've plugged in everything I can understand from those symbols, but I can't get us to a point where our transports can simply cease all motion while still warping space-time in a way that shields them from external threats. Our ships keep drifting and shifting position, and the bubble doesn't stay stable enough to avoid detection. The only good news is that we've been able to control the process of collapsing the warp-field bubbles in a safe and predictable manner. It doesn't help us though, if we still can't control where we want the ships to go when they're in a bubble."

It was now Turner who pushed the images away as he concluded, "I still believe I can work it out, but I need more time to do it." He chuckled without humor. "Funny thing is this was once just an interesting intellectual exercise for Bret and me. It feels a hell of a lot different now, knowing that lives depend on what we do."

The room settled into a low buzz of sound, as people muttered their own views on where things stood. Austin finally moved back toward the display, a sign he wanted to be heard. "We don't have any more time, Alan, so let's figure out what to do."

The buzz faded as everyone waited.

"Our basic problem is that we can't keep everything stable in all directions at the same time. That's not unlike the problem we had years ago when we tried to develop the first warp-field generators. It seems to me that we need to make the best of what we *can* do."

"What's that?" Albretti asked.

"If we stop trying to control movement in *every* direction and allow for movement in *one* direction that we choose, we can warp space-time to move at very slow speeds. While that happens, a transport can still avoid being affected by what's happening outside the warp-field bubble." Austin gestured toward the display. "Anyone see a barrier that would no longer be a barrier in that situation?"

Yabuno practically leaped up as he said, "The radiation field! We could get through it without getting fried."

"What about the leaks we've been having?" Lambert asked. "Why wouldn't they still be a problem? If a ship can be detected while using this approach, then wouldn't the radiation still get through and poison us?"

"That's Sam's point," Yabuno said. "By trading a completely stationary approach for a little movement, we get most of what we wanted, including no more leaks. If we start moving from outside the field, then by the time we reach it, our ships will be fully within their bubbles. That means no radiation to worry about, and nothing giving away our position, at least until we're ready to move back into normal space-time."

"It means we can't just sit in front of one of their ships in a warp bubble though," Lambert said. "It also means that forming and collapsing those bubbles may take longer, or at least be kind of fuzzy at times. We'll be facing increased vulnerability during those times. I'd rather that we be able to enter into fixed positions around one of their ships and take them out at our convenience."

"I think we can arrange some solutions," Austin replied with a grin as he looked over at Albretti.

"Hell yes," Albretti enthused. "We can work out some maneuvers that will give us what we need when we want to take on those bastards. It'll be a tricky dance at times"— he grinned—"but we can figure out the steps."

"We'll start working on those dance steps right away, Joe," Austin said.

Albretti's expression sobered as he walked over to the display and motioned toward their position and the alien ship. "Before we celebrate our victory, we'd better keep in mind that our transports won't be moving very fast at this speed. It'll take hours just to reach their ship from here." He looked around the room hopefully. "I don't suppose we could try to shorten that trip by hauling ass to the edge of the radiation field and then launching our transports with their new, improved warp-field generators?"

Austin shook his head. "They'd see us coming and would know we had something in mind. The benefit of the greater distance is that it must be hard, even for them, to get good readings on our operations, considering the interference from the radiation. Let's use that interference to our advantage. However," he continued, "this isn't something that we can set up in ten minutes."

All eyes shifted to Curly Stephens, who brushed an unruly lock of red hair out of her face. "It'll take us more like ten hours to get our transports ready with the new configurations."

"We may not have ten hours to spare, Curly," Austin replied. "Our time is practically used up as it is; we have to get the hell out of here and at that ship before Harrington and her friends get around to doing whatever they have planned."

Stephens brought up an enlarged image of the alien ship. "I know all of that, Sam. We have to get it right though. For obvious reasons, we won't be able to do any field-testing. Radiation field or not, they'd smell a rat—assuming they even have noses—if they saw us checking to see if it functions properly. For it to work, this whole thing has to be a surprise.

"I just hope to hell it won't be the wrong kind of surprise, because we won't have any other options." She shook her head slightly. "It'd take us hours just to bring the generators back to their current configuration if something goes wrong. Depending on the nature of any damage, it might take closer to forever to fix things." An anxious look passed across her face as she looked at Turner and Yabuno. "Your numbers *have* to work."

Austin's gaze took on a hard look that wasn't directed at Turner, even though Austin was looking at him. "There's one other thing that we haven't yet addressed, Alan, that you shared with me a short while ago. Tell us where things stand regarding your efforts to understand the aliens' language."

Turner brought up some unfamiliar images on a display as he began. "As you know, thanks to Bret's mirroring protocols, we were able to review the efforts of Harrington's people to understand the aliens' language. We managed to combine that information with the information that Melody's people retrieved from the communications array."

His voice took on an apologetic tone. "I wish I could say that I now understand the language as well as Harrington's people, but I've been focusing on other alien symbols, as we've already discussed. I've been spending what time I could spare in developing a series of algorithms to delve more deeply into their language to make up for our lack of time. The algorithms are crude so far, but with some refinements, we may be able to catch up in far less time than it took Harrington's people to work it out. I've run into a big problem though; some of the information I've been able to download has been corrupted by the radiation field, so even my efforts to improve the algorithms are taking longer to produce results than I'd hoped."

Turner had a worried expression. "What I think I've learned so far is unsettling, to say the least. It appears that the aliens have an interest in meeting humans, although it isn't clear why, considering that they've never shown much respect for human life. It's even possible that Harrington has come to believe that the aliens have relatively benign motives toward us. Anyway, in addition to an exchange of technology for the derelict, the aliens have insisted on meeting some humans.

"However, I can't tell whether Harrington plans on meeting the aliens herself or whether she wants to send some ambassadors. While she has people of her own who could serve as ambassadors, there are others aboard that ship that she might intend to use instead. If she does,

I doubt she plans on asking them to volunteer for the honor."

Austin summarized the issue for them. "In short, her hostages may be more than just hostages. If they're more than just hostages, considering how she feels about us, she probably wouldn't lose much sleep over anything happening to our people."

Seven hours later, everyone was standing by for a message from Austin, who had stayed aboard *Pathfinder*, which had once again become his flagship. As he stood on the bridge of the tough ship, receiving the latest reports on the status of each transport, he thought back over the previous hours.

Just before Turner and Yabuno had headed off to work with Stephens's people to reconfigure the transports, Austin had cornered Turner. "Alan," he'd begun, "I know you'll be in for some of the toughest hours you've ever known as you work with Curly and her people, but there's something even tougher I'd like you to do after the transports are ready to launch."

Turner had actually chuckled slightly as he'd replied, "I already know what you're going to say. You want me to continue to refine my algorithms for understanding the language of our alien enemies. You also want me to keep working on the problem while we head out toward the alien ship, in case I have some brilliant insight that will save the day."

Austin had grinned. "Yeah, something like that. Sounds kind of desperate, doesn't it?"

"It doesn't matter, because I was going to do it anyway."

Austin's grin had faded. "I wish we knew more about what Harrington has in mind for our people."

"So do I," Turner had said. He'd pulled up several images of the derelict symbols, stared at them for a few moments, and then closed them again. "Getting back to the derelict, it still feels like I just about have enough of it worked out to do what we wanted to do. The problem is that our generators are already pretty damned complex, and maintaining a stable warp-field bubble around these behemoths is nearly impossible as it is. If only we could start from a simpler point." Austin had missed the momentary flash of inspiration on Turner's face as he'd moved to join the others.

Now, at a nod from Austin, his face appeared on displays throughout the Citadel transports. "To all of you on our transports," he began, "I've always been impressed by how our people can do incredibly difficult things that others can't do. In this case, as dramatic as it sounds, you've done things that go beyond incredibly difficult. Alan Turner and Bret Yabuno have worked side by side with Curly Stephens and her people to try to give us a chance to save the lives of our loved ones on board *KT-2*. Amazingly, they did it in only seven hours.

"While some of you were involved with the reconfigurations of our transports' warp-field generators, the rest of you have been doing equally vital things necessary to get ready for the encounter. Melody Lambert and her people have been working on ensuring that no one outside this system learns about our attack on the alien ship until we choose to let them know about it. Our ships' captains and I have been choreographing the 'dance steps,' as Joe Albretti has put it, that may mean the difference between success or failure with the new warp-field generators. The rest of you have been doing thousands of other things that need to be done, including setting up onboard anything we can use as weapons against our adversaries.

"Finally, as important as is the objective I've already mentioned, which is to save our loved ones, there is another objective that is hugely important. We need to keep our human enemies from handing over to our alien enemies technology that may mean the extinction of the human race. That may lead to some tough choices relating to the derelict.

"We will start in five minutes. Good luck and Godspeed." At a nod from Austin, the transmission ended.

Hours later, Austin met with Albretti and Yabuno in his stateroom. Austin noted that Turner was missing and asked, "Where's Alan? We need to know if he's come up with any other insights."

"He's working on something he wants to run by me," Yabuno replied. "He'll be here as soon as possible."

Albretti stood before a display, pointing at an image of the alien ship that still waited just outside the radiation field. "I wish to hell we could see something while in this bubble, Sam," he complained. "For all we know, they've already figured out what we're doing and have shifted, so that they can blast us with an EMP in short order."

Yabuno shrugged as he brought up an image of the communications array. "They can screw us without firing a shot, just by telling everyone at the other end about us. We know Harrington well enough not to expect anything other than a lot of dead people if that happens."

"Too bad we have to wait to block the array from relaying any communications traffic until after we get clear of the radiation field," Albretti mused.

"We didn't dare try anything like that before we left," Austin reminded them. "It would have been way too long to risk some kind of unscheduled call that wouldn't get through or receive a response. We can't monitor that traffic while we're in a warp-field bubble, and any kind of problem like that would be sure to tip them off."

The images on the display faded as Turner's face appeared. He made a gesture, and the image split to reveal new mathematical symbols. There was excitement on his face as he spoke. "Sam and I talked about trying to start from a simpler place to solve the problem. In a way, I've done just that, by setting aside the problem as it relates to the transports and just working on it for *Pathfinder's* generators. As you know, there're some interesting differences, including the fact that we don't need to maintain as massive a bubble as for a transport. Bret, take a look at these figures and tell me if they mean what I think they mean."

There was a moment of confusion on Yabuno's face as he sought to take in the figures. The confusion changed rapidly to understanding and then hesitated at the brink of elation as he manipulated the figures and said, "If I understand what you just showed us, the changes I made should give *Pathfinder* the ability to become motionless while maintaining a stable warp bubble. How the hell did you figure it out?" He held up his hand and laughed as Turner started to answer. "You have no idea how much I want to have that conversation, but we need to make some modifications to the new configuration to accommodate these changes." He looked at Albretti. "Joe, tell the Chief I'm heading to engineering and we're going to play around with his warp-field generators again."

"Got it, Bret," he replied. "While you're taking care of that one, Sam and I need to talk about some new dance steps that may be possible with this news."

As Yabuno prepared to leave, he looked back at the display. "Are you coming over to engineering, Alan?"

Turner shook his head. "I'd really like to be there, but you understand the figures as well as I do."

Yabuno snorted. "I doubt it."

"You understood them well enough to improve upon what I did, and that's more than enough to do what needs to be done." He looked back at Austin. "Besides, I still have work to do on another project for Sam and not much time to do it."

Austin nodded, and the display went dark.

CHAPTER THIRTY-SIX

Everyone was back on the bridge, with minutes to spare before they would collapse the warp-field bubble and launch their attack on the alien vessel. Despite the good news about the new generator configuration, their faces all reflected the tension from the long hours leading up to that moment.

"What's the status of the warp-field generators, Bret?" Austin asked.

Yabuno's expression was wistful as he said, "The chief and his people did everything possible while the generators were in operation, but not all of the changes could be made while they're hot. The moment the bubble collapses, his people can complete the changes."

Albretti spoke up. "Fortunately, *Pathfinder* can maneuver under normal propulsion while the changes are being made. I just hope it won't be too long before we're ready for some of our dance steps." He looked at a chronometer. "Speaking of time, we're down to thirty seconds, so let's get ready."

The moment the final seconds ticked away, the image on the main display dissolved from an indeterminate darkness to a familiar view. Although there were plenty of stars breaking up the endless swathes of black, people focused on the horror of the ship that had served both as their warden and a sentinel over the previous thirty-three days.

The rest of the transports maneuvered toward the enemy vessel from different directions as the transport carrying Lambert closed on the array, to eliminate any chance of a warning being issued to their enemies, human and alien. The predator was now the prey, as multiple EMP weapons were deployed, seeking to destroy their common target. However, that common target was far larger than any of its would-be attackers and could still inflict death, as its own EMP weapon was deployed and sought a target.

In short order, the images on the displays deteriorated under the bombardment, and targeting by either side was complicated significantly.

As a vessel passed to the side of the alien ship, the EMP probe shifted position in pursuit. By the time it caught up, however, the transport had managed to reestablish a warp-field bubble. Austin resisted the urge to comment on how long it seemed to take for the ship to move fully outside of normal space-time.

The good news was that while the EMP probe was occupied with its elusive target, other ships blasted the enemy vessel with enhanced pulses. When the aliens sought to direct their lasers toward these attackers, others materialized out of their warp-field bubbles from different locations and commenced further attacks. Although everything was happening at a fairly quick pace, it still seemed to take too long to complete the changes into and out of normal space-time. Austin felt like cursing as he saw several transports fail to escape into a warp bubble quickly enough to avoid damage from the EMP weapon or the lasers. However, he was pleased to note that the alien ship was clearly sustaining massive damage, as the lasers were losing their effectiveness. The engagement continued and even the EMP weapon, as terrible as it was, didn't seem quite as destructive.

The aliens were adapting to the situation, however. They took note of the amount of time it took for the transports to escape into warp-field bubbles and realized that the human ships had to stay in motion in one direction as they escaped. Because of the dangers inherent in these maneuvers, no one would try to move into space that another transport was trying to vacate. They began to anticipate locations where the transports might reappear.

Albretti received a message from the chief. "We're ready to roll, Captain."

"Great news, Chief," he replied. He nodded to his pilot on the bridge as he pointed to a spot on the display. "That's where we need to be when we materialize into normal space-time. Chief, take us into a warp-field bubble, and get our EMP weapon online."

The image had barely faded into the usual indeterminate darkness before it dissolved back into normal space-time. At an order from Albretti, they blasted their enemy. However, after just a few seconds, they moved back into a warp-field bubble, stretching it out to match what the other transports had done.

"If we've figured this out," he said, "the aliens will now assume that no one will try to move into this space for a while, so they'll shift their focus to a different direction." After more seconds had ticked away on a chronometer, he gave the order to move back into normal space-time.

The first thing they saw was an enemy ship now completely out of position to deal with them. This time, the fire from the scout ship was sustained. Although the aliens tried to bring their lasers to bear against their unexpected attackers, *Pathfinder* shrugged off the damage and maintained fire.

Upon noting that *Pathfinder* had positioned itself to keep blasting their enemy without an effective response, several of the other transports stopped skipping in and out of normal space-time. While some of them kept up the pressure from their EMP weapons, others deployed a familiar weapon—in practically no time, large rocks smashed into the alien craft from different angles as multiple rail guns launched their deadly payloads. Some of the rocks almost seemed to fade from view as they rushed toward the indeterminate outlines of the hull's brown-and-black surface.

Whether the repeated assaults from the EMP weapons had damaged the quasi-organic functioning of the alien craft was impossible to know. However, the ragged edges from the holes that had been blasted through the body of the ship looked less like lacerated tissue than in previous encounters. It still didn't look anything like traditional structural damage though.

Moments later, the attacking ships abandoned their fixed positions as the besieged ship shuddered from internal explosions that began to rip it apart. What started as almost delicate tendrils of flames were subsumed by the dazzling fire that burst forth from what now looked more like a carcass than a ship.

Fortunately, the transports had made it into warp-field bubbles safely. They stayed within those protective embraces as the ship that had served as their jailer went through its death throes. Normal space-time moved easily past them as they sought a safe distance before reappearing. Up until now, their encounters with their enemies had always meant human deaths, even when they'd won. Now, thanks to the new technology, they'd avoided any casualties. Austin gave a silent prayer of thanks.

There wasn't any time to savor their victory, however, since destroying the alien ship was only part of their plan. Their attacks had kept the enemy from keeping tabs on the ship containing Lambert and her people. Hopefully, the other ships had bought enough time to ensure that the communications array hadn't been used to warn the other aliens, or Harrington, about the breakout.

As they all moved back into normal space-time, Austin contacted Lambert's ship, noting that it continued to maintain a defensive position near the array. "Melody, open up a private channel back to Citadel and the rest of our transports that can't be detected by Harrington; everyone needs to hear this. Where do we stand?" he asked. "Tell me they didn't get a message through."

Lambert brought up an image of the array, along with various technical readouts. She breathed a small sigh of relief as she replied, "Just as you expected, they were too distracted by our transports to send out a warning before we'd reestablished control of the array at this end. All of the EMP activity helped as well. We started monitoring the traffic even before taking control, so we're pretty confident that their friends don't know what happened."

"Are we still sure there's no way for them to have sent a warning to their friends some other way?" Albretti asked.

"It looks like they were using our array, which would make sense. We'd have detected anything they'd have tried to set up and become suspicious." Lambert expanded the image to show the distance between Citadel and the estimated end point of the trip with the hostages. "That means that even if they managed to send out a warning with their own equipment during the attack, it won't reach the others until after we've caught up with them."

Lambert pointed to an image of the radiation field as she turned to Albretti. "You asked whether it would have been worth the risk to try to take control of the array before we left. Here's another reason why that wouldn't have been a good idea. It's one thing to get information from the array for study; we'd just try to work with the corrupted files. It's another to deal with complications from the corruption screwing up our efforts to control the array from our end. There's too much interference from the radiation field for us to risk everything on getting it done from there. If we'd failed, we'd never have gotten to the alien ship in time to take them out."

Lambert brought up an image of Sara. "This message arrived while we were making our way through the radiation field." At a nod from Austin, Lambert played the message for everyone.

Sara stared at the display with a shell-shocked look on her face. "This is Sara Albretti. As you can see from the chronometer readout, this is day thirty-three. I've been taken on my usual rounds of the ship and confirmed that every one of our people is unharmed. As you know, today is a special day, and Harrington took me on a tour of the bridge, with an amazing set of images on the display. There's a remarkable complex here, with a dozen alien ships moored nearby. While we haven't seen any physical images of the aliens yet, Harrington's people have made contact with them." Her expression darkened. "Speaking of Harrington, she wants to say something to you."

Harrington stepped into view. "I want to remind you that we've kept our part of the bargain, Sam. As Captain Albretti has acknowledged, your people are safe and unharmed. That means it's time for you to send the codes to release control of the derelict and your encrypted files to me, so we can complete our transaction with the aliens. When you've done that, we will tell the aliens to forward the technology promised to us. Once we've confirmed that the technology works on the transport we select, we will release the derelict to the aliens. Your people will be free to take the other transport back to Citadel or wherever else they care to go; by that time, it won't really matter to us," she concluded with a malicious look.

"Keep in mind what will happen to your people if the release codes don't arrive as promised," she warned. "If you try to make a fool of me with the aliens, I will make sure this is the last transmission that Captain Albretti will ever send to anyone." The message ended after she nodded briefly.

"When did that message arrive, Melody?" Austin demanded.

"It arrived just over three hours ago," Lambert replied.

"Damn," Austin said. "They'd have to know the message arrived here, wouldn't they?"

"That's right." Lambert nodded. "That also means that going this long without replying to their message wouldn't have been viewed by them as anything other than calling off the deal."

A terrible sadness appeared on Austin's face as he said, "Sara and the others may have paid the price for my gamble."

"I don't think so, Sam, although you won't like the reason why," Turner broke in, appearing on another display.

Austin swiveled quickly to face Turner's image. "You've learned something more about what Harrington has in mind?"

Turner's expression was angry with a touch of something Austin couldn't quite identify. "Harrington won't kill our people, at least not yet."

"Why not?"

"She's going to give them to the aliens."

A chill ran down Austin's spine as he said, "I take it our people aren't going to act as ambassadors."

Turner shook his head. "When I said, 'give,' I meant 'give,' like lab specimens. From what I can tell, they want to figure out how human bodies work." Austin now knew that the look on Turner's face was horror. "The best description I can think of is that they want to take our people apart. Nothing's been said about what it would be like to be taken apart or whether they would be put back together."

Liz had been listening from their stateroom. "It's hard to believe all of the scientists working for Harrington would agree to be a part of such crimes," she said. "I'd have thought Earth history dating back at least to the Bio War aftermath would have reminded people about what to expect when these crimes are brought to light."

"Harrington was never a student of history," Austin replied, "except as it related to the willingness of some presidents to abuse their powers."

"I don't think her scientists understand what she has in mind," Turner said. "While they'd have to know what the aliens want, I think she's been telling her people, at least the scientists, that while they have agreed to the aliens' demands, Harrington won't honor that part of the deal. A certain amount of subterfuge, both with respect to the aliens, as well as to Sam, will lead to true peace, plus a new relationship with the aliens. The aliens will overlook the part of the deal relating to providing human lab rats once they realize that they'll have the real treasure, the derelict."

"You really believe her people could be that naïve, to stand by while Flynn, Powers, and the rest of her thugs take over *KT-2*?" Liz asked.

"Even intelligent people can be extremely stupid," Turner said. "By the time they realize what she really plans on doing, it'll be too late, and everyone will consider them in on it with Harrington."

Lambert was still skeptical. "How do you know this? I can't believe Harrington would be foolish enough to send messages that show her real plans."

"People have been careless about their communications for centuries," Turner said. "Harrington thought she was being clever in how she worded her messages to people, but she never dreamed we'd have access to all of her communications to the aliens and would be able to figure out her intentions from what she said in some messages but not in others. Ultimately, she must believe that she can make a deal with President Lee that he and the rest of their solar system would be bound to honor. She doesn't seem to care whether Lee knows what she thinks of him, either; she thinks he'll roll over anyway."

"That's where she's wrong," Austin said, a cold fire stirring in his gaze. "No one can make a binding agreement to overlook crimes against humanity. While I hope that it never gets to the point where Lee has to decide whether to accept such a deal, it won't matter to Citadel. I've already sent a message to him emphasizing the folly of being on the wrong side of history where Harrington and the aliens are concerned. I hope that he pays attention to it."

Joe Albretti had remained quiet during the conversation but wouldn't any longer. "I don't give a damn about what might happen down the road; I just want to know when we're going to finish our mission and get our people out from Harrington's reach." The fury in his face matched the fire in Austin's gaze. "I'm not going to pretend I don't have a special interest in getting Sara out of there, although all of our people are important. As far as I'm concerned, Harrington is a dead woman if anything happens to any of our people. However, we need to work out our next moves quickly if we're going to have any chance of saving them."

Lambert spoke. "Sam, I've located another message on the array, but it isn't from Harrington. Whatever it is, I can't understand it." She looked at Turner. "I just forwarded it to you, Alan. I wonder if it's from the aliens to the ship we destroyed."

"When did it arrive?" Turner asked.

"It came in around sixty minutes after the one from Sara arrived."

A faint gleam appeared in Austin's glare. "It probably was to check on whether we were trying to pull a fast one on them. The timing works for us, since we were still making our way through the radiation field undetected. There weren't any alarms to raise then. I'll bet there's something that might be a response back to them."

Lambert nodded. "There's something like that, but I can't understand it either."

Austin looked at Turner's image. "What about it, Alan? Is there any chance of our translating those messages immediately?"

"There's no way," he said with a shake of his head. He pulled up the new images and gestured at them. "Since they don't have to worry about tailoring those messages to a human audience, they're almost certainly using some symbols we haven't seen before. Who knows how long it might take my algorithms to show results? For all we know, it might take days or even months to make some sense of what they're saying. It wouldn't surprise me if they've made a deliberate choice to use symbols humans haven't seen, to preserve the privacy of their communications with each other."

"In that case, we're heading out to meet Harrington as soon as we've completed our damage assessment. I saw several of our transports take shots. Since we don't have the luxury of waiting for repairs, we need to know what they can do going forward."

Albretti spoke. "As much as I want to get there even sooner, Sam, I'd like to make sure every captain knows how to take advantage of the fact that *Pathfinder* can maintain its position in a warp-field bubble. It may be what keeps Sara and the others alive."

"I have something to share with you and the other captains as well," Austin said, "but I need you to wait a moment while I send a message to Curly."

Stephens's image appeared on a display. "That was a hell of a show, Sam," she began, before Austin cut her off.

"Sorry to be so abrupt, Curly, but we don't have much time."

Stephens was all business. "What do you need?"

"I need you and your people to do whatever it takes to cobble together replacements for the rail guns the aliens destroyed. Beef up the rear guns, and get them as close as possible to your side of the radiation field. Strip the mining operations if you need anything, but get it done. Make sure you have a hell of a supply of asteroids available. Also, get started on permanent replacements, even though that'll take longer to complete. Deploy them as soon as you complete them."

"You can count on my team," she replied proudly.

"I know. I'm counting on you for the survival of Citadel in case we don't come back," he said grimly.

Austin signed off and turned back to the main display. "We know how much minutes count right now. We'll have to cover everything while we're getting ready to head out of here. Everyone had better be ready to go in fifteen minutes, or I'll want to know the reason why."

CHAPTER THIRTY-SEVEN

Harrington's face had an unpleasant expression as she met with Flynn and Powers in her quarters. "It's hard to believe that Austin may have written off Captain Albretti and her people." She nodded toward Powers. "You have confirmed that the message arrived back at Citadel. Is there any possibility that we could be wrong about that message?"

Powers shook her head. "No, the fact that we received confirmation shows that nothing got in the way of their getting it."

"What about interference from the radiation field? Could the message have gotten to the array itself but become corrupted when transmitted through the radiation field to the Citadel planetary array?"

"Receipt of message from the planetary array has also been confirmed. The confirmation protocols would let us know if there was any significant corruption in the message." Powers made another small gesture as she continued. "You're probably going to ask if their reply with the release codes might have been garbled. *Something* would have gotten through to us, since the confirmation from their planetary array got through."

Harrington turned to Flynn. "Have we received any updates from the aliens? It would be just like Austin to find a way out of their system."

"As you know, the aliens have contacted their own ship in the Citadel system and confirmed that nothing has happened back there," he replied. "They've promised to let us know if anything changes. There's been no word from them since then."

"We should check with them again," Harrington said in a tone that showed a lack of confidence in her new ally.

Flynn shook his head. "We've been through this before, Ms. Harrington. They interpret it as an insult when we check up on something they've said they'll do. We already know they don't regard us as being their equals, and they don't react well to comments that suggest they have to answer to us for anything.

"Besides, they'd spot a fleet of transports from far away, and we know humans can't survive the exposure to the radiation. Austin's the only exception, and even he needs time to recover. He isn't likely to get that recovery time, and his ship would be pretty much useless anyway," Flynn said emphatically.

"All right, we can't go back to the aliens," Harrington said reluctantly. "We can still send a demand to Austin directly and say that he gets to see one of his people die as a reminder of what will happen to the rest if he keeps stalling." Her expression grew malicious as she said, "I can think of someone in particular whose death would hit him very hard."

"If he sees us kill Captain Albretti, there's the risk that Austin would assume his people are going to die anyway," Flynn said. "All cooperation might end at that point. Also, we promised those people to the aliens. They probably won't accept any shortages of the deliverables."

Harrington was growing increasingly frustrated. "Hasn't Austin already made that call by refusing to send the codes to us? It's either that, or he's playing a game with us. Besides, all I'm hearing are reasons why we can't get what we want. I want to hear how to get what we want, despite Austin's stall tactics. Let's start with figuring out what happens when we tell the aliens we don't have the release codes for the explosive devices on the derelict. To say they'd be furious would be an understatement."

Powers snorted. "Yes, so let's use the radiation field to our advantage. We'll tell the aliens that the codes were corrupted during transmission and won't work. We can play to their vanity by suggesting that they should be able to bypass the explosive devices that have been attached to the derelict. Our only condition is that they don't get to work on the derelict until they've transferred their technology to us. They shouldn't have a problem with that, since the ship is here and we can't take it anywhere else. This shows we're not trying to back out of the deal."

"Won't they know there wasn't any response from Austin?" Flynn reminded them. "Catching us in a lie wouldn't work out well for us," he warned.

"They've never bothered to try to learn our language or how we communicate internally, which means they aren't monitoring the communications network for our traffic in our language," Powers said. "They don't respond to anything we do unless we're using their symbols."

Powers continued. "Even though we don't understand how the Citadel generators work, the aliens have told us that the technology is so transformative that there won't be anything of the old technology left anyway. While a complete understanding of the new technology will take some time, we should be able to use it for maneuvering purposes, including heading back to our solar system."

"I hope we can rely on the files that they've promised to explain everything about their technology," Harrington said. "How do we deal with the fact that they still want the humans we've promised? While I don't care about them, I want to be sure we can get the hell out of here before Citadel finds out about it. I don't have any illusions about what will happen to us if we're anywhere near this solar system."

"I have an idea," Powers said. "Let's tell them the humans will remain on board this ship, which we'll release to the aliens once we've confirmed that their technology works. We'll be modifying the other ship; they already know we don't understand the Citadel technology, so we wouldn't be able to use the warp-field generators on board this ship to move the people to safety."

Flynn's expression was noncommittal as he said to Harrington, "You realize that we could still try to do this deal without turning the people over to the aliens. Once we confirm that their technology works, we could leave on the other transport. While the aliens wouldn't be happy with us, they would still have what they really want—the derelict. Taking that approach would make it much easier for us to come to terms with people like President Lee."

"All of this is a series of calculated risks," Harrington replied. "The aliens have already threatened to destroy us if we back out of any part of the deal. It took some work on our part just to get them to take their damned EMP weapon offline during this trip. I'd much rather avoid the risk that their threat is real, regardless of what it might mean for the people on Earth. Lee is sufficiently weak that he'd have to make a deal with us anyway." Her gaze flashed with a spiteful chill. "Besides, Sam Austin has been sure I'd receive his punishment for what happened when I was president. While he was able to kill everyone else, I'm still standing. I want him to know that *I* won, not Citadel, and that he's receiving the punishment I've chosen for him. He'll have to live the rest of his ridiculously long life with the guilt of losing all these lives, while I get to remain in our home solar system under the protection of Austin's former friends and allies.

"Now," she continued, "how do we send them over to the aliens? We only have a limited number of people that we can trust, and they might be overwhelmed by trying to keep everyone in line."

"The answer is to lie to them," Powers said. "Sara Albretti thinks I'm being misled by you into believing that the people from Citadel won't be in any danger if Austin fulfills his part of the bargain."

"What did you have in mind?" Harrington asked.

"We should tell them that we are all moving from this ship to the other one for reasons of safety, since Austin didn't send the release codes. As we know, Austin insisted on ensuring that this ship be subject to destruction if it were to be separated from the derelict. Let's tell them part of the truth, which is that Austin has written them off and the aliens are going to try to remove the explosive devices from the derelict. Since this transport can't be moved far enough away from the derelict for safety, we all need to move to the other transport."

"What good would that do us?" Harrington asked impatiently.

Powers brought up an image of one of the airlocks for the transport. "One of the benefits of a ship this large is that at times it can carry many people. There are enough airlocks on this ship to accommodate everyone who is on board currently. Likewise, there are also enough shuttles available to accommodate everyone on board."

"I see where you're going with this," Flynn said with a hard laugh.

Powers nodded as she continued. "We would make sure that only our people are in certain airlocks and only their people are in other airlocks. The shuttles would be keyed to the individual airlocks, so that once they have their passengers, certain ones will head toward the other shuttle." Her expression turned colder as she said, "The others will head straight for the aliens, at whichever location or locations they want."

"Excellent plan," Harrington said approvingly. "However, while I wonder what's to prevent the Citadel people from taking control of the shuttles or the airlocks, for that matter, and going wherever they please, there's a more basic issue to address. If I were from Citadel and only saw others from Citadel nearby, I wouldn't be willing to enter an airlock that might be instructed to vent directly to outside the ship."

Powers mulled over Harrington's objections. "To answer your first point, everything on this ship can be set up to require the captain's authorization codes in order to be operated, which is why we haven't worried much about someone like Albretti getting loose. With respect to your second point, you'll note that the airlocks can be configured to be sets of double airlocks, with each compartment separated by a bulkhead. We can arrange things so that people from Citadel enter into one of the compartments and some of our people enter into the adjoining compartment. Displays would confirm the people in each compartment."

"Wouldn't they suspect a trap anyway? We could always rig things so that our hatch stays shut while theirs opens directly to space."

"That's why we're going to have to allow them to link the two hatches, so that what happens to one happens to the other. Neither hatch will open unless they confirm that a shuttle is on the other side. Fortunately, the shuttles can accommodate the double compartments."

"How does that help us?" Harrington asked skeptically. "Our people will still have to share their shuttles with the Citadel people."

"They won't be expecting another trap once they see that we are allowing them to join us on the shuttles. They won't know, of course, that we will lock the controls for their compartments in the shuttles, so that they are trapped there while the shuttles take our people to the other transport. This means that our people will exit from the shuttles into the other transport, but the Citadel people will be stuck on board. The shuttles will already have been given remote instructions to head toward the aliens with our friends from Citadel."

"If we allow them access to the controls for the airlocks, why couldn't they do something similar to our people?"

"They still need the captain's codes, which they won't get. We will enter those codes into the airlock controls to allow for the limited purpose of linking the airlocks."

Harrington provided the conclusion. "We'll send a message back to Austin, telling him that he's playing with the lives of his people. Later, we'll claim that we were trying to protect the hostages by taking them with us, but the aliens captured them in retaliation for Austin's failure to abide by the deal to send the codes. We'll then be free to head back to Earth with our new technology and shift the blame for the loss of the Citadel people to Austin. How long will it take to send a message to the aliens to let them know what we want to do?"

Flynn shrugged. "It's hard to say for certain, but it would be at least an hour, perhaps longer. We'd have to wait for a reply and then translate it. It might be three hours all told, maybe a little less if we're lucky."

"Go ahead and do it," Harrington ordered. She turned toward Powers. "Make sure Albretti doesn't do anything stupid in the meantime."

CHAPTER THIRTY-EIGHT

"We're ready to come out of our warp bubble," Joe Albretti said.

"How certain are we about our location?" Austin asked.

"We have a better idea than we would have had if Sara hadn't had the foresight to include star images with her report," Yabuno said. "We were able to keep track of their position each day by noting the changes. Since we know Sara's last report was after they stopped and had seen the alien camp, we know pretty damned closely where they have to be and where we should be to check things out."

"All right, let's do it, and be prepared to move back into a bubble right away if we're discovered."

Albretti sent word to the chief, and moments later, the featureless gray-and-black landscape dissolved into a familiar black backdrop speckled with countless stars. In the distance was a combination of the familiar and unfamiliar, none of which was a welcome sight. The familiar consisted of various alien ships largely identical to each other, but each seemingly with its own deadly personality, described by the brown-and-black shadows stretching across their misshapen hulls.

The unfamiliar consisted of multiple structures of various sizes, some of which were similar to the ships and some of which were larger or smaller. Each structure was connected with nearby structures with what looked like passageways, and each looked like the same type of semi-organic creature as the ships. As was typical with the alien architecture, it was difficult to determine both the precise size and shape of the structures. The only guide they had was to compare the structures with the alien ships that were moored to them.

There was no sign that the aliens had taken any notice of them. There was also no sign of either of their transports or of the ancient ship that had meant so much to the aliens. Austin nodded toward a display with an image of the nearest module from their sensor network and asked, "Is there anything more from Harrington or the aliens since we left Citadel?"

Yabuno nodded. "We have something from Harrington."

Austin nodded for Yabuno to play the message. Harrington's image appeared, looking as unfriendly as ever.

"You have failed to keep your part of the bargain, Sam. I won't take any action against your people, because I never intended to; they were just a means to ensure your cooperation as we sought peace with the aliens. For the same reason, I've been playing the bad guy, even though I never meant any of those words." She gave a disappointed sigh. "Unfortunately, the aliens may change their minds about peace once they learn about your treachery, which makes whatever happens next your responsibility. We are probably all in great danger, but I'll do what I can for your people. I don't know how you will be able to tell the families of your people that it was worth playing with the lives of their loved ones instead of supporting a bid for peace." The image ceased abruptly.

"That bit of theater was obviously intended for the people back on Earth," Austin said with disgust. "When was it sent?"

"It was sent through the network shortly before we arrived," Yabuno replied.

"That means she may not realize where we are," Austin said. He pointed to an image on another display. "Can you take us around to this point on the other side, Joe? That looks like a good spot to search for the derelict and our transports without ending up on top of them."

Albretti nodded and spoke with the chief. As the view faded once again to gray and black, Austin was surprised to see, for the first time, a hint of the structures they'd been watching a moment earlier. As they began to move, the faint image vanished.

"Alan," he called, "did you see that?"

"Yes, but it's gone now."

Austin felt a surge of excitement. "Were we really seeing their facility while inside a warp bubble?"

"It's possible," Turner admitted, "although it might have been some kind of visual echo relating to the last thing we were watching when we formed the bubble."

"Why wouldn't we have seen something similar when we took on the ship after we came out from the radiation field?"

Turner gave off a subdued chuckle as he replied, "We're still doing fine-tuning on this thing. I hope like hell that what we're doing with *Pathfinder* will someday translate to something similar for the transports."

"What will it mean if we see something from within the bubble before we go back into normal space-time?"

"I hope it means that we can watch them from a place where they can neither see us nor do anything about us."

"We're nearly there," Albretti called out. He counted the seconds down. Just as they reached zero, a faint, distorted image appeared; then, the scene dissolved into normal space-time.

This time, the scene included familiar images that weren't unwelcome, as the two transports plus the derelict came into view. *Pathfinder* had materialized at some distance away from the other ships and at an angle that enabled them to take in much of the alien facility as well. Austin called for the display to focus on the derelict.

"Zoom in, Joe, and let's see if the explosive charges are still in place."

A moment later, they were able to confirm that everything was as it had been over a month earlier. However, Albretti was watching a different display and said, "There's something happening over here." They shifted to the other display and watched as one of the alien vessels moved toward the derelict.

"What the hell is that?" Yabuno asked as they saw things seem to grow, snakelike, from the exterior of the enemy vessel. "It looks something like the lines they used on the derelict when they captured it the first time."

"I'd bet Harrington made the best of the situation when she didn't hear back from us and told the aliens to get the derelict themselves," Austin said. A worried look flashed across his face. "While that probably means her deal is still on with them, I'm not sure what that means for our people." He glanced at Yabuno. "Can we confirm whether everyone is still on board the original transport?

Yabuno shrugged. "There's no way to know for sure. I don't see any recent energy signatures from multiple shuttles, although someone went to the other transport not long ago, probably to get it ready to receive the alien technology."

"What are the chances that the aliens simply took our people off the transport directly, Bret? We still have the information from our previous encounters with them to tell us about their energy signatures."

"We'd recognize their energy signatures, either because, like you said, they'd match what we've seen before, or because they wouldn't match any of our own signatures. Keep in mind, we might not be able to tell whether they made contact with the transport or just approached to within a short distance." He thought for a moment. "However, they probably haven't even approached the first transport yet."

"Why not?" Austin asked. A moment later, he chuckled as the answer came to him. "That's right—they're deadly, but they aren't stupid."

"Can someone explain it to me?" Albretti asked.

Austin nodded to Yabuno, who replied, "Harrington would have to have told them about the explosive charges on the derelict and the fact that the first transport is linked in with those charges. If they screw up with the charges on the derelict, they might find that there wouldn't be much left of the transport, which means there might not be anything left of their ships that are nearby. It also means they wouldn't have the human lab rats."

"Couldn't they have just taken the people off the transport first and then worried about the derelict?"

"Harrington might not have been willing to give up the leverage she needed to make sure she got the technology from the aliens," Austin said, "or it just might be that the aliens didn't want to wait to get their hands on the derelict as soon as possible. Whatever the reason, we'd better transmit our findings and data to the others, with a reminder to get their asses here right away. For all we know, the aliens might only need a few minutes to remove those charges, and then it'll be time to pay the rest of the bill."

"There's another reason for our people to haul ass," Yabuno said in a tight voice. "I'm seeing an energy signature from the second transport that looks nothing like what should be there." He looked at the others with alarm. "I think they're importing the new technology directly into the warp-field generators. Once that's complete, Harrington can get out of here at any time. She might just leave our people on the first transport, to be picked up by the aliens at their leisure."

"Send the message now," Austin ordered. "Let's keep an eye on things until our ships get here."

Albretti confirmed that the message had been sent.

"I'm not sure we can wait for reinforcements," Yabuno said. "I'm getting energy signature readings from multiple shuttles on the first transport. They're consistent with powering up a small fleet of shuttles transporting everyone on that ship, our people and Harrington's."

"*Everyone?*" Austin was puzzled. "That doesn't make sense. Harrington would never place her own people in jeopardy like that." Understanding flashed across his face. "Harrington's protecting her ass, and the aliens want to be sure the human cargo won't be lost if something goes wrong with the efforts to defuse the explosives on the derelict. Harrington will get to confirm that the new technology works, the aliens will finish with the derelict, and Harrington will then send our people to a fate not fit for any human."

"That's smart of them for another reason," Yabuno said. "So long as everyone is on the shuttles, we'd never dare attack them even if we could get free of the Citadel system, because we'd end up killing our own people."

Albretti gestured toward the display. "Whatever we're going to do, we'd better do it fast, because the aliens are almost at the derelict now."

"That will be our target," Austin said. He pointed to a location on the display. "Joe, head for this spot near the derelict at high speed."

Albretti shook his head. "We won't be in position to take on the aliens from that angle; the derelict will be in the way. Also, we can't get into a warp bubble and move there as fast as we need before the aliens have shifted position."

With a predatory expression, Austin explained his plan. "We're going to proceed in normal space-time the whole way. We're not ready to reveal the warp-bubble trick just yet, and I want them to sweat over the derelict being in the way. Work the course so that we move around the derelict and come up behind the aliens."

Albretti grinned. "I get it, Sam. They won't have their EMP weapon in proper position, but we'll bring ours online as we move behind the derelict. We'll come out and blast them hard, and then move back behind the derelict before they can react. The interference may allow us to do the same from the other side."

Austin nodded, and *Pathfinder* raced toward the enemy vessel. As anticipated, the alien ship deployed its EMP weapon and sought to bring it around to bear on the tough scout ship. At the last moment, *Pathfinder* swung hard around to the other side of the derelict, deploying its own weapon as it raced past the ancient ship.

The alien weapon was still trying to react to the sudden course change when *Pathfinder* emerged into view. At a word from Austin, their weapon launched a ferocious attack on the alien ship, neutralizing much of its ability to use its lasers in retaliation. Austin was also counting on the aliens being somewhat tentative in their response, out of concern over damaging the derelict.

Whatever the reason, *Pathfinder* sustained minimal damage as the enemy ship continued to perform a lateral move to aim its EMP weapon at the human adversary. The aliens had to correct the maneuver in order to avoid inflicting damage on the derelict, allowing *Pathfinder* to maintain a steady surge of destructive pulses without letup. Finally, at another word from Austin, *Pathfinder* was able to surge forward but stay behind the derelict, as it moved back around to the other side of the ancient ship.

When *Pathfinder* appeared again, the aliens were once again out of position, allowing for another sustained attack on the heavily damaged vessel. The satisfaction the humans felt from the attack was cut short, however, as Yabuno warned, "We have company heading this way, people."

"How many?" Austin asked.

"Three have left their moorings, and their EMP weapons are all pointing in our direction. I think they're pissed," he said with a hint of satisfaction in his voice.

Austin was calculating another move as he asked, "How long before they reach us?"

"The first one will be in range in about a minute."

"It'll have to be enough to do what we want." Austin pointed at the main display. "Bret, the exterior of that ship looks even uglier than usual, thanks to our barrage. Zoom in on this point. Let's see if the semiorganic nature of those structures has failed enough for us to use something else."

A moment later, they saw lines in the hull that looked like lacerations, as if the flexibility of a living organism had been compromised.

Austin turned back to Albretti and said, "Joe, it's time to use some of our modified torpedoes. Launch the first one for detonation at this point; then, launch another one, targeted at the same place, right after the main pulse from the first torpedo has passed us." He looked at the other display and saw the new danger closing on them. "Get ready to haul ass once the second one's been launched."

Although they knew the first torpedo had been launched, there was nothing to see as it raced toward its target in a mini-warp bubble, detonating as it reached the damaged surface of the enemy vessel. They had a brief moment to savor the obvious breach in the hull before the main pulse reached them and the second torpedo was launched in another mini-warp bubble. This time, it entered the target before detonating. A fireball erupted within the dying ship and burst outward in multiple directions.

The other enemy ships tried to shift course to avoid the destruction, each of them veering around different parts of the derelict to head off any escape by *Pathfinder*. Austin nodded at one display while he gestured at several points on another one and spoke to Albretti. "Let's head out this way at high speed, and send a signal to detonate the explosives at these places on the derelict. Keep the yield at a low level. Take the rest offline until we're ready to change them back."

Albretti stared back at Austin in shock before noting the locations of the explosive devices and replying, "That's a hell of a calculated risk, Sam."

They watched as minor explosions erupted on three separate locations on the derelict. The derelict came to life, just as it had once before, when the aliens had taken possession of it. What had been a smooth surface in blue, gray, and black was transformed into massive sheets of cold-blue energy, reaching in anger for the source of the attacks.

As before, they'd managed to trick the ancient ship into concluding that the aliens were responsible for the attacks and were, therefore, the ones to be punished. However, the derelict had destroyed a single, heavily damaged alien ship the first time. This time, the enemy consisted of three tough, undamaged ships.

The cold-blue fire seemed to roil over the surface of the derelict for a moment, and then three separate sheets of energy burst out toward the attacking ships. The energy almost seemed alive as it surged around each ship, causing some of the surface architecture to tear or wither away and opening vast rips in the hulls. With the new pathways formed, there was no stopping the energy as it inundated every crevice of each ship. The destruction caused even the indeterminate outlines of browns and blacks to shine brilliantly for an instant.

Once Austin was sure the three attacking ships were no longer anything except ruined hulks, he turned his attention toward the first transport. Incredibly, because it had been out of position relative to the paths of the alien ships, it didn't appear to have suffered any damage, although there was no way to be sure at that distance. The waves of fire gushing from the derelict finished overwhelming each of the would-be attackers and were gone. In an instant, the derelict was quiet again, with only the late ships serving as reminders that anything had happened.

Austin noted with alarm that multiple shuttles had launched from the transport, but before he could react, Albretti spoke. "Remember what I said about a calculated risk, Sam? The good news is that the derelict appears to be OK." He gestured at the display. "The bad news is that we don't need to worry about bringing any of the explosive devices back online, since the energy surge seems to have eliminated all of them. If the aliens want to capture that ship and even start to take it apart, there isn't anything stopping them any longer."

"Our game of dodging around the derelict is over too," Yabuno reported. "Take a look." They saw multiple alien ships bearing down on them at high speed from various directions, eliminating any possibility of using the derelict as a shield. As Austin prepared to give orders to maneuver, the images from the displays deteriorated rapidly. Six transports materialized from warp bubbles and attacked the nearest of the alien ships, forcing the enemy to come about to face the new threat.

The humans began a deadly dance, where the transports moved in and out of normal space-time, materializing where an alien ship was out of position. Initially, the humans used the tactic of isolating and engaging a single enemy vessel and swarmed around it. A transport would deploy its EMP weapon and pound its target, while a sister ship used its weapon from another angle to rake the alien flanks and degrade any lasers or other weapons. As the alien craft sought to maneuver to meet the threat, the transport that was threatened by the move would shift back into a warp bubble to reappear where the aliens weren't prepared. In rapid order, the flanks had been raked repeatedly, and the ship was reduced to relying on its EMP weapon for defense.

The enemy was confused by the new tactic, and their other ships made only token, ineffective moves against the humans. In their momentary disarray, the aliens were unprepared for another weapon that the transports had on hand. Unlike *Pathfinder*, the transports had significant capacity for storing small asteroids and could switch to deploying their rail guns. Now that the secondary weapons on the alien ship had been degraded, there was no effective way to resist an onslaught from a large rock.

A transport materialized into position behind the target vessel, where the dreaded EMP weapon was out of position to counter the move. A rock hurled toward the enemy at extreme speed, obliterating a structure on a portion of the ship's hull and carving a gash into the surface. Moments later, the breach in the surface was exploited by a conventional torpedo, its progress toward the alien ship no longer threatened by other weapons. The device entered through the gash, and a massive ball of fire burst outward through the same opening, with new holes blasted from within.

Two more torpedoes were launched from different angles and passed into the ship's interior through the newly blasted openings. More fireballs followed, and portions of the hull simply failed. It looked vaguely similar to ragged scraps of flesh. Although a few small pockets of safety may not yet have finished collapsing, there was no effective structure remaining to provide any protection against the harsh environment of space.

The aliens had studied the actions of the humans and prepared to face a new onslaught against the next vessel nearest the one that had been destroyed. However, Austin saw them and contacted the other transports. "Look at them. They're getting into position to take us on when we attack the ship nearest the one we just destroyed."

He reached toward the images on the display and pointed to a vessel near the rear of the alien fleet and said, "Let's screw with them and head for this one instead. They'll have to waste precious time getting over to it and even more time getting their weapons into position. While you're heading over there in your warp bubbles, *Pathfinder* will be the decoy and draw them even farther away by attacking the one they think we're going for. Make sure your tracks from your bubbles don't look like you're heading over toward the real target."

Austin gazed at the display and analyzed the area around the decoy target. He showed Albretti where to materialize, and they vanished into a warp bubble. They moved into position and appeared in normal space-time. While they were away from the target's EMP weapon, they found themselves facing an immediate threat from other alien vessels. After a token burst from their EMP weapon, they vanished back into a warp bubble only to reappear within range of the alien EMP weapon.

As Austin had anticipated, the aliens had been caught off guard, expecting to find the scout ship in a different position and surround and attack it before it could retreat. As the deadly alien weapon began to glow in anticipation of launching an attack, *Pathfinder* launched a specialized torpedo that raced toward the target in a path that couldn't be tracked. Not even the enemy ship's lasers could respond to the torpedo in time before it detonated in front of the EMP weapon. *Pathfinder* took careful aim and used its EMP weapon to blast the damaged counterpart on the enemy vessel.

"They're right on top of us, Sam," Yabuno warned. "I think they're too pissed to care if we're a decoy."

Austin grinned. "Take us back into a bubble. Let's see if they've learned anything; if not, we might get another opportunity to stick it to them once the action picks up elsewhere and they figure out we're just a decoy."

As *Pathfinder* vanished, the transports materialized into normal space-time at multiple points around the new target, attacking much as they'd done with the first vessel. As the enemy ship shifted position, two transports appeared where they couldn't be reached and opened fire in a pattern that degraded the weapons on the alien ship's right flank. The aliens anticipated a similar move on the other flank and opened fire with their lasers on that side, only to find that the attack came from above. While they were reacting to the pressure from the unexpected direction, the transports began to vanish once again as others appeared. One launched a small asteroid from its rail gun, which tore a hole through the ship. With the hull compromised, the follow-up EMP blast from the other ship caused massive damage.

The aliens knew they had to stay in motion, or else the humans would use their rail guns to target the EMP weapon from a safe distance. However, two of the transports positioned themselves at locations where they could keep track of the aliens as they moved. One of the captains saw her opportunity and launched a rock that streaked toward its target.

Even if the alien ship had been able to fire at the incoming missile in time, it would only have resulted in multiple projectiles piercing the enemy ship's hull, instead of the single hole caused by the brutal impact. The blast checked the rotation of the ship, leaving it virtually dead in the water. There was now no way to prevent the other transports from finishing off their target.

Once again, the Citadel ships had to scatter as other enemy ships converged on the area. The aliens had finally begun to learn some of the tactics the humans were using. They realized that keeping their ships far apart from each other would give humans more opportunities to pick them off, and they grouped together accordingly. The humans could see the change in approach as well, and Austin gazed at the display to work out new targets.

"I don't think the aliens will provide us with any more opportunistic targets," he said.

Yabuno pointed at the display. "They know they can't have their EMP weapons all pointed in one direction, or we'll attack from the rear. Look at how they have their weapons positioned to address that issue. We might be able to exploit it with an attack from this location. I don't think they can respond quickly enough to stop us from inflicting a lot of damage."

Austin frowned. "You're right, but it worries me that they wouldn't have thought about it as well."

"They don't have the same options now as they did when they had more ships available. Other approaches have weaknesses too."

"All right, we'll give it a try." Austin contacted the other transports. He pointed at the images on a display as he said, "Take a look at the positions of their EMP weapons; they're clearly trying to keep their options open in case of attacks from multiple directions. However, that makes these two vessels potential targets, using the maneuvers we developed to deal with this enemy lineup. While you're doing that, *Pathfinder* will try to create confusion with the ship we attacked before, so they don't get the idea they can gang up on you. Get ready to move in twenty seconds."

As the transports materialized to commence their attack, *Pathfinder* appeared behind the alien ship with the useless EMP weapon. Austin sought to draw the attention of the enemy by launching another EMP blast against one of their ships.

The transports moved in and out of normal space-time around one of the enemy ships and then around the other. They pounded the ships with heavy EMP bursts, followed by projectiles launched from their rail guns. For a moment, both targets had their EMP weapons facing the rest of their ships, leaving their aft sections exposed.

Two of the transports saw the opportunity and vanished into warp bubbles. To their surprise, when they rematerialized into normal space-time, they found their targets moving away from them at high speed. A moment later, they understood why, as they found themselves on the receiving end of an EMP attack that was more powerful than anything they'd encountered from an alien vessel.

Austin cursed. The aliens had manipulated the transports so they knew where the humans would be at a particular moment. He looked toward their complex and realized that one of those misshapen structures had a powerful EMP weapon of its own. There had been no opportunity to use it until now, as the alien ships would have been threatened by their own weapon. However, by getting the transports to position themselves on the edge of the alien fleet, there was the chance to blast the Citadel ships with little risk while their own fleet was moving away from the point of attack.

Even though they'd made huge strides in protecting their transports against EMP attacks, the ships couldn't withstand the terrible onslaught. The horrified people on board *Pathfinder* and the other transports watched as the ships drifted, no longer under control—and perhaps not even capable of supporting life.

In a moment, what had been a devastating fleet of six transports, guided by the scout ship *Pathfinder*, was only four. With a third of their fleet taken away in brutal fashion, no one was certain whether they could even carry out any more attacks. The alien ships closed in on the surviving transports.

CHAPTER THIRTY-NINE

Harrington walked onto the bridge, demanding, "What's so urgent? Are there problems with the alien technology?"

Flynn pointed at the main display. "We have unexpected company, Ms. Harrington."

Harrington stared at the display, a shocked look replacing her earlier irritation. "How did Austin get here, and why haven't the aliens notified us?" She looked at the images in confusion. "What's wrong with the display? Some of their transports seem to be fading in and out of view. Is that part of the interference from the EMP weapons they're using?"

Dr. Farmer replied, "It looks like they've solved the problem, at least partly, of how to control a warp bubble so they can make slow maneuvers."

The irritation returned to Harrington's face. "What does that mean?"

"It means that they can move into a warp bubble and pass through territory without being affected by it and then materialize nearby."

"Can't we do that?" Harrington asked.

Farmer shook her head. "No. Even if we had full understanding of the warp-field generators on this ship, which we don't, we could only do extensive warping of space-time, to travel significant distances. While doing it, we would have to be careful about the impact of gravity on our movements.

"That's one of the reasons why they've been trapped in their star system; the impact of the gravity from the planets in their system, plus their home star, would make it potentially suicidal to try to leave their system via a warp bubble directly. They always begin a journey from outside their system. Thanks to the radiation field, we took that option away."

Farmer gestured at the display. "I've no idea how they did it, but they've slowed down the warping effect. Note that they haven't been able to slow it down to a full stop, outside of simply dissolving a warp bubble. Look at how they seem to pass into and out of our space but never truly stop while maintaining a bubble."

An admiring look flashed across her face. "They're now even further ahead of us where practical warp-field generators are concerned. We still can't move past the dead-end approach that they used in their first ships to reach Citadel."

"What does this mean for us?" Harrington demanded. "Austin is fighting the aliens, but they outnumber his ships. We should just sit back and let them take care of our problem for us," she said with disdain.

"Austin is still one of us!" Farmer protested. "Besides, he's only here because of us. While we don't mean any harm to his people, it's understandable that he would want to help them. Besides, if he's able to defeat the aliens, we might not need to deal with them at all. At the least, we owe it to him to try to give him some assistance."

"You still don't understand things, Dr. Farmer," Harrington replied. "While I don't want the aliens around anymore than you do, we still need to make a deal with them to make it happen; I want that deal to be on my terms. At this point, the aliens may not be willing to trust us. They probably either think that we aren't reliable, or they might even believe Austin and I lured them here as part of a trap."

"That will happen anyway, once they learn you don't intend to give them some of our people," Farmer replied.

A nasty gleam appeared in Harrington's eyes. "That's where you're wrong. We've long planned on giving them some of our people." Harrington nodded toward the display. "We'll never get out of here alive if we don't do what we agreed to do. Are any of you volunteering to take the places of the people from Citadel or at least join them in solidarity as they meet our allies?"

To emphasize her point, she nodded at several of Flynn's people, who had moved into position to cover the exits. While their weapons were held in a relaxed manner, they could easily be brought to bear in an instant.

Farmer and the others looked back at Harrington in shocked silence. Porter looked at Raffles, who wouldn't meet his gaze. Porter looked down at his feet, shame radiating from his face.

A smug look appeared the former president's face as she said, "I didn't think so. If any of you truly had the character you like to think you have, you would have quit in protest before we ever left our star system."

"You didn't give us any choice!" Farmer protested.

Harrington gave a dismissive shrug. "Didn't I? No one pulled a weapon on you, so you still had a choice. I'm happy to note that not one of you chose to insist on following your alleged consciences, so I'll thank you hypocrites to stay out of the way while we work on our survival."

"We may not survive much longer if we don't do something," Flynn warned.

"What's the problem?"

"That damned cat-and-mouse game they're playing around the derelict could turn deadly for us quickly if any of their shots is off. This ship is linked to the derelict. If those explosive devices detonate, we may find the same happening to us. As you know, we can't just move this ship away from the derelict, thanks to the proximity link Austin had installed."

"We've already powered up the shuttles. Will our plan still work?"

Flynn nodded. "I assume that you still want to bring the Citadel people with us."

"Of course," Harrington said emphatically. "We can't leave them behind unless we want to deal with aliens that are probably already angry with us over what Austin's doing. Notify the people that are already on board the other ship that we're coming aboard, and round up everyone else. Be sure to send a message to the aliens explaining that we will be sending the shuttles to them *after* we've transferred to the other ship." Her expression turned slightly unsettled. "The last thing we want is to become part of the offering."

Porter and Raffles were in a heated discussion as they headed toward an airlock with several of their colleagues.

"Keep your voice down, Gerry!" Raffles implored in an urgent whisper. "You heard what Harrington said. There isn't anything we can do about the people from Citadel. Let's just go along with the program and make sure we get back to Earth in one piece."

"How can you say that?" Porter replied, nausea rippling through his stomach. "We've sold them out like they were something other than human beings."

"We didn't know what Harrington had in mind," Raffles reminded him. "Like she said, we thought we wouldn't have to do anything else once the aliens had the derelict."

"We were stupid to ever go along with a plan like that without questioning it." A streak of red flashed across his face. "I'm still ashamed that we didn't stand up for them when we could have. I don't know if I will ever be able to look in a mirror again."

"You'll find a way to live with yourself once we've returned to our solar system, rich, famous, and with no way for Citadel to reach us," she said, her true nature showing itself. "Imagine the accolades when you tell the world about how you found the artifact that made everything possible."

Porter looked away from Raffles as he muttered, "I'd be ashamed to tell them about my part in this. I wish I'd never done it. I wish you'd never come to me."

Flynn and Powers and the rest of Flynn's people collected the men and women from Citadel and marched them toward the airlocks. Powers was responsible for getting Sara to her destination. As they walked along the passageway, Powers explained the reason for the move.

"Since Austin didn't come through with the release codes, we didn't have any way to remove the explosive devices from the derelict. The aliens have taken on the challenge of removing the devices. As a precaution, we're all leaving this ship while they try their magic, just in case things don't work out and the link between the two ships is triggered."

"You're foolish to believe the aliens will honor any agreement with you," Sara said. "Now that they've gotten their hands on the derelict, without any way for us to get it back, you no longer have any leverage."

Powers didn't mention that the remaining leverage involved Sara herself. Instead, she said, "They've already transferred their technology to the other transport, Albretti. They wouldn't bother doing that if they weren't going to honor their deal. So long as everyone sits tight and doesn't try to do anything stupid, we'll all get out of this in one piece."

Although Sara was surprised at the news, the skepticism remained on her face as she approached an airlock.

"There's not enough room for your people and our people in the same airlock; therefore, we've set them up as double compartments, separated by a bulkhead. After you've entered one compartment, we'll enter the adjoining compartment."

Sara made a derisive noise. "There's no way I'm going to enter an airlock where I don't know what's on the other side, Powers. If you want to kill us, then you can do it right here."

Powers rolled her eyes slightly. "We thought you might feel that way, so we'll give you temporary control of the airlocks, so you can confirm that a shuttle hatch is on the other side of each of your hatches, keyed to the same command that will activate our hatches. Once you've confirmed the arrangement, you will lock it so that nothing can change it. You will then confirm to your people that they can enter their airlocks. We will then activate the hatch controls, and everyone will enter the shuttles. Naturally, your compartments will be segregated from our compartments, for purposes of security."

Sara was still troubled by the plan and replied, "I'll go along with your approach, with an important change. At least half of your people will enter their airlocks before any of my people enter theirs. The other half can stay outside as our guards. Harrington, Flynn, and you must be among the people that are in the airlocks before we enter, and I'll need the displays activated in all of your airlocks to confirm everything, including the fact that the rest of your people have entered your airlocks after we've entered ours."

Her gaze grew colder as she said, "Since I know you'll be sure to protect your own asses, my way will make sure that you still haven't set up a way to screw us once we're in the airlocks. I'm still not convinced you're telling us everything; you haven't given us much reason to trust you."

Powers admired the plan, even though she knew it wouldn't save them. "All right, Albretti, we'll go along with your changes. Be careful not to try any stupid moves of your own," she warned, "or some of your people might get hurt or worse."

Powers spoke into her link to advise Harrington and Flynn about the change in plan. Within a minute, the rest of the Citadel people had arrived, escorted by some of Flynn's people. To Sara's surprise, the former president herself walked up with Flynn.

Just before she stepped into the airlock, she turned to Sara and said, "While I'd like to take a moment to talk with you, Captain Albretti, we need to leave this ship immediately. I'll look forward to talking with you another time." Before Sara could think of a response, Harrington had entered the airlock. Flynn walked up and spoke into his link. A moment later, he nodded at Sara and walked into Harrington's airlock with Powers.

Sara looked over her shoulder at the guards that remained nearby, their weapons ready in case of trouble. The passageway was quiet as she entered her airlock. She brought the airlock controls online and confirmed that they accepted her commands. After a few entries plus a review of various displays, she had confirmed that there was, in fact, a shuttle in proper position outside each airlock. She reviewed the displays again and conformed that half of Harrington's people had already entered their airlocks.

Finally, she brought online the display for her own airlock and spoke. "People of Citadel, this is Sara Albretti. Under an agreement with Ms. Harrington and her people, I have confirmed that all airlocks have been linked together so that we can all leave this transport while the aliens are engaged in removing the explosive devices that have been placed on the derelict. The shuttles will take everyone to the other transport, which is at a safe distance from the derelict.

"Under this arrangement, I have made a visual confirmation that half of their people have already entered their airlocks. It is now time for all of our people to enter their respective airlocks. Once the interior hatches for our airlocks have closed, the remainder of their people will enter their airlocks, and their interior hatches will then close as well. Please enter your airlocks now, and leave them the moment the hatches open; there isn't any time to waste. I hope to see you shortly. Good luck."

The airlock was filled in no time, and the hatch closed. Sara received word from her console that the rest of Harrington's people had entered their airlocks and that all hatches had closed. All hatches then opened, and everyone moved through them quickly.

Harrington gave a cursory glance around the interior of her shuttle. Her gaze lingered on the bulkhead to one side, where she knew Sara and her people were now imprisoned. She waited until her hatch closed and asked for confirmation that all of the other hatches were closed as well. Flynn verified that the shuttles had all left their docking stations and were heading toward the other transport. At a nod from Powers, Harrington had Sara paged to come to the display.

Sara appeared, the background filled with her people. Harrington's expression turned triumphant. "Now that we've left the ship, Captain Albretti, we can talk, although there won't be much time."

Sara didn't respond, so the former president continued.

"It seems that our destinies have been linked more than once, Captain. Because of your actions, Sam Austin still lives, I am no longer president, and my freedom and very life are threatened. It only seems right that you help restore both my freedom and my life."

Sara spoke scornfully. "I don't know what you've been smoking, Harrington, but you've managed to forfeit your right to both your freedom and your life, and I doubt very much that anything I do will serve to prolong either one."

"The nice thing about it is you've already done everything needed to ensure me a long and free life. All you had to do was enter the shuttle, and the rest will play out without any further need for your cooperation."

"You're selling us out somehow, aren't you?" Sara asked wearily. "Why do I have the feeling that the shuttles aren't even heading toward the other transport?"

"You're wrong about one thing—we *are* heading toward the other transport," Harrington said. "However, the only shuttle hatches that will operate once we get there will be *our* hatches. Yours won't operate, which means you and your people will stay aboard, sealed in your compartments."

"I'll bet you have another trip planned for our shuttles."

"That's right. The reason why the aliens didn't simply tell us to get lost once they got ahold of the derelict is that they also want to meet some humans."

"After talking with you, I'd have thought they'd never want anything to do with humans again."

Harrington's gaze turned colder. "On the contrary, they insisted on it after we began to communicate. This is just as important to them as getting the derelict."

"You're the politician; you revel in attention, so why didn't you volunteer for the job?"

"One of the important things about being a politician is being able to delegate difficult tasks," Harrington replied. "Besides, the aliens aren't looking for ambassadors; they want to understand how humans work." A queasy look flashed across her face. "From what we've been able to understand, a certain amount of taking humans apart is involved. They haven't been clear about what that entails or whether the humans will be put back together afterward.

"The good news for you, if you can call it that, is that the aliens only want live humans, so we've actually had a strong interest in keeping you and your people alive. All of Austin's elaborate precautions to protect your lives during the trip out here weren't really necessary." Harrington paused for a moment as Flynn said something. She turned back to the display and said, "We're just a few seconds away from docking with the other transport, so I'll have to leave in a moment."

She continued in a mocking tone. "For what it's worth, your lives might really buy us a lasting peace with the aliens. There won't be much point in bothering with us once they have the derelict under their control." Her expression turned malevolent. "I'm looking forward to seeing Austin's face when he learns what's happened to his people. He'll know that he's the one responsible for everything. I won't bother signing off; you can watch as we leave you behind." Harrington and the rest of her people turned their backs on the display as they prepared to step through the hatchway to safety.

CHAPTER FORTY

The hatch that would let them gain entry to the other transport remained closed, and Harrington looked annoyed as Flynn and Powers checked the controls. Their movements became increasingly frantic as they realized the shuttle was once again underway. Harrington turned back toward the display in terror.

"What the hell have you done, Albretti?" she practically screamed. She settled down slightly. "I don't know how you got control of the shuttle, but you're still in the same boat as we are, just stuck in a different compartment. I'll make a deal with you. Bring this ship back to the transport, and we won't hold you as prisoners. You'll really be free to leave and return to Citadel this time."

"What makes you think we're in the same boat?" Sara asked. At a nod, the rest of the people around her backed away. For the first time, Harrington realized that the background didn't match what she could see from looking around her own compartment. It had the bare look of a passageway.

"In the first place," Sara continued, "we're not on the shuttle at all; we never left our transport." A look of contempt flashed across her face. "Too bad for you that you don't know more about ships or you would have recognized that the background was wrong. Instead, you spent the last seconds of your freedom—or perhaps I should say the first seconds of your captivity—gloating about your plan to murder us and sell out the rest of humanity to serve your own interests."

"How the hell did you get control of the shuttle?" Powers practically hissed. "Everything was preset; you couldn't have overridden the controls."

"Remember how your boss thought she was being clever in anticipating Sam sending a special command code to the transport that would override the codes you took from the captain?"

"I'd bet my life that nothing ever got through from Austin," Powers insisted.

"Interesting thing to wager, considering the circumstances," Sara noted wryly. "However, you'd lose that bet. What you didn't know was that after the original encounter with you and the rest of Harrington's creatures, Sam changed the protocols to allow a former transport captain to enter command codes as well, under certain special situations. I won't go into the details, but this sure qualified as a special situation. Sam simply reminded me of these facts."

"He never said anything like that!" Powers protested.

"He did, when he reminded me I was a former captain of *KT-2* and said I needed to act accordingly."

"If you could have done this at any time, why wait until now?" Powers asked suspiciously.

"I couldn't have done it before," Sara replied with a shake of her head. "I was locked out of everything. You gave me an opportunity when you turned the airlock controls over to me. They link to the hatch controls aboard any shuttle. It only took me a moment to confirm that the hatches to our shuttle compartments were programmed to remain sealed upon docking with the other transport.

"I assumed that you simply planned on keeping us aboard the shuttles until we weren't needed as hostages anymore," she continued. "I only had a few seconds available, so I programmed *all* the hatches on the shuttle to remain sealed upon docking. I also reprogrammed our airlocks so that the passageway hatches, rather than the shuttle hatches, opened. I sent a message to the rest of the Citadel people letting them know what I'd done. We just stepped back into our original transport."

Sara had a determined look on her face as she said, "We're still in danger here, but we'd much rather face that danger instead of whatever combination of death, mutilation and other unspeakable acts the aliens had planned for us."

Harrington spoke. "All right, you've made your point; you've outplayed us and this round goes to you. Obviously, you control the command codes for the shuttles. I expect that you'll send the commands for the shuttles to return to whichever transport you want." Her expression was less than contrite as she continued. "You'll find that you still need us to deal with the aliens, however, since we're the only ones who can communicate with them." Her expression hardened. "What we tell them will depend on how you treat us. You'll need to make it worth our while to persuade them that they're getting a good deal even without adding you to the ledger."

Flynn spoke. "We're getting too close to the aliens; we need to turn around *now*."

Harrington looked at Sara. "Let's stop wasting time. Regardless of whatever you may think of me, you won't leave fellow humans to whatever you believe the aliens have in mind."

Sara looked at them with a mixture of contempt and sadness. "If history ever records your actions, you'll be remembered as someone who has committed and sought to commit crimes against humanity on a truly horrific scale. It isn't my place to give you another chance and place more lives in jeopardy. Others have already done it, in some cases through their lack of courage to do the right thing.

"However, what you've said about being a fellow human isn't something I take lightly; I'm not sure what kind of person I'd have to be to arrange for someone to be subjected to the kind of treatment that we'd never allow a human to perform on another human. In short, I truly couldn't say what I'd do in these circumstances, Harrington.

"I had a few seconds at most to make a decision on how to arrange for our escape without tipping you off, and the way I chose was simply to lock all of the shuttles' controls to be the same as what you'd set up for us."

Powers gasped as Sara continued. "I see Powers has already figured it out. As a precaution, you set up the controls in our compartments on the shuttles so that they couldn't be overridden by anyone. You expected your own hatches to open once you docked, but I instructed those hatches to follow the same commands as ours. The shuttles are therefore continuing on to the next stop, still unable to accept override commands from any of the compartments, even yours.

"What this means is that even if I wanted, which I'm not sure I do, I can't send an override command to your shuttles until after they've visited their next destination and their cargo has been unloaded." Sara gazed at them with a melancholy expression. "By that time, if the shuttles were to obey the codes at all, they'd return as devoid of passengers as you are of a conscience.

"There isn't anything else to say, other than you've confirmed that we'd better regain control of this transport if we want to avoid your fate. There's also the question of avoiding detonation of our ship if the aliens aren't as capable as you hope in removing the explosives." The transmission ended.

As Harrington began to scream incoherently, Flynn struck her hard in the face to silence her.

With the former president sprawled in a pathetic heap, Flynn turned to Powers and demanded, "All right, we only have a short time before we reach the aliens. What can we do to keep this from being a one-way ticket? Can we send a message to the aliens that a mistake has been made?"

Powers shook her head. "We can't establish an external link with anyone."

Flynn was puzzled. "Why not? We spoke with Albretti even after they moved back into the transport, so that was an external transmission."

"Albretti established the link when she had temporary control of the airlock. She just maintained that link when they stepped back into the transport. We no longer have the ability to establish communications with anyone because that was one of the protocols for their compartments that she imposed on ours."

Flynn gestured at the control consoles. "Can we use these to reestablish control over the navigation or propulsion systems, or at least disable them so we won't continue on this heading?"

"No," she answered in a bitter tone. "If we hadn't been so clever about segregating the compartments to maintain control over them, we could have had access to those systems. Besides, disabling the navigation or propulsion systems wouldn't do us any good at this point; the course is set, and we're heading straight for the aliens. We'd just drift toward them anyway."

"What about the environmental ducts? Can we get through them to the systems themselves and change course?"

"That's just science fiction, Flynn. On a shuttle, there's no reason to have ducts that are large enough for people to crawl through." She thought hard for a moment. "While there's no way to get direct access to the engines, there are service access ports under the decks." She scanned the area quickly and moved toward a handle that was concealed in the deck. "Fortunately, these systems can be operated manually in an emergency, in case of a problem with the power or the control consoles." She raised the handle and gave it a turn, and they removed a hatch. She pointed toward what looked like a relay station located below the deck. Multiple lines ran into and out of the station. "This allows for manual control of the navigation and propulsion systems if you know what you're doing."

The opening was large enough for her to slide in next to the station. A moment later, she was working on bringing the station online, so she could check on the status of propulsion and navigation.

Flynn said, "It doesn't really matter now, because they outsmarted us anyway, but once Harrington started to spill the beans about what was really going to happen, we should have shut her up. Albretti's bright and knows these ships and their systems better than we do. She'd have done the same thing that you're doing."

Powers shook her head. "No, she wouldn't. When we set up everything, I reviewed the plans for the compartments that Albretti and her people would be using. There weren't any points of access other than two hatches, which means that there aren't any access ports in those compartments. I put it out of my mind until just now." Powers looked away from the station for a moment. "No more chatter," she snapped. "It's a distraction I don't need while I try to figure out whether I can even do anything with this thing. I'm not a damned engineer."

She turned back and continued wresting with the unfamiliar layout. After what felt like more than enough time for them to have reached the alien complex, the vessel lurched slightly. She allowed a small look of relief to flash across her face as she turned to face the others. "This is a cumbersome way to do it, but I think I've managed to change our course. If I'm right, then that movement we felt a moment ago was the engines kicking in to pull away from the complex. I think I've managed to send us on a course back toward the second transport."

"How can we be sure about that?" Flynn asked.

"This is a relay station, so there isn't a visual display down here. I'll try to restore the use of a display that can show an exterior view. Right now, we're flying blind, but just about any direction other than toward the complex is a good direction to take."

"Can we notify any of the other shuttles about what we've done?"

Powers gave a hard stare to the others. "There's no way for us to tell anyone else what has happened, let alone how to avoid the complex. Unless someone has some exceptional luck, we're the only ones who will avoid meeting the aliens face to face."

Flynn's expression darkened. "While I'm glad we've dodged that bullet, there aren't enough people on this shuttle to run a transport. How the hell can we return to our solar system, assuming we can even get back to the other transport?"

"We're going to have to take a risk that the new warp-propulsion system is every bit as simple to operate and maintain as the aliens have led us to believe. I'll have an even harder job setting up the right protocols to keep the transport running for three months in a warp bubble than I've had getting us here with normal propulsion." Powers frowned as she noticed some odd readings from the relay station. A familiar voice spoke as she moved closer to the station.

"I'll hold you to that, Powers," Harrington said, having recovered her composure. She was barely able to control the anger in her voice as she said to Flynn, "I won't forget that you hit me."

She flinched slightly as Flynn's look became more dangerous. "I've warned you before not to threaten me. Unless you have something useful to add, I suggest you stop while you still can."

"Here's something useful; now that we can control this shuttle again, can we send a message to the aliens, telling them about the mistake?" A malevolent look appeared. "At this point, I wouldn't mind if they went ahead and destroyed Albretti's transport; we certainly don't need it anymore."

"Having access to it right now would help a lot," Flynn replied. "If you hadn't been lying there in a daze, you'd have heard what Powers said a moment ago. Without the information that's at either transport, we don't have any way to create a new message to get us out of this mess. We're stuck anyway though, since we can't send out any external communications." Harrington's face flushed at Flynn's words.

"Both of you, stay quiet!" Powers hissed as she kept working on the systems below the deck. "Something's not right with these readings. It's as if the engines are working much harder than they should, and I don't know why. I'm trying to establish a connection with an emergency external warning system and post the images to the display. There! I think I've done it. What do you see?"

Powers struggled to her feet as commotion erupted around her.

CHAPTER FORTY-ONE

As Austin pondered the loss of part of their fleet, Yabuno called out, "The shuttles have launched from the transport."

"Where are they headed?" Austin asked.

"They're making straight toward the second transport." Yabuno's expression was a mixture of apprehension and relief. "It's the smartest thing to do, even though it helps Harrington. The first transport is too close to the fighting; they can't maneuver, and a stray shot could kill some of our people. Also, we don't know what's going to happen if something goes wrong with the derelict."

Austin suppressed a sigh. "OK, the aliens are closing in on us anyway, which means we can't help our people now. We'll have to deal with them later."

"What's the plan?"

Austin's expression turned cold as he opened a link with the surviving transports. "Two sides can play at misdirection," he said as he nodded at a display. "See how they've opened the gap between their ships and the EMP weapon at their complex? They're trying to rush us into doing something stupid, by making it seem they're about to descend on us. They hope we'll try a desperation move with our rail guns and come in close again. They'll be ready to blast us if we try it, or they'll pounce on us if we're too near the ships." He pointed to a specific spot as he continued. "This is the place where we can screw with them."

"That's right in the middle of them," Yabuno said in surprise. "They could come at us from all sides."

"That's probably what they think too. However, they'd be like a circular firing squad if they tried," Austin replied. "Any shots they tried with their EMP weapon would hit their own ships. That just leaves lasers and any other projectile-based weapons they have.

"Taking those weapons out will be *Pathfinder*'s job. It'll be a hell of a distraction, because the transports will still be making hit-and-run moves to confuse them. It'll also leave us with only one type of weapon to handle. It means that the time has come to use *Pathfinder*'s ability to come to a full stop in a warp bubble. Doing this will be the stepping stone to taking out their big EMP weapon."

Austin looked over at Yabuno. "What're they doing now?"

In spite of the moment, Yabuno grinned. "They're still heading toward us, which means there's more of a gap between their rear vessels and their complex than before." His grin faded. "They're trying even harder to get us to move into that space."

Austin nodded. "That tells me they probably have another EMP weapon set up in one of the adjacent structures, just waiting to get us as we materialize near the one we know about. If we're going to do anything about them, we need to do it now."

The Citadel vessels disappeared en masse, leaving the aliens with no way to be certain where the ships would appear next. Two transports appeared in the gap between the forward and rear groups of alien vessels, targeting a forward ship that was out of position to attack them immediately. Another alien ship was maneuvering to get into position for an attack when *Pathfinder* materialized and inflicted a flanking EMP burst, blunting the attack. In the meantime, a transport rail gun delivered its deadly payload to the original target, followed by an EMP burst from the other transport.

While the targeted ship was kept off balance from the attack, the other two transports materialized behind the enemy vessel that *Pathfinder* had raked with the EMP burst. Yabuno called out, "The other two forward line ships are heading our way!"

Austin took note of their approach and sent a message out to the transports.

Pathfinder and the first two transports moved into warp bubbles, while the other transports took the opportunity to target the side of the enemy vessel that had been raked by the scout ship. With the alien ship's ability to direct laser and projectile fire reduced, both transports were free to use their rail guns to blast large holes in the enemy vessel. *Pathfinder* reappeared and delivered a conventional torpedo into one of the ragged openings. The scout ship quickly shifted back to its EMP weapon and used a sustained attack to ensure that the alien ship would be unable to deal with the massive damage.

As the two forward enemy vessels appeared, *Pathfinder* vanished again. The alien ships made a quick, radical course change and were in a position to attack the two transports that had planned on appearing behind them. They concentrated their fire on one of the Citadel ships and drove off the other transport with lasers. The transport receiving the EMP bursts was unable to escape into a warp bubble and couldn't withstand the attack. The radio silence and lack of any maneuvering by the stricken vessel was ominous.

Austin lamented the fact that the loss of three vessels meant that his fleet, not counting *Pathfinder*, had been reduced by half, with no way to know whether any of the drifting transports even had any survivors. He knew they needed to move quickly to bring the odds more into their favor. He noticed that the enemy ship that had sustained massive damage was still somehow maneuverable. He also took note of the other ship that had taken significant damage but still seemed capable of inflicting further destruction.

At a word from Austin, *Pathfinder* disappeared into a warp bubble. The two forward alien ships moved quickly to take positions to attack the rugged fighter when it made its expected appearance near the crippled enemy ship. However, *Pathfinder* didn't appear next to the easy target but the harder one. Austin had their ship approach their enemy more closely than usual, pausing in front of the flank that had already been attacked and delivering a searing blast. While the enemy was reeling from the attack, *Pathfinder* switched over to a conventional torpedo to follow up where lacerations had appeared in the hull.

As the two enemy ships bore down on the Citadel craft, the torpedo made its way to its target, and the resulting explosion ripped the lacerations into large gashes. The scout ship followed up with a specialized torpedo that made its way unopposed in a warp bubble, entering the craft before detonating and tearing the interior apart. *Pathfinder* began to feel the sting from the approaching EMP weapons but was able to move back into a warp bubble.

While Austin had kept the two forward ships engaged, the two transports that had been in warp bubbles made their way toward the damaged alien vessel and reappeared. As one of the transports deployed its rail gun and launched its payload into the heart of the damaged vessel, Austin was shocked to see all three ships appear to reel from an unseen force. He realized that the aliens had sacrificed a ship they'd concluded would be destroyed anyway in order to attack two Citadel vessels. The transports began to drift, and didn't respond to messages from *Pathfinder*.

At that moment, Austin received more bad news from Yabuno. "All of the shuttles that reached the transport have left it and are heading straight for the complex." His look was bitter. "Harrington must have sacrificed our people in order to save her own ass!"

"Can we recall those shuttles?"

Yabuno shook his head. "Not a chance. There's a lot of interference in the way, and even if that weren't a problem, someone, probably Harrington, has set it up so that the shuttles aren't accepting outside commands."

Albretti spoke, the desperation plain in his voice. "Can't we get over there before they reach the aliens?"

Yabuno pointed to a display. "Not now. One of the alien ships that was guarding the complex is moving toward the shuttles to collect them." His expression was sad. "We don't dare use our weapons near them. It's too late anyway."

They watched in horror as tentacles seemed to grow from the giant ship and reach toward the shuttles. One by one, each shuttle was collected and pulled inside the enemy ship. Albretti let out an awful scream, knowing his wife was aboard one of the shuttles—if she was still alive.

Yabuno pulled their attention back to other dangers. "We need to stay sharp and deal with the danger that's still out there. The two forward ships are approaching us again. Even with one of their ships out of the picture while it captures our shuttles, there are three of their ships, plus that damned weapon at their complex against *Pathfinder* and one transport."

"That transport has the last rail gun in our arsenal," Austin noted. "We're going to need that gun to blast the hell out of that complex, assuming we can even get close enough to launch anything. The problem is they've figured out how to track our ships as they move out of warp bubbles. That means our transport might not have enough time to materialize and fire the rail gun before they can blast it. We also have to be careful where we end up out here, because they're tracking us in hopes of taking us out with their big weapon."

"What do you want to do?" Yabuno asked.

Austin's expression darkened. "I want to make them pay for what we've lost, which I hope doesn't include more lives, by going to the one place where they won't take shots at us. The others nodded as he sent a message to the transport with his plan.

They materialized near the derelict. At Austin's direction, the transport deployed its rail gun, taking direct aim at the EMP weapon at the complex; the projectile was launched, racing toward its target at a speed that was breathtaking to watch. EMP and laser weapons were useless, and even if projectiles could have been launched, they would have been brushed aside by the rock that hurtled relentlessly toward the enemy. Before the first rock smashed into its destination, a second was launched, followed shortly by a third. Each rock destroyed a different part of the structure that housed the weapon, with the damage combining to reveal large portions of the structure directly to space.

While the transport used its rail gun to deadly effect, *Pathfinder* launched a specialized torpedo, which raced into a gaping hole, blasting the structure so violently that adjacent structures suffered major damage as well. The rear ship abandoned its position, racing toward the Citadel ships, determined to finish the humans for good.

The two forward alien ships arrived near the derelict, approaching with great speed. While they had already seen what would befall them if they were careless, they had to bring the conflict to an end, even if their ships were endangered. Their speed was such that the humans were unable to prepare fully for the attack.

The transport had time to bring its rail gun around to bear on a new target. However, as another rock hurtled toward one of the enemy ships, the other was in a position to launch an EMP attack without drawing retaliation from the ancient vessel.

It was of little comfort to note that the rock did considerable damage to the alien craft, as they were about to lose their last functioning rail gun. *Pathfinder* had been unable to get into position and couldn't bring its EMP weapon to bear on the enemy ship. As Austin prepared to order *Pathfinder* into the line of attack to offer scant protection for the rail gun, everyone was surprised by an EMP attack from a new quarter. The transport that had been the original prison for the people from Citadel had somehow deployed its own EMP weapon and was now unleashing a bombardment against the unprotected front and sides of the would-be attackers.

The attack degraded the effectiveness of the weapon severely, giving *Pathfinder* time to move into position and bring its own weapon into play. As the enemy ship withered under the crossfire, the transport with the rail gun was free to continue to bombard the other alien vessel, rendering it useless in a shockingly short time. As the transports moved out behind the derelict for safety, the scout ship finished off each of the enemy ships with specialized torpedoes. Fortunately, the resulting fireballs didn't reach the ancient vessel, so they managed to avoid rousing the sleeping giant.

The key issue was figuring out how the original transport had come back to life when it had been presumed abandoned. As the displays between the ships were linked, the people on *Pathfinder* were stunned to see friends and loved ones they'd given up for dead. Neither Albretti nor Sara bothered to hide their tears of joy at seeing each other.

Austin spoke in an urgent tone. "I'm really sorry to intrude on a hell of a reunion, but we aren't finished yet. Sara, I'll be happy to yield to Joe being the most glad to see you, but I'm not far behind. Right now, if you can maneuver, you need to move your ship so the derelict is between you and the alien complex. Although you might be beyond the reach of their weapons from the complex, we don't want to take any chances."

Sara surprised Austin by replying, "No, thanks, Sam. By my count, your fleet of transports is down to one. Ours will double that number. Two transports plus *Pathfinder* should be able to give the aliens hell." Her expression became fierce. "Besides, we owe them something for what they've put us through."

Austin chuckled. "Fair enough, although the concern about being within range of their weapons is valid." His expression turned grim as he continued. "We can't be certain that we've dealt with all of their weapons in that complex; we've already seen what can happen if we aren't careful."

The enemy ship continued heading toward the humans and was now joined by the one that had captured the shuttles. For the first time, neither side had a clear advantage in the sizes of its fleets, although they still didn't know to what extent other weapons were within the mass of misshapen structures the aliens had created.

Austin noted that the alien craft continued to approach at an angle that moved them farther away from the derelict, probably in the hope of drawing one or more of the Citadel ships away from the ancient vessel. That only mattered if they had at least one other major weapon to use against the humans.

Yabuno opened a link to the other ships and pointed out the new grouping of the alien ships. "They're using the one with the shuttles as the lead vessel, probably assuming that we won't want to fire upon it and risk hurting our own people." He looked at Sara. "How many of our people were aboard those shuttles, Sara?"

To his surprise, her expression turned cold. "None." Upon seeing Yabuno's quizzical look, she explained. "Harrington planned on maintaining control by segregating the Citadel people in separate airlocks and compartments on the shuttles. She said that we'd all end up on the other transport, still in separate compartments, and safe while the aliens did their work.

"I had access to the airlock controls for a moment, I managed to have the settings for their compartments match the settings she'd set up for our compartments. I also programmed our airlock hatches to open back onto our transport."

One of Sara's hands gripped a nearby rail until her fingers were white. "She couldn't wait to get underway, so she could gloat about her real plans for us. She was fine with the notion of sacrificing fellow humans to advance her own interests. Her attitude changed once she realized that she'd placed herself in that trap. Too bad for her that she doesn't have any way of sending a message to the aliens that they have the wrong people; that technology is only on board the two transports."

Her gaze at Yabuno was hard. "No one else among her people ever had the courage to help us, so as far as I'm concerned, there aren't any humans on board that ship. There certainly isn't any reason to place any of our people in jeopardy in order to preserve those lives."

Yabuno noticed the same look on Albretti's face.

Austin's expression turned thoughtful after a moment. "Sara's transport can't make the kind of transitions into and out of a warp bubble that our other ships can. Also, she doesn't have a rail gun or any torpedoes. However, you have a powerful EMP weapon that they'll respect, so we'll make use of it."

"What's the status of the other transport, the one that the aliens have supposedly retrofitted with their warp-field generator capabilities?" Yabuno asked. "It hasn't moved since we arrived."

"There's never been more than a tiny crew aboard her, perhaps only a few technicians at this point," Sara answered. "I'm not sure they've even been able to test the new propulsion system yet." She shook her head. "They wouldn't have a clue how to run that ship to be of any help."

"All right," Austin said. "We'll leave them alone for now." Austin sketched out his plan as the alien ships closed on their position.

Harrington's screams joined with the cacophony of horrified noise that flooded the compartment as they watched the image on the display. An impossibly long and flexible tentacle had reached out from the alien ship and seemed to caress the shuttle's exterior as it encircled the craft. The tentacle drew the smaller ship toward a hole that grew in size as they neared it, like a mouth opening to receive a meal.

Harrington whirled to Powers and demanded frantically, "You said we were heading away from these monsters and back to our transport!"

She sought to grab Powers's neck, only to find her hands blocked by a quick movement, followed by another one that hurled her toward the deck in a heap. Harrington was stunned into silence.

"Don't try to hang this on me, Harrington," Powers said with a mixture of fear and anger. "What I did with that relay should have worked, although we might have been too close to the aliens anyway to make a difference. I don't understand what happened."

They heard another voice through the shrieking, and they whirled to a different display, where Gerry Porter was speaking, and they heard the phrase "good news." Flynn slapped several people with brutal efficiency to bring the noise level down enough to hear the message.

"Repeat your message," Flynn said. "It sounded like you were telling us you had some good news."

Porter began talking again. "Yes, I do indeed have good news. As you know, our compartment has the same displays as yours. I've done quite a lot of reading on technical topics during our trip here. Since access to a lot of the systems was restricted, I had to be satisfied with some lesser topics, including the workings of some of the systems of the shuttles.

"What does all of this have to do with the good news you mentioned?" Flynn asked impatiently.

Porter remained calm as he continued. "It actually has everything to do with it. I was familiar with the workings of the shuttle and knew about the access ports to things such as navigation and propulsion relay stations. As it happens, we have a port in this compartment as well. While Ms. Powers was working from her end, I was doing the same at this end."

"Is that the good news?" Harrington asked, still sprawled on the deck. "Can you get us out of here?"

Porter smiled. "Of course not; the good new news is that I made sure Ms. Powers wouldn't be able to turn the shuttle around."

People in both compartments were shocked. "What!" Harrington was back on her feet, although she was too stunned to demand an explanation.

Porter gave her one anyway. "You called us cowards and worse, Ms. Harrington, on account of our refusal to do the right thing when we should have, and you were right. While nothing can change that fact, we can at least ensure that people who were entirely innocent pawns in this transaction aren't sacrificed as part of a deal to satisfy your personal ambitions. If someone has to pay the price, it should be the people who made it happen in the first place.

"Who knows?" he said ruefully. "Maybe humanity will benefit from the alien technology after all. That was always the rationale you gave us." His tone became sarcastic. "Please don't tell me you didn't mean it."

The last image they saw on the display was Raffles in the background, sobbing uncontrollably, before Harrington leaped up and smashed at the unit with her fists. They stared back at the main display and noticed that they could no longer see any stars, as the mouth continued to open to receive them. Flynn stopped trying to silence the screams.

CHAPTER FORTY-TWO

The enemy vessels had given up trying to lure the humans toward the complex, and approached the derelict with the one with the human cargo slightly in the lead as protection for the other ship. At the last moment, they veered hard over, to go the other way around and catch Sara's transport from the rear. They had to break off their attack at the last minute when *Pathfinder* appeared suddenly in their paths from a warp bubble, its EMP weapon already deployed. *Pathfinder* vanished a moment later, after having delivered a burst from its weapon that barely reached its target.

During the moment of distraction, the transport turned around and pursued the enemy vessels. The aliens sought once again to turn back for an attack, only to find that the other transport had appeared out of a warp bubble with its rail gun deployed. The projectile barely missed colliding with one of the enemy ships. As they sought to counter the new threat, the transport disappeared back into a warp bubble, only for *Pathfinder* to appear from a different direction.

Austin saw that the two enemy ships were determined to support each other while maneuvering constantly, hoping for a chance to damage a Citadel vessel without exposing them to attack. They assumed that the humans weren't prepared to expose themselves to further attack from the complex, which limited their mobility.

He opened a link to the other ships. "This game of cat and mouse is pretty damned complicated when we aren't sure where their big weapon is located." He pointed at a spot on the display. "The only way to pry the two of them apart is from the inside. They don't have their EMP weapons pointed at each other."

"They have their other weapons available though," Yabuno said. "Although projectiles are probably not a good idea for them here, they can fire their lasers at us from both sides."

Austin nodded. "This is where it's going to be tricky."

Moments later, *Pathfinder* appeared between the two enemy vessels, using its EMP weapon to blast the ship that didn't have any humans aboard. Just as enemy lasers threatened the scout ship, she disappeared back into a warp bubble. A transport materialized from a different angle, out of reach of the deadly EMP weapon, and sought to rake the flank of the same enemy ship with an EMP burst. Sara's transport moved in from the other side, equally out of reach, and sought to inflict the same damage on another location.

Visuals were degraded significantly by the EMP bursts in the same area, so it took a moment for the aliens to react to the reappearance of *Pathfinder* in the same location, just as the transports stopped firing. This time, the scout ship was able to maintain a sustained burst, largely wiping out the rear weapons on the alien ship, adding to the damage it had already received.

Pathfinder vanished again just as the other enemy ship arrived to close the gap. With the ships engaged, a transport reappeared out of a warp bubble with its rail gun deployed and launched a rock at the damaged vessel. As the rock tore a hole through the hull, *Pathfinder* materialized and launched a specialized torpedo that began a race toward its target that could only have one outcome.

A satisfied look flashed across Austin's gaze as he surveyed the destruction. They'd finally broken the two ships from their defensive strategy, as the undamaged one raced away to avoid being consumed by the angry fireball that erupted from deep inside the wounded craft. Austin wasn't about to rest on his laurels, however.

Suddenly, the ship reeled from an EMP attack. As *Pathfinder* struggled into a warp bubble, Austin made a quick check of a display. After getting confirmation that they weren't in position for an attack from the complex, he was shocked to notice two things. The first was that a ghostly, distorted image had appeared again on the display. The second was that he could have sworn that it was the transport with the alien propulsion!

"Alan," he called to engineering. "What the hell am I seeing on our screen?"

"We've been tweaking things," Turner replied. "You remember how we saw an image before. We're now able, at least sometimes, to see what's around us in real space-time as we stay in a warp bubble."

Just then, the image faded, leaving the usual grays and blacks on the display.

"Can you get the images back?"

"Sorry," he replied. "We've taken some damage from their EMP weapon, which will take time to repair. At best, the images will come and go, if we can see them at all."

"Can we still maneuver?" Austin asked.

"Other systems are still functioning."

"We'd better get moving," Yabuno warned. "Sara's ship needs some help."

After shifting position, *Pathfinder* materialized from its warp bubble. Sara's transport was making a desperate attempt to avoid being trapped between the last enemy ship and the new adversary. Their other transport continued to keep the alien ship off balance for the moment.

"Are they insane?" Albretti wondered out loud.

Austin ordered a link opened to the attacking transport. "*KT-20*, this is Sam Austin. Are you out of your mind? I don't care what your orders are from Harrington. Break off your attack, or I'll blast your miserable hides out of space!"

A terrified voice replied. "Don't fire, Austin! The ship isn't under our control. The propulsion, navigation, and weapons systems are under the control of the aliens. We can't stop it; the systems won't respond to our commands."

"All right," Austin replied. "You'd better be telling me the truth, because you won't get a second chance to lie to me. Keep this channel open." Austin spoke to Yabuno quickly and then turned back toward a display. "This is Sam Austin, opening a direct link to *KT-20* controls.

Under my authority, all previous command codes are hereby canceled and wiped. Only my instructions are to be accepted until further notice. Confirm instructions."

There was only silence as the ship continued its pursuit of the other transport.

Austin turned to an internal link.

"Alan! How do we deal with the fact that the alien technology is keeping that transport from accept my commands?"

"I'm not sure we can deal with it, short of destroying that ship." He thought for a moment. "How are the commands being provided?"

"I don't know. I'll link in the guy on that ship." A moment later, he said, "Go ahead, Alan."

"OK, *KT-20*. How are the commands reaching your ship's systems?"

"I'm not sure," a hesitant voice replied. "The display keeps showing symbols like the ones we translated, plus some we don't recognize at all."

"Are there any audio signals coming from the aliens?"

"No, we've never been able to communicate using anything other than the symbols."

There was a sound of a sigh of relief from Turner. "That's the key. *KT-20*, can you disable all of the nonaudio inputs to the ship?"

"What good will that do?"

"It will cut off the aliens' ability to control your ship. So long as there are any data inputs that aren't audio in nature, the information can be converted into the symbols needed to control your ship."

"I wouldn't know where to begin to cut off access."

Yabuno broke in. "Even a trained engineer would have trouble catching everything, especially with no time to spare, and it doesn't sound like this guy fits that description." He glanced at a display and warned, "We need to move fast, Sam. Our other transports are on the edge of disaster as it is. If the aliens can time things just right, they only need one or two more EMP blasts to take out our last rail gun and then turn on Sara's ship."

Austin spoke. "*KT-20*, you'd better listen carefully. I'm not about to jeopardize the well-being of the people on our ships to help you and anyone else aboard *KT-20*, so you have sixty seconds to get into a shuttle and launch it. Stay the hell out of my way while the fighting continues; you can surrender later. If you try anything stupid, I'll just leave you out here, where you can rot for all I care. Go!"

Austin opened a link to the transport with the rail gun. "You're too close to the aliens. You're also getting too far out of position to be sure they can't blast you from the complex." He pointed to a display. "The moment we go into a warp bubble, do the same, and move to this spot. That'll put you out of range of their weapon and let you fool them into thinking you're going to pound them with your rail gun. If they value their lives, they'll try to shift position to place Sara's transport in the way. When that happens, target and destroy *KT-20*. *Pathfinder* will deliver a follow-up shot, and then we'll tackle them as a team. Sara, once the aliens start to move, you'd better move away from them, to open up some distance.

"Joe, launch a couple torpedoes at the aliens to get their attention; then, let's move into a warp bubble. After that, let's get the hell over there, so we'll be ready to deal with *KT-20*." The scout ship launched the torpedoes and then vanished. The other transport vanished as well, leaving Sara's transport alone.

The transport appeared where Austin had indicated and made a show of bringing its rail gun around to bear on the enemy ship. However, the enemy ship sought to approach Sara's ship directly, without regard for its own safety.

Austin spoke to the Citadel ships. "They may be bluffing, but it doesn't matter. Stay with the plan, and take out *KT-20*."

For the first time, Austin was sad to note, a Citadel transport opened fire on another one. Even as the rock streaked toward its target, the rogue transport changed course to continue its pursuit of Sara's ship. The rock missed by a few yards. As the rail gun was reloaded, *Pathfinder* launched a torpedo, which raced across the distance to inflict destruction on what should have been a kindred ship. The rogue transport wasn't equipped to deal with such weapons and found itself with a major breach in its hull. Propulsion and navigation weren't affected, and with no cargo or personnel to take into consideration, the ship continued with the chase.

However, a remote-controlled pursuit vessel wasn't suited for outmaneuvering much faster rail-gun payloads. The ship shuddered from another impact that tore through much of its cargo area, exposing large areas as targets. *Pathfinder* didn't waste any time, and another specialized torpedo headed toward the rogue transport. Not more than an instant after ripping into the ship, the torpedo sent an unstable warp bubble rippling through the interior, destroying most of the ship and bringing that part of the pursuit to an end.

The scout ship plus the two surviving transports doubled back toward the last enemy ship, attempting to encircle it. The aliens retreated back toward the complex. Austin sent a message to the other ships.

"It looks like they either want to lure us back within range of a weapon that we still haven't located, or they just want to know that they won't have to worry about an attack from the rear."

"It's probably both," Yabuno replied. "Having another weapon that can blast us from a distance is the best explanation for some of their maneuvers."

"We'd better figure it out pretty quickly," Albretti said. "We're running out of rocks to throw at them. Trying to salvage some from one of the drifting transports would be tricky, since there's no way to stay shielded from another weapon. The same thing goes for trying to rescue our people from those transports."

"Also, the derelict isn't far from that complex," Yabuno said. "They may be able to bring it even closer, now that the explosive devices have been destroyed. We'd never be able to get close enough to it again to mine it. They know that we can't stay here forever. Eventually, we'll have to leave, without the derelict and without the people they've captured. While their complex has been hit hard, major portions of it are probably still usable. Since it looks like they still have everything they wanted, this may be an acceptable deal as far as they're concerned."

"Also, they may be able to call for reinforcements," Turner said with a worried expression. "The longer we wait, the greater the danger for us."

"We still have one advantage, and we need to use it," Austin said. "*Pathfinder* can go right up to their front door and knock on it without their seeing us coming."

"If we do that in front of the wrong door, they could knock back hard, and there would be no more *Pathfinder*," Yabuno warned. "There just isn't any way to be sure where their weapons are located."

Austin brought up an image that included everything in the area that had been built by human and alien hands. "While that's true, there *is* a way to be sure where their weapons *won't* be." He looked at Albretti.

"How many rocks do we have left, Joe?"

"Three, Sam."

Austin turned to Turner. "Can three points cover everything, and if so, from what locations?"

Turner's eyes widened as the implications sank in. He moved toward the display and pointed. "Who knows if it's even possible, but if I had to do it from just three points, these are the ones I'd choose." He gave Austin a hard stare. "This is insane, Sam. I could be wrong about the number of points or the locations or both."

"We don't have any choice." Austin turned back toward the entire group. "You need to know what I have in mind, because most of you don't need to be on this ship when I carry out the plan. *Pathfinder* can materialize next to one of the other transports, and you can transfer to a safer location."

"Why would we do that?" Yabuno asked.

"Because this is the last place you'll want to be," Albretti said. "Our transport with the rail gun is going to target the three spots Alan picked out and pound them with our last three rocks. After that, this ship is going to pay those sites a visit." He looked at Austin with a grin. "No arguments about whether I'll be here; you know I'm staying on my ship to see it through. Anyway, even if we've picked places where the aliens have weapons, they won't be there after we've blasted the hell out of them."

"That's what Sam meant about knocking on their door," Turner said. "*Pathfinder* is supposed to materialize right next to each of those spots and then fire a torpedo at the derelict. Since you can't be in three places at the same time, this ship will need to move in a warp bubble from spot to spot, with a torpedo ready to launch each time she rematerializes. After the last torpedo launches, *Pathfinder* will go back into a warp bubble and vanish from the derelict's reach while it pounds the hell out of this complex."

His expression became more alarmed. "You're assuming that they won't be able to target the torpedoes in time to stop them from reaching the derelict. You're also assuming that the derelict has enough energy to destroy something as massive as this complex. You also can't be sure that *Pathfinder* will be able to get into a warp bubble fast enough to be safe from the effects of the derelict's attack."

"All valid points, Alan, but we have to take the chance while there's still time."

"There may be less time than we think," Yabuno called out. "There's movement of some kind on the surface of the complex. Tentacles are starting to appear all over the place." He had an unsettled look on his face. "It looks like their organic components are starting to repair some of the damage."

"That settles it," Austin said with a grim expression. "If they get very far with their repairs, we might not able to coax the derelict to take them out."

"OK, we're with you," Yabuno said. "We aren't leaving *Pathfinder*."

"There isn't any reason for all of you to be in danger. If this goes wrong, someone will need to come up with another plan."

"If you want to talk about danger, we shouldn't expose ourselves to an attack while in shuttles from *Pathfinder* to a transport, for one thing," Yabuno pointed out.

Austin's grim expression softened slightly. "Since you're so damned determined to stay on this ship, I doubt you're all that concerned for your personal safety."

"How about a practical consideration, then?" Yabuno replied. "We'll be tipping them off that something major is going to happen if they see us abandoning *Pathfinder*. Face it; if we're going to do it, we'll need to haul ass right now."

CHAPTER FORTY-THREE

The scout ship made its way toward its target, the usual gray-and-black background present on the display. It moved into position and waited as the countdown reached zero. Outside, the rail gun transport launched one of its dwindling supply of rocks toward the complex. Although Austin would have preferred to follow up each rock with a specialized torpedo to enhance the damage, there wasn't time to allow for switching from one weapon to the other and back.

Preparations had been made for a rapid firing of the projectiles, so the second rock was fired almost immediately after the first one. The final rock was set in place and launched as well, exhausting the supply of ammunition and leaving the weapon useless.

Since the rock was launched at extreme speed at a relatively close distance, it was nearly impossible to react to it, and the aliens had no effective means of intercepting it anyway. Moments after the rock ripped a massive hole through the alien structure, *Pathfinder* appeared from its warp bubble. It only took an instant to launch another torpedo toward the derelict. There was no reaction from the complex as the scout ship moved back into a warp bubble.

In no time, *Pathfinder* was over to where another gaping hole had been ripped in the structure. Once again, the vessel launched a torpedo, although the aliens had taken notice of the path and tried to intercept it. The attempt failed, because the path was too close to the derelict itself, and the aliens didn't dare try another shot.

Pathfinder moved across to another section of the enemy structure, secure within a warp bubble. However, when it appeared back in normal space-time, the aliens were waiting. They had analyzed the timing and locations of the first two torpedoes and realized what the humans intended. Moments after the third torpedo was launched, the aliens managed to destroy it in flight, without drawing a response from the derelict.

The people on *Pathfinder* were in a desperate quandary. Austin called to engineering. "Bret! They caught our third torpedo. Since we've been staggering the speeds of the torpedoes, impact of the first two will both be in thirty seconds. We can't fire another one and have it reach the derelict in time. Can we launch a specialized torpedo instead?"

"Not without modifications; we can't take a chance on getting it wrong and having the warp distortions throw everything off, Sam."

Austin looked at a display. "Get a conventional explosive in a specialized torpedo with the warp distortions disabled, and launch it the hell out of here."

"We're putting it in place now. We can't duck and hide after we launch this one; we're going to have to watch to make sure it reaches the derelict and detonates, since we're detecting EMP countermeasures to throw things off. That'll make it pretty damned difficult to get back into a warp bubble before the derelict sends something really nasty in our direction."

"You could have stayed on a transport," Austin muttered, mostly to himself. Because the specialized torpedo would move toward its target in its own mini-warp bubble, launch would need to take place only a split second before the impact of the other two torpedoes to bring on the full fury of the derelict. This meant that the scout ship couldn't try to move away from the complex, as they had to ensure that the launch would be from the correct location.

While the countdown continued, the aliens employed EMP bursts from their unseen weapons, in hopes of throwing off any technology-driven measures. Visibility suffered tremendously. When it seemed they couldn't wait any longer, the specialized torpedo raced away from the complex, down an unreadable path. They worried over whether the torpedo been able to enter its warp bubble before feeling the effects from the alien weapons.

The answer came virtually immediately, as Austin was barely able to make out an image of the derelict seemingly consumed by a cold-blue fire that burst out in three separate torrents. The force from the energy was so great and swift that *Pathfinder* found itself buffeted by a massive geyser of all-consuming energy.

After a moment, Austin realized that the geyser hadn't gone away, but they had somehow made it safely into a warp bubble. They watched as the eerie, distorted images of fire flowed around them and overran the insane architecture. The outlines of the structures seemed to burst away, still pursued by the cold inferno.

Austin knew they needed to get out of there, for rematerializing within that inferno would destroy them instantly. They moved carefully through the warp bubble toward their transports and reappeared safely into normal space-time. They caught a glimpse of the blue fire that continued to rage from the derelict and engulf the strange structures, and then the outpouring ceased, as if a spigot had been closed.

There was little to be seen of what had once been a community that sustained a dozen alien vessels, plus possibly many others of their kind. The browns and blacks that had marked the structures and vessels were now almost entirely black scorch marks; various embers were already fading from an impossibly bright white.

As they linked with the transports, they were reminded by their friends how narrow their escape had been. It was Sara's turn to cry for joy as she saw that her husband was safe.

They were alerted by Yabuno that the fight still wasn't over. "They're not giving up," he warned, as the remaining enemy craft closed on their position. "They may still believe we won't attack that ship, so long as they have humans as hostages."

"We can discuss this later when we have more time, but while all humans have inherent value, Harrington and her people have truly made themselves outlaws—proper punishment for their actions cannot be grounded in the law because there is no proper punishment for what they've done and tried to do.

"While I won't say whether they deserve their fate, I will say that their fate is of their own making, and their lives aren't worth the sacrifice of more lives," Austin said, his expression darkening. "That means we will attack the aliens to destroy them."

"What's the plan?" Sara asked.

"Your ship will be the bait, while we jump in and out of warp bubbles along the sides, where they can't reach us easily, and give them a taste of an EMP pounding. Once we've degraded their own EMP capability, you will turn back on them and give them another blast."

As Sara acknowledged the plan, the other two ships vanished in their warp bubbles, seeking contact with a still-deadly enemy. The scout ship materialized first, catching the aliens off guard by moving close to the larger ship and opening a fierce barrage. *Pathfinder* was out of position to be reached by the larger ship's EMP weapon, so lasers and projectiles were the weapons of choice.

Pathfinder moved back into a warp bubble for a moment, as the projectiles passed by harmlessly, only to reappear in a slightly different position and reengage the enemy. The closeness of the smaller ship's approach, plus the strength of its own EMP weapon, degraded the weapons of choice rapidly, leaving the side exposed, with no effective means of answering the attack.

The other transport had moved into a comparable position on the other side of the enemy vessel, concentrating its fire in a similar manner. The attack also affected the enemy weapons, although not quite as effectively, due to the less-precise nature of the transport moving into and out of warp bubbles.

Austin looked at the display with great satisfaction and pointed to it as he spoke to Albretti. "We're finally ready to attack the EMP weapon from this location, where they still can't get at us."

"We're just seconds away. We'll start the attack once we're in position," Albretti said.

The scout ship opened fire as the enemy ship continued to fight the transport on the other side. At a word from Austin, the Citadel ships opened up some distance from the aliens. Suddenly, the bait transport reversed course, its EMP weapon deployed and firing, joined by the other ships. The aliens maintained fire with their own weapon, but Sara and her people were determined to bring the fight to an end. They accepted some damage as the price for going on the offensive, and the alien weapon continued to lose effectiveness.

Pathfinder switched over to a torpedo as it completed its maneuver and faced its enemy again; the giant ship was unable to avoid the impact or the resulting hole that resembled a laceration. As *Pathfinder* made ready to launch a specialized torpedo into the breach in the enemy vessel's hull, the target reversed course, moving away in full retreat.

As the Citadel ships continued the pursuit, Yabuno said, "I guess they've figured out not to expect to hide behind human hostages anymore."

Austin opened his link to Turner. "It's time to broadcast the message, Alan."

"What message, Sam?" Yabuno asked.

"The message that makes it clear we can speak for ourselves from now on," Austin replied.

"The message has been sent," Turner confirmed.

"Something's happening with the aliens," Yabuno reported. "We may want to back off a bit, in case they're about to lose it, and they're trying to take us with them."

As Austin had the pursuing ships put more distance between them and the enemy ship, they watched as their adversary's vessel tried to form a warp-field bubble. They saw unusual distortions around the holes in the ship's hull.

"They can't escape this time!" Albretti cried triumphantly. The feeling of triumph that was shared by others changed to frustration as the holes filled rapidly with what looked like organic tissue. A bright light spilled out from within the ship through what looked vaguely like pores. The light was extinguished quickly, as if the holes had been sealed. This time the craft seemed to distort only slightly before finally moving into a warp bubble and vanishing.

"It looks like they cauterized their wounds, so they could maintain the integrity of their ship and make their escape," Yabuno said.

"Where'd they go?" Albretti asked, pounding a display in frustration. "They couldn't have another base like this one, could they?"

"There's no way to know for sure," Yabuno replied, "but they left without the derelict, and that looks like they cried uncle."

"I hope they left for home, wherever that might be," Austin said. He gazed at the display. "We'll have plenty of time to talk about it later; right now, let's see what we can do about rescuing our people.

CHAPTER FORTY-FOUR

They'd been relieved to discover that while their ships had been crippled by the alien weapons, there were no fatalities among their transport crews. The fighting had taken place during a relatively short period, meaning that the lack of life support had not yet become critical. While Yabuno and the transport engineers were jury-rigging systems to sustain them for the trip back to Citadel, Austin had *Pathfinder* return to the ruins of what had once been a deadly enclave.

Although they made a thorough visual and sensory inspection of the devastated base, they could find no signs of life or even of anything that looked like a corpse. They made similar findings when inspecting the ruins of the alien ships.

"We never seem to find their stuff in any form other than complete destruction," Turner commented. "While I get it as far as being deep fried by the derelict is concerned, we can't seem to stop them by any means short of total destruction.

"What about finding any useful artifacts?" Austin asked.

"While it's possible that some components from their ships might have been ejected, there's no way to track anything now. Unlike the location of the one artifact that was discovered in Earth's solar system, there aren't any planetary bodies where anything could have been lodged."

"The complex wasn't that far from the ships that were destroyed," Austin pointed out. "Couldn't something from the ships have ended up there?"

"There's no way to know now," Turner said with a shake of his head. "The complex was destroyed after their ships, and we've already seen what the place looks like. The only thing we've picked up is the shuttle that escaped from *KT-20*."

"Let's have a talk with those people," Austin said in an unfriendly tone.

Two men who had been among those on board the shuttle in question faced Austin and others from Citadel.

"Let's go over the technical issues first," Austin said, nodding at Turner and Yabuno.

"I won't validate your actions by referring to the transport as your ship, since it was ours, so I'll call it by its name," Yabuno began. "Why did *KT-20* attack our transport?"

The men squirmed in their chairs as one of them replied, "We didn't have anything to do with it. The alien technology seemed to take over our—the ship and handled all its operational aspects."

"Just what was this technology?" Turner asked. "Was it something physical, or was it entirely in the form of data?"

"All we ever received were more of those crazy symbols they use to communicate with us. However, after a while, we saw something that was roughly a sphere in shape, about the size of a basketball, that was next to the warp-field generators." He shuddered slightly. "It was creepy to watch; several tentacles seemed to grow out of the thing and embed themselves in the generators. We don't know if the thing made its way over from the aliens or if it was created once those symbols started going to work.

"We looked at the displays for propulsion, navigation, and weapons, and all they showed were those symbols. None of the usual information relating to the operation of the generators was visible."

"Did you record any of the symbols?" Yabuno asked. "Can you recall any of them?"

The man shook his head. "I never knew much about the symbols. We had people who could understand them enough to work out how to communicate with them."

"Where are those people now?" Austin demanded.

"They were aboard the shuttles," he replied.

"All of them? They didn't leave anyone at home to read their damned language?"

"No, they made us all come with them to Citadel."

"They 'made' you come? Did you pull a gun on you?" Austin asked sarcastically.

"No, they just told us to come, and we did," he replied weakly.

Austin didn't bother hiding his revulsion. "Why were you here, then?"

"We're scientists. We hoped to be able to learn about their technology, especially since they promised that it would actually be much simpler to use than the Citadel technology, but it just didn't relate to anything we understood."

"What do you know about running a transport?"

"Not much," the man admitted.

Turner looked at Austin. "We'll interview them further during the trip back to Citadel, but there isn't much more to be learned on the technical side for now."

Austin faced the men directly. "Tell us why you became Harrington's lackeys."

The men blanched. "We didn't know that Harrington was involved," one of them protested. "We were told by Flynn that a project was underway to find a way to communicate with the aliens and try to find a peaceful solution to the conflict. It was supposed to be a behind-the-scenes effort, since Citadel couldn't acknowledge being on good terms with Earth."

"Why would you believe that Citadel was involved?"

"Flynn gave us data that Citadel shared with Earth. We assumed Citadel wouldn't have allowed it if you weren't OK with what we were doing."

Austin looked at Yabuno, who said, "That would have been from when we were still cooperating in the aftermath of the original attack. Harrington must have managed to keep that data or get it under her control after she was impeached."

Austin's expression was cold. "President Lee told us that that project had stopped its activities, although he may have been misled. Let's make it a priority to get that data back, so this can't happen again." He looked back at their prisoners. "You are going to help us get that data back from wherever it may be. You'd better act as if your lives depend on it, because they do." He nodded at Yabuno and Turner as he continued. "I'll leave it to Bret and Alan to talk with you about the specific technical aspects of your activities. What I want to know is when you knew what the aliens wanted in exchange for the derelict and how you could have possibly gone along with it."

"We've known since before we left our solar system about what the aliens wanted. Flynn convinced us that it was a reasonable price to pay, considering that no one could understand the technology behind the derelict and everyone would be able to understand the new technology the aliens would provide."

Austin was shocked. "It didn't occur to you that giving that advanced technology to the aliens might have been the worst thing to do, considering the power they would have?"

The man shrugged. "That wasn't really our concern. That was for the governments to work out."

"Did you think that trading human lives for the derelict was also not your concern?" Austin asked in a dangerous tone.

"We were assured that we'd never actually go through with that part. We were told that once the aliens had the derelict, they wouldn't be interested in humans anymore."

"We found a recorded message left behind by one of your colleagues," Austin said. "His name was Gerald

Porter. As you must already know, he was the one who figured out where to search for the artifact that led to this nightmare in the first place. He painted a damning picture of your acquiescence to Harrington and to her plan to go through with the deal involving the humans from Citadel. Porter acknowledged his own culpability and cowardice in not trying to do anything for the hostages, not even trying to warn them about their intended fate." Austin's expression made it clear that he had the same view of the men in front of him.

"There wasn't anything we could have done about it anyway!" the man protested. "By that time, Harrington's people were armed. Besides, no one would have believed that we hadn't been associated with Harrington from the start anyway, so our only option was to go along and take advantage of the amnesty that everyone would receive in return for the alien technology."

Austin's gaze turned as cold as the blue fire from the derelict. "You're sorry excuses for humans, to be willing to sell out your fellow men and women for personal convenience. You're also quite a fool to gamble on Citadel accepting any amnesty bought with the blood of our people."

Austin left the room in disgust.

CHAPTER FORTY-FIVE

The damage to several of the transports had been extensive, and it had taken over three weeks to patch them up enough to make the trip back to Citadel, where they'd receive thorough overhauls by Curly Stephens and her people. Although *Pathfinder* and several of the transports could have used their warp-field generators to return home in a wink of an eye, that option wasn't available to the more severely damaged vessels or to the derelict. Austin had been touched by the fact that all of the crews had volunteered to stay together to support each other as needed during the trip home. Messages had, of course, already been sent ahead, letting everyone know they'd been successful.

Sara, Albretti, Yabuno, Turner, and Liz had joined Austin in his stateroom on the scout ship. With a twinkle in his eye, he asked Sara if she wanted to resume command of *KT-2* for the return trip. She grinned, taking Albretti's hand.

"*Pathfinder* has the bed I share with my husband, Sam." A mischievous look appeared on her face. "I suppose I could try to commute between two ships, running a transport by day and commuting back to this ship at night to sleep with Joe, but I don't think it would work out." She became more serious. "Besides, Wash can take care of things for now. If he doesn't want it, there are at least a couple of number twos from the other transports who can take over *KT-2* for now. Most of the issues that arise over the next month will be technical ones, and we have plenty of technical talent among our ships to handle practically anything that comes up."

Yabuno looked at Turner and asked, "Any thoughts on where the aliens went, Alan?"

Turner shrugged. "It's hard to know, but I've been making out what I can of their messages to Harrington's people. While there's still a lot to review, I think Harrington was right in believing that the complex we destroyed was something akin to a forward base and that their home world is much farther away."

"Couldn't they have built another forward base somewhere else?" Albretti asked.

Turner shook his head. "Think about all of the effort that had to have gone into building and getting that complex up and running. It supported at least a dozen of their ships and probably had a sizable population dedicated to keeping it running. Bases like that would be few and far between. It's more likely that they went home or at least back to a base much closer to their home, if their home is truly too far away to make a direct trip feasible."

"I wonder if Harrington or any of her people is still alive," Liz mused with a shudder. "While I'll never forgive her for her crimes, I wouldn't wish what's going to happen to her on any human."

"I'm still struggling with that one, Liz," Sara said. "In one sense, I agree with you. However, speaking as one of the intended sacrificial victims, I'd say she got what she deserved. In spite of the fancy words she used about what it would mean to the security of two star systems, she was never operating from anything but her own self-interest. I should know, since she was happy to gloat about it when she thought she was in the clear and I couldn't do anything about it."

She looked at Austin. "She was looking forward to being able to hide behind the agreement she planned on working out with the nations back in her neck of the woods. It was important to her that you be punished and that you understood that the loss of our lives was your fault for having crossed her."

"In a way, I don't disagree with either of you," Austin replied in a melancholy tone. "I'd agree that Harrington deserves everything that's coming to her, but I would have been OK with destroying the ship that captured her, to prevent her from actually meeting that fate." His expression darkened.

"She turned out to be every bit the fool I feared. The aliens were happy to do a deal where their technology would be incorporated into all of the ships in that solar system. They could just show up one day and instruct our own ships to destroy us. Ironically, the humans' only hope for survival would have been Citadel, since we'd never have agreed to incorporating that infernal technology within our ships. In light of the delay when sending and receiving messages between the two systems, we would have had to rely solely on whatever Citadel ships were already in their solar system to defend against that threat."

He looked at Yabuno and Turner. "Speaking of communications, are we sure there's no way Harrington could have communicated with the aliens once they were in their shuttles?"

"Yes, we're sure," Turner replied. "We've located the technology they set up on *KT-2*, and Harrington's scientists confirmed that they had similar technology set up on board *KT-20*. There wasn't any reason to take the technology with them on the shuttle; it takes a while to create a message of any significant length, possibly longer than the trip from one transport to another to create another message, and they'd already sent the message they needed from *KT-2* before they departed."

"Speaking of technology," Liz said, "I'm so glad we stopped the aliens from getting our files on the derelict. Have we recovered all of them?"

Austin looked at Yabuno, who answered slyly, "Funny thing about those files; they seem to have become thoroughly corrupted. They wouldn't have been of any help to the aliens, or to Harrington's people either, for that matter."

Liz laughed. "I take it those files were already corrupted before transmission?"

"What do you think?" Yabuno replied, grinning. "Considering the extent of the corruption, there's no way for anyone to tell. That's the problem with transmitting complicated information through intense radiation. Anyway, that's our story, and we're sticking to it."

"What about the work you were doing on the warp-field generators?"

"You mean the work that's based on the picture I drew?" Yabuno asked. "None of that stuff was in the files on the analyses we performed on the derelict, and there wasn't a reason to connect any dots for them."

"I see. What's going to happen to Harrington's scientists?" Liz asked.

"When we return to Citadel, they'll appear before a tribunal and face judgment for their actions," Austin replied. "I'm not a fan of people trying to look the other way while they sell out human beings. I thought we'd settled that one after the Bio War or even further back, at Nuremberg. Anyway, regardless of what the judgment will be, whether it is carried out or not may be influenced by their cooperation with us in ferreting out and locking down all information relating to communicating with the aliens."

His expression hardened. "One thing we'll make sure they know is that if we take them back to Earth to locate this information, Citadel will not recognize any efforts by them to hide within any Earth-based jurisdiction. That's another reason why the judgment will be in place before anyone returns to Earth—it avoids any arguments over their guilt, assuming for the moment that things won't look any better for them once we've reviewed all the facts. With their guilt established, there won't be any questions about our jurisdiction over them." He let out a small sigh. "If some of them had stopped to ask whether this project was even a good idea, we might never have had the further loss of life."

"The only one who stopped at all to ask any of those questions, even though it was too late, was the guy who left behind his message owning up to his part in what happened," Turner said with a thoughtful look.

"What is it, Alan?" Austin asked.

"That message wasn't the only thing he left behind. He mentioned being caught up in the excitement of writing a paper describing his work and results. I found his paper. Bret and I have spent some time reading it."

Austin was curious. "What did you think of it?"

Turner grinned. "It wasn't bad. In fact, he did a pretty damned fine job of it. He took another look at things we'd already concluded meant nothing and figured it out. It would definitely have been worthy of being published."

Austin shook his head. "The two of you are welcome to it, and I'll be interested in reading it as well, but that paper will never see the light of day. The last thing we need is for people to start a treasure hunt, looking for more relics and getting into more mischief. We'll have to make sure to look for any copies of that paper when our people collect the rest of their information and files." Austin stopped when he saw the anxious look on Yabuno's face.

"It was a closer call than any of us realized," Yabuno said with relief. "Porter only finished the paper the day they were 'persuaded' to leave for Citadel. If they'd waited another day before rounding Porter and the other scientists up, he'd have submitted it for peer review. That reminds me, Alan," he continued with a puzzled expression, "what was that message you sent out right before the aliens headed out of here for good?"

Turner looked at Austin, who nodded. "Sam asked me to create a message to the aliens using the information I'd gleaned from my review of Harrington's people's communication."

"What did the message say?" Liz asked.

Austin spoke. "We sketched out all the space between Citadel and Earth, plus a huge buffer around each system, and told them that space belongs to us and that they are never again to visit it. If they try, we will destroy them, as we destroyed them today. It also said that human lives are important and warned them not to treat those lives lightly. We made it clear that Harrington never had any right to speak for any group of humans in the first place and that we speak for ourselves, especially where this system and the derelict are concerned."

Upon noticing the questioning looks, he chuckled. "You're probably wondering where Earth fits in. Our message was a bit ambiguous on that point, which was necessary. Let's face it; Earth isn't going to be able to talk with them directly because they don't have the communication technology, and we aren't going to share it with them."

He looked more sober as he continued. "I'm tired of people from Earth taking actions that have an impact on us without our consent or even knowing about it. If at all possible, we won't speak for Earth without talking with them first, but delays in communication may not make that possible. If it becomes necessary for communication to take place in Earth's solar system, I'd rather trust in

Citadel's embassy handling the communications with the help of the Citadel Group than leave it to any political authority. J. W. Preacher has much better judgment than just about anyone else there."

"I understood from some of my talks with Powers that it takes some time to create a message," Sara said. "You would have had to create the message that we sent out before we knew we'd won. Weren't you taking a gamble?"

"Not really," he answered. "This was a situation where we didn't have any choice except to win, even if that meant no one would be returning to Citadel."

"One thing Harrington's people shared with us is that when they created messages to the aliens, they had to do it in a deferential tone," Yabuno said. "It seems their friends went nuts anytime they felt a lack of respect from an inferior race."

"Alan picked up on that too," Austin agreed. "I didn't give a damn about their sensibilities, however. We didn't have the time to work that approach into our message, and it wouldn't have been consistent with the message we wanted to send anyway. We made it clear we were talking to them as equals." He grinned. "We would have told them what they could do with themselves if they didn't like it, but we weren't sure they would have understood it."

CHAPTER FORTY-SIX

Pathfinder and the rest of the convoy from Citadel were now only a day out from their home. Thanks to the deep-space network, everyone had been able to stay in touch with their loved ones. Sam and Liz had finished sending a message to their sons and were enjoying a quiet moment in their stateroom.

"We haven't seen much of Joe and Sara during this trip," Liz noted with a smile. "They seem to be spending a lot of their time alone in their quarters. That's a pretty good idea, considering everything they've been through."

Austin chuckled. "I don't blame them at all; they have some time to make up for, especially since they weren't sure if they even would see each other again. Besides, Sara's suggestion about Wash was a good one. He's doing a fine job looking after things for now. He's already a hell of a pilot and knows the rest of the ship well. He'll end up with some experience as a captain, which will be great in case he ever wants to take up the job. He knows he can come to me with any questions, rather than bother Joe or Sara."

She gave Sam a mischievous look. "I'm glad he hasn't come to you with too many questions, since Joe and Sara aren't the only ones that have needed time for themselves during this trip."

Sam was interrupted from returning her look by his link. He kept the device on audio only, considering what Liz wasn't wearing at that moment. "What is it, Wash?"

"A message has come through from J. W. Preacher, Sam."

"Great!" he exclaimed. "Send it through to my link."

"Already done. Have a good evening," he said with a hint of smugness.

Liz turned onto her side to face Sam and propped herself up on one arm. "If I didn't know better, I'd say from his tone of voice that he knows what we have in mind. At least, what *I* have in mind," she said pointedly.

Sam laughed. "I have the same thing in mind, my love, and we'll confirm those thoughts as soon as we hear what J. W. has to say."

They watched as Preacher's face came into view with a warm, welcoming expression. "Sam, I was so glad to receive your message after your successful rescue of our people. Although I mourn the loss of Jose Benitez, I'm deeply grateful that the rest of our people were unharmed." The warmth faded as he continued. "While I take seriously my duty to pray even for people like Harrington, I find that I believe she got what she deserved.

"In a way, it's just as well that there wasn't anything left of any of the alien ships or structures. I truly believe we are better off without the temptation of something based in evil." He made a small gesture of waving away a protest. "Although I understand the aliens may not relate to the concept of evil, I sometimes find that efforts to excuse evil on the basis of cultural differences show a lack of understanding of evil. In my view, those arguments don't make their actions any less evil."

He chuckled. "Here I am, venturing into philosophy when I wanted to bring you up to date on events back here. Pete Lee sent me a message to be forwarded to you. As we've discussed before, I've reviewed the message so I can offer my thoughts, which I will do following Lee's message."

Preacher's face faded and was replaced by Lee's. "Greetings, Sam," he began. "I'd like to start by congratulating you and everyone else from Citadel on your success in rescuing your people from the aliens and recovering the derelict. Once again, you have demonstrated that Citadel was founded by people with an intense desire to defend their lives and their freedoms and the abilities to back up that desire."

Lee's expression turned somber. "You had some pretty tough words for me in your previous messages, and I've given a great deal of thought to them. While I hope we can get together someday for a face-to-face conversation, I want you to hear some of my thoughts.

"It is important to keep in mind where the responsibility for criminal acts lies. Courtney Harrington and the people who carried out her instructions, and no one else, are responsible for her criminal actions.

"That sounds like I'm trying to absolve myself from all responsibility for what happened, doesn't it?" he asked ruefully. "While I stand by my statement, I'm well aware that some of the actions of my administration didn't help the situation. While I still believe a legal process had to play itself out under extraordinary circumstances involving an impeached and convicted US president, I know you feel very strongly otherwise. In any event, we could have been more diligent in keeping tabs on Harrington's actions while she was under house arrest. If we had, we would have known about her efforts to communicate with the aliens and been able to prevent it from going as far as it did.

"It didn't help that she made us look like fools when she evaded her house arrest and had herself smuggled on board your transport," he noted. "Because we hadn't been keeping close tabs on her activities, we never considered that she would be hiding outside our solar system. After all, under normal circumstances, there's no way she would have traveled to Citadel voluntarily. It therefore seemed to be a matter that we could handle within our system and not something that needed to be passed along to Citadel."

Lee seemed uncomfortable as he continued. "There's probably also the fact that I didn't want to have to admit to you that house arrest was inadequate for Harrington, and I hoped to have her captured before discussing what had happened.

"Hypothetical questions are always tricky, since one can never be sure about how they would have truly played out. I'd like to hope that I would have never considered accepting a proposal along the lines of what Harrington suggested. However, I have to be honest and note that the answer might have been different if, for example, Citadel had been destroyed and the derelict were in the possession of the aliens. Sometimes we make deals we wouldn't normally make when we feel we don't have any other choice. I shudder over the prospect of having accepted Harrington's deal, since we know that that would have been a deal with the devil.

"Fortunately, we don't have to worry about what might have been," he said. His tone again turned somber. "I have concluded that nothing good can come from what Harrington was doing, so I have ordered that everything relating to those activities be collected and turned over to Citadel for safekeeping. That includes the alien artifact, plus all files relating to the translation and use of the alien symbols. No copies will be retained of any of these materials.

"I have issued a presidential finding that subjects these items to special national-security restrictions, which will make violations subject to the death penalty. I hope that will impress upon people that I am deadly serious about the dangers associated with them. I suggest that you jettison these materials into the Citadel sun, but that's your call," he said without humor.

"J. W. has shared with me the substance of your warning to the aliens to stay away from our respective solar systems. I appreciate your continuing to look out for our interests. In light of the distance between our solar systems, which makes communication slow, and the advanced state of technology Citadel possesses relating to dealing with the aliens, it makes sense for Citadel to take the lead on any issues relating to the aliens. For obvious reasons, that includes any direct communications with them. I don't mind saying I hope we never hear from them again.

"I want to close this message with my profound regrets over the fact that we allowed our problem to become your problem, with tragic results. I hope the gestures I've mentioned will be taken as a sign of my sincerity. I hope one day to be able to say these things to you face-to-face. God bless, to you and everyone else on Citadel." Lee's image faded.

Preacher's image returned to the sound of chuckling. "Lee is probably still smarting from the words I shared with him after seeing your message to him. One thing he's learned about Citadel is that we don't put up with bullshit.

"I let Lee know that we will be sending some people to Earth to help track down every last file Harrington and her people developed in connection with the aliens. Also, the reason he decided to make that information subject to death-penalty sanctions is because I let him know we would insist on it. At this point, we aren't in any mood to deal with any more nonsense from anyone over this information. It's always interesting to see how the prospect of having one's neck stretched can get the attention of people who might otherwise be tempted to withhold information. Lee doesn't know it," Preacher continued slyly, "but I already have some extremely savvy people within the Citadel Group getting ready to track down information that might end up in some hard-to-reach crevices.

"Lee would have liked us to make a commitment not to publicize Harrington's actions, especially as they related to communicating with the aliens, in view of the potential for unrest. I let him know that wouldn't happen. We need to make it clear that Harrington wasn't some kind of martyr who met her untimely death at the hands of the aliens while trying to protect the two solar systems. People will be reminded that Harrington was a fugitive from justice who met her end as a result of trying to make a deal with the devil. The collateral for her deal was human lives. That won't make Lee look particularly good when people start asking questions about his not having done much about it, but he brought it on himself.

"Besides, secrets like that can't remain secret; they can only fester over time, with sometimes tragic results. That's when the finger-pointing starts, and we don't want to jeopardize our own credibility when it comes to the aliens."

Preacher shook his head. "While I believe Lee to be an honorable man, I wouldn't be surprised if he ends up a one-term president. That means there is a limited shelf life on any promises he makes to us, especially the ones that don't have the force of law behind them. You'd better not lose any time in getting anyone out here that you want to deal with the Harrington situation."

It was now Preacher's turn to look somber. "That brings me to my final thoughts for now. Although we've continued to stay out of Earth politics, we're going to need to do a better job of keeping tabs on the political landscape around here. While I've always done that to a certain extent, as part of running a DC law firm back in the day, we should take a greater interest in the people who are good prospects for sitting in that office after Lee is gone. We'll also need to keep better tabs on other significant political figures as well.

"I'll follow up with some additional thoughts, but the nature of the relationship with Citadel is such that it is likely to be a personal one between the respective presidents for some time to come. We need to find a way to broaden our influence, so that the foibles of one person don't keep leading to so much trouble for us." Preacher signed off.

As Sam mulled over the messages, Liz said, "Ironic, isn't it? A big part of why we left Earth was to start over and get things right that couldn't be fixed back there. I think we've made a great start, as far as the work on Citadel itself is concerned. It's Earth that keeps screwing things up for us."

Sam grinned. "The problem is that we want to have it both ways. On the one hand, we want to maintain ties with them due to loved ones, friends, trade, etc. On the other hand, we want to be able to tell them to leave us the hell alone."

A mischievous look returned to his wife's eyes as she pulled him next to her. "Are you interested in being left the hell alone right now?"

"Not a chance," he replied. "I want to maintain some special ties with a loved one."

"Good answer." She didn't give him a chance to say anything else.

COUNTDOWN CITADEL

The story continues in the next novel by Robert Adrian, *Countdown Citadel*. Time has passed since renegade former US president Courtney Harrington attempted to form an alliance with a hostile alien race to force Earth to grant her amnesty for her past crimes. She found herself facing something worse than death at the hands of her unreliable allies.

A new group called Phoenix has arisen in Earth's solar system and claims to be able to do everything the Citadel Group can, including traveling to another solar system. Another planet in the Citadel system is habitable, and Phoenix has claimed the right to colonize it. Austin finds there is little support in Earth's solar system for denying a group the right to do what Citadel has already done. If ships from Phoenix arrive and seek to colonize another planet peacefully, can Citadel refuse?

The competition with Citadel is personal for Phoenix, and the upstarts don't see eye to eye with Citadel on much of anything. Sharing the security of the system with such a group could be deadly. Austin may be forced to decide how far Citadel is willing to go to avoid being placed at the mercy of hostile interests.

Robert Adrian is the pen name of an attorney with more than two decades of experience working primarily with Silicon Valley technology companies. He grew up reading Robert Heinlein, Isaac Asimov, Ray Bradbury, Andre Norton, and other giants of science fiction. Now, as the author of the Sam Austin Chronicles, he blends his passion for science fiction with other interests, such as historical and futuristic writing. Book three of the series, *Checkmate Citadel*, is the sequel to *Target Citadel*, which is the sequel to the first book, *Destination Citadel*. Adrian enjoys completing projects in his workshop and participating in local music events, which is how he met his wife. They live in the San Francisco Bay Area with their three children.